Disney
Tangled
The Series

The Friendship Mix-Up

WITHDRAWN

By
NEW YORK TIMES
Bestselling
author

Jimmy
Gownley

Illustrated
by

Veronica
Di Lorenzo,

Caroline
LaVelle
Egan,

monica
catalano,

and
Jeffrey
Thomas

Colors
by

Anastasia
Belousova

and
chintsova yana
Konstantinovna

Random House 🏠 New York

Lettering by
Chris Dickey

Designed by
Kurt Hartman

Edited by
Lauren A. Burniac
and Holly Rice

Managing Editor:
Cathryn McHugh

Copyright © 2018 Disney Enterprises, Inc. All rights reserved.
Published in the United States by Random House Children's Books,
a division of Penguin Random House LLC, 1745 Broadway,
New York, NY 10019, and in Canada by Penguin Random House
Canada Limited, Toronto, in conjunction with Disney Enterprises,
Inc. Random House and the colophon are registered trademarks of
Penguin Random House LLC.

rhcbooks.com

ISBN 978-0-7364-3848-3 (trade)—
ISBN 978-0-7364-9023-8 (lib. bdg.)

MANUFACTURED IN CHINA

10 9 8 7 6 5 4 3 2 1

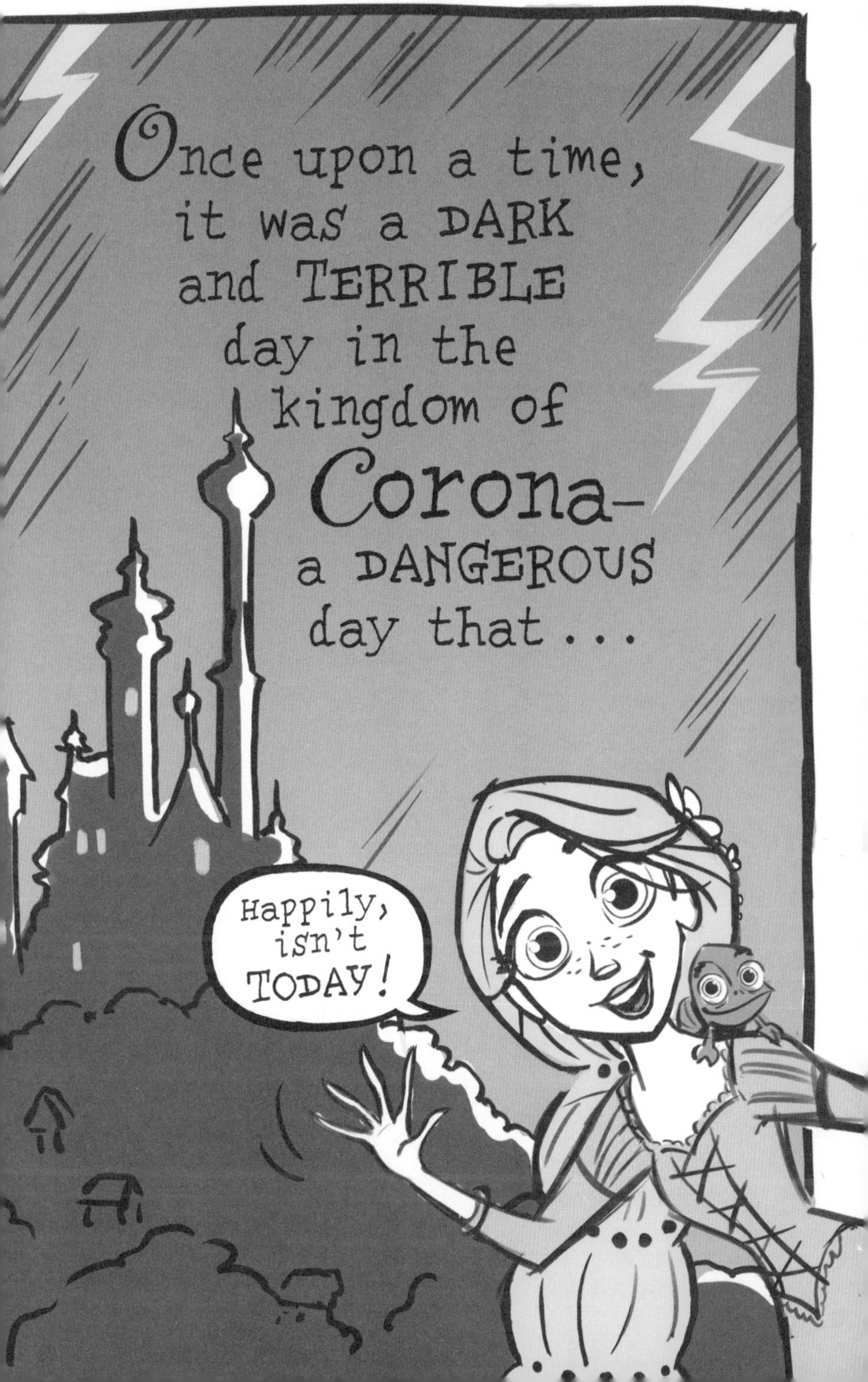
Once upon a time, it was a DARK and TERRIBLE day in the kingdom of Corona—a DANGEROUS day that . . .
Happily, isn't TODAY!

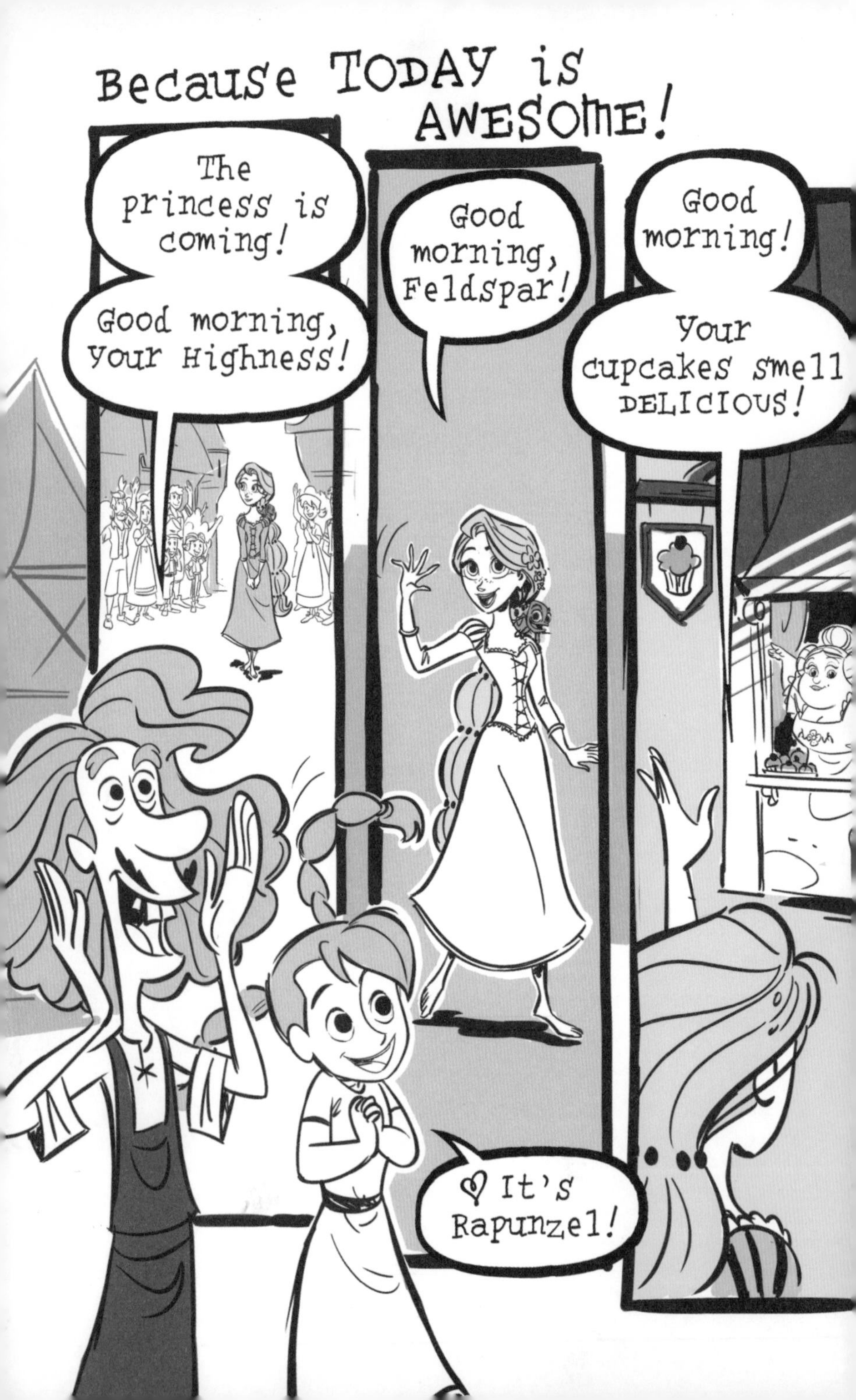
Because TODAY is AWESOME!
The princess is coming!
Good morning, Your Highness!
Good morning, Feldspar!
Good morning!
Your cupcakes smell DELICIOUS!
It's Rapunzel!

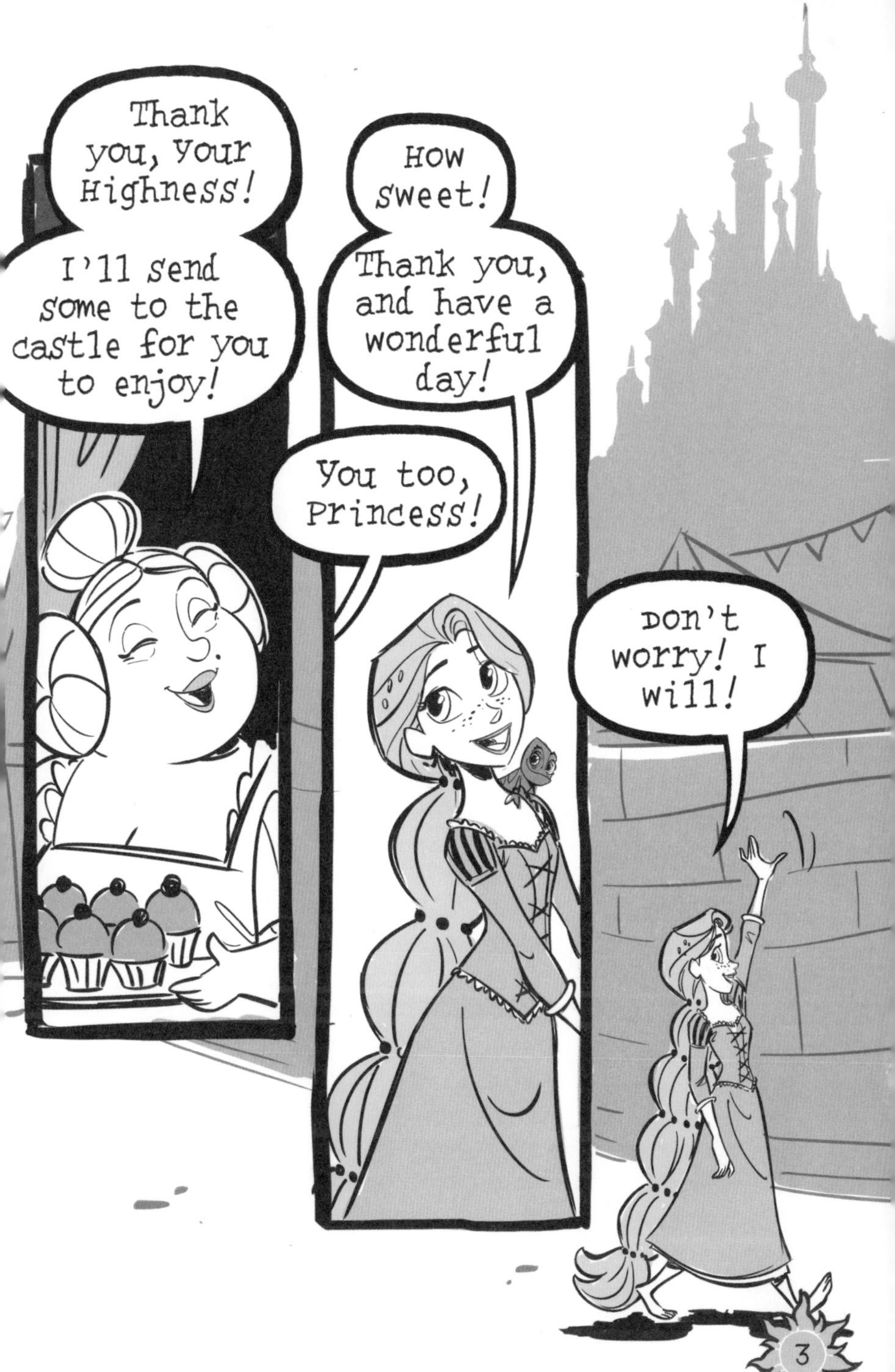
Thank you, your Highness!
I'll send some to the castle for you to enjoy!
How sweet!
Thank you, and have a wonderful day!
You too, Princess!
Don't worry! I will!

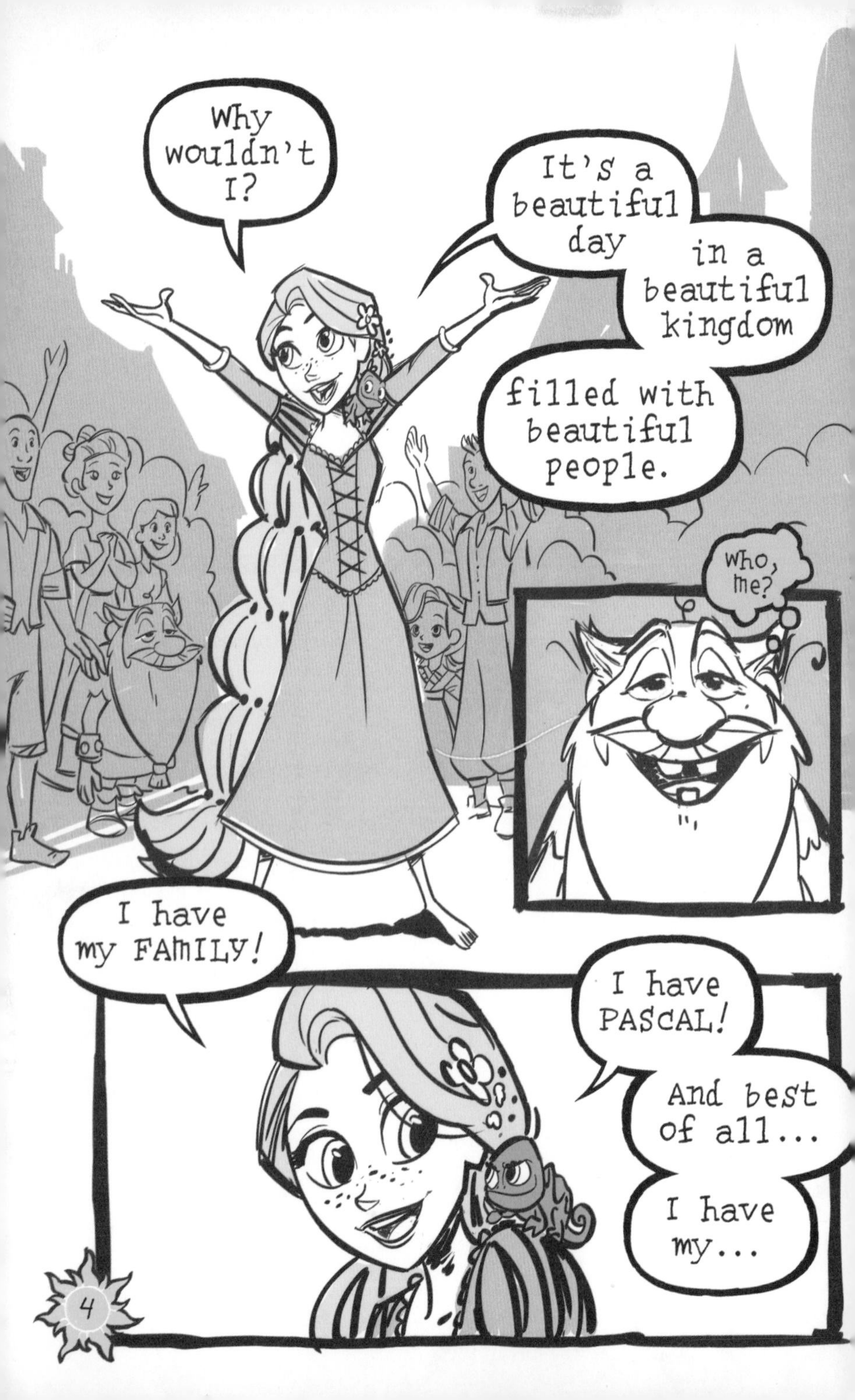
Why wouldn't I?
It's a beautiful day
in a beautiful kingdom
filled with beautiful people.
Who, me?
I have my FAMILY!
I have PASCAL!
And best of all...
I have my...

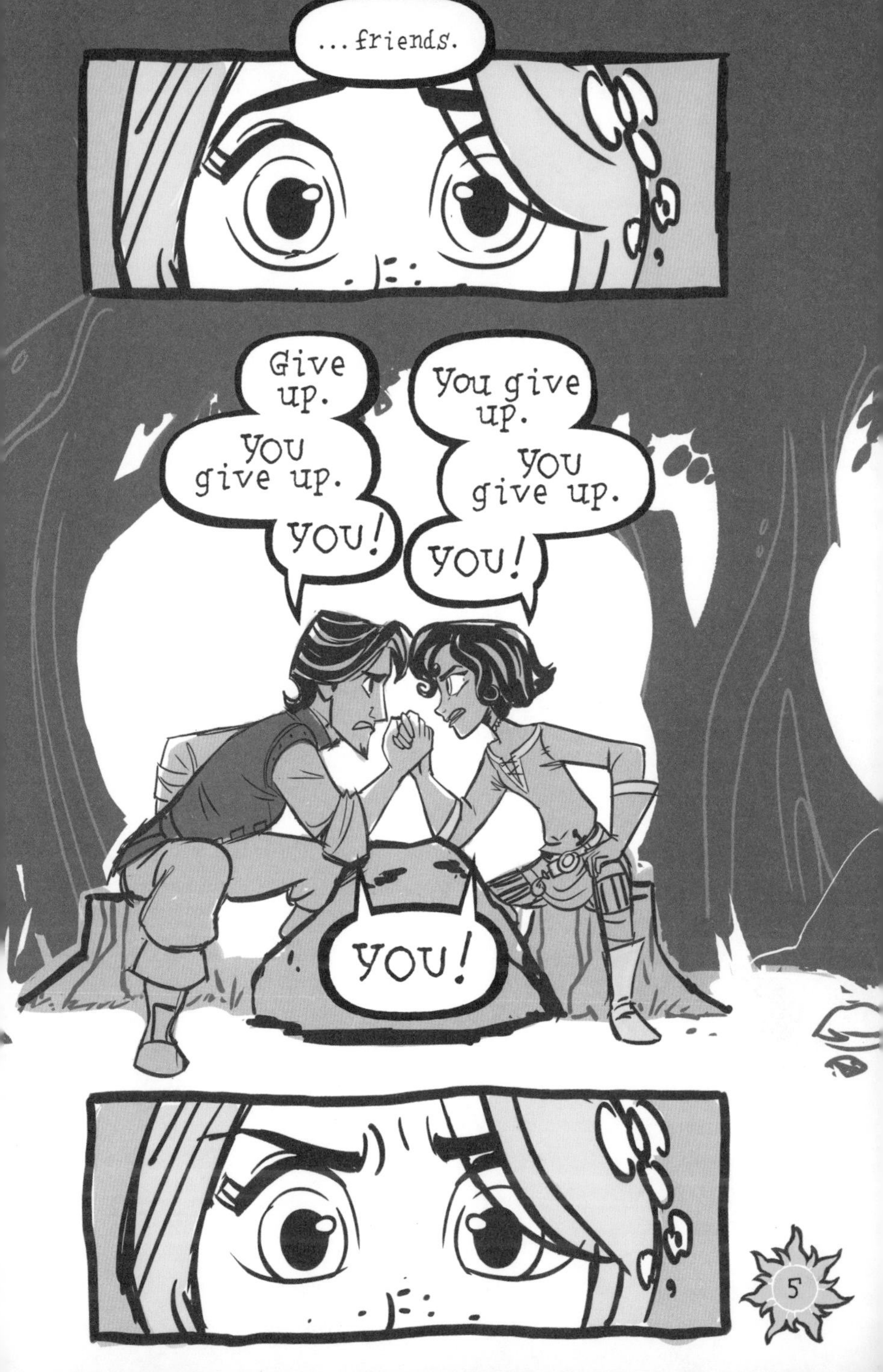
...friends.
Give up.
You give up.
YOU give up.
YOU give up.
YOU!
YOU!
YOU!

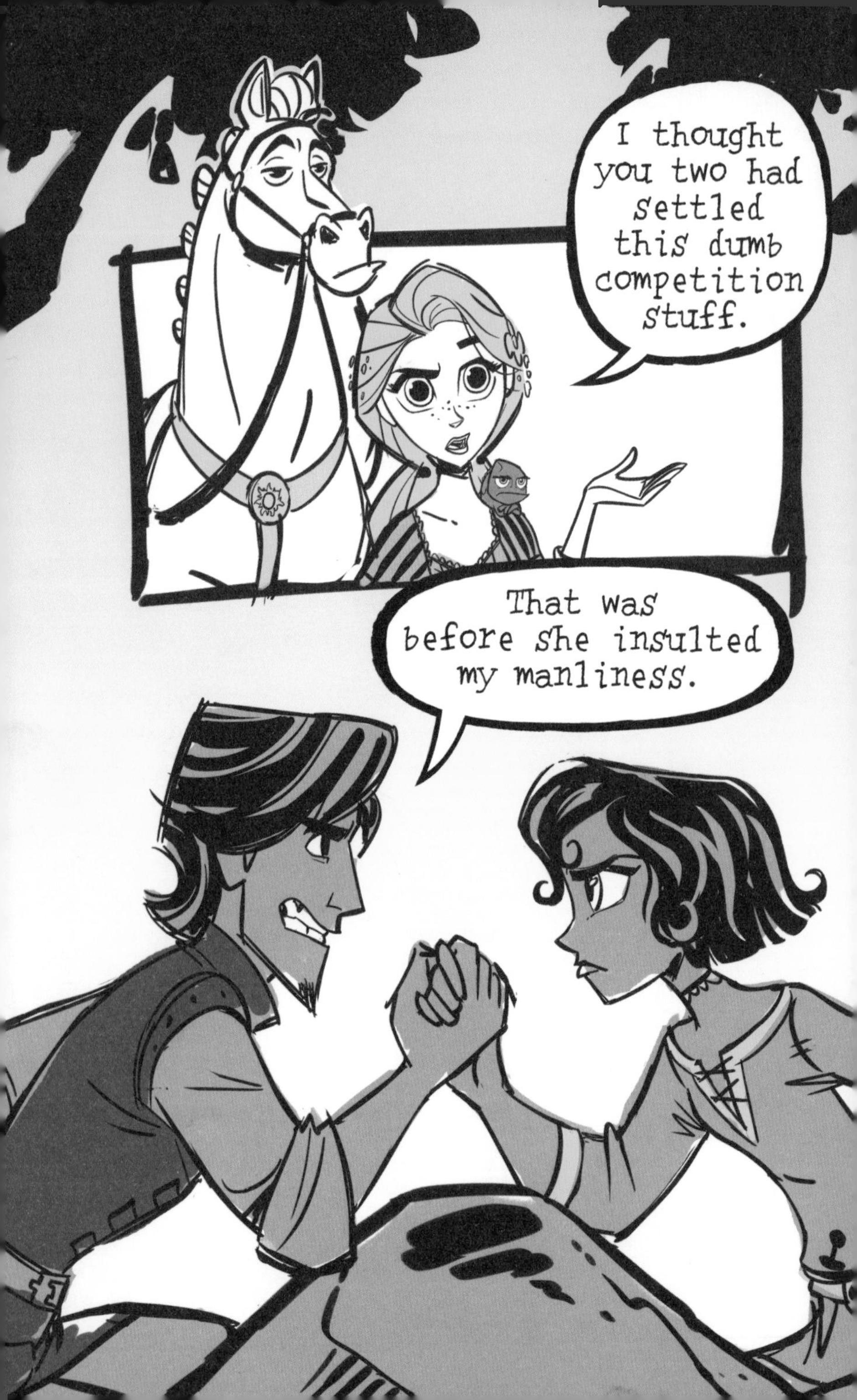
I thought you two had settled this dumb competition stuff.
That was before she insulted my manliness.

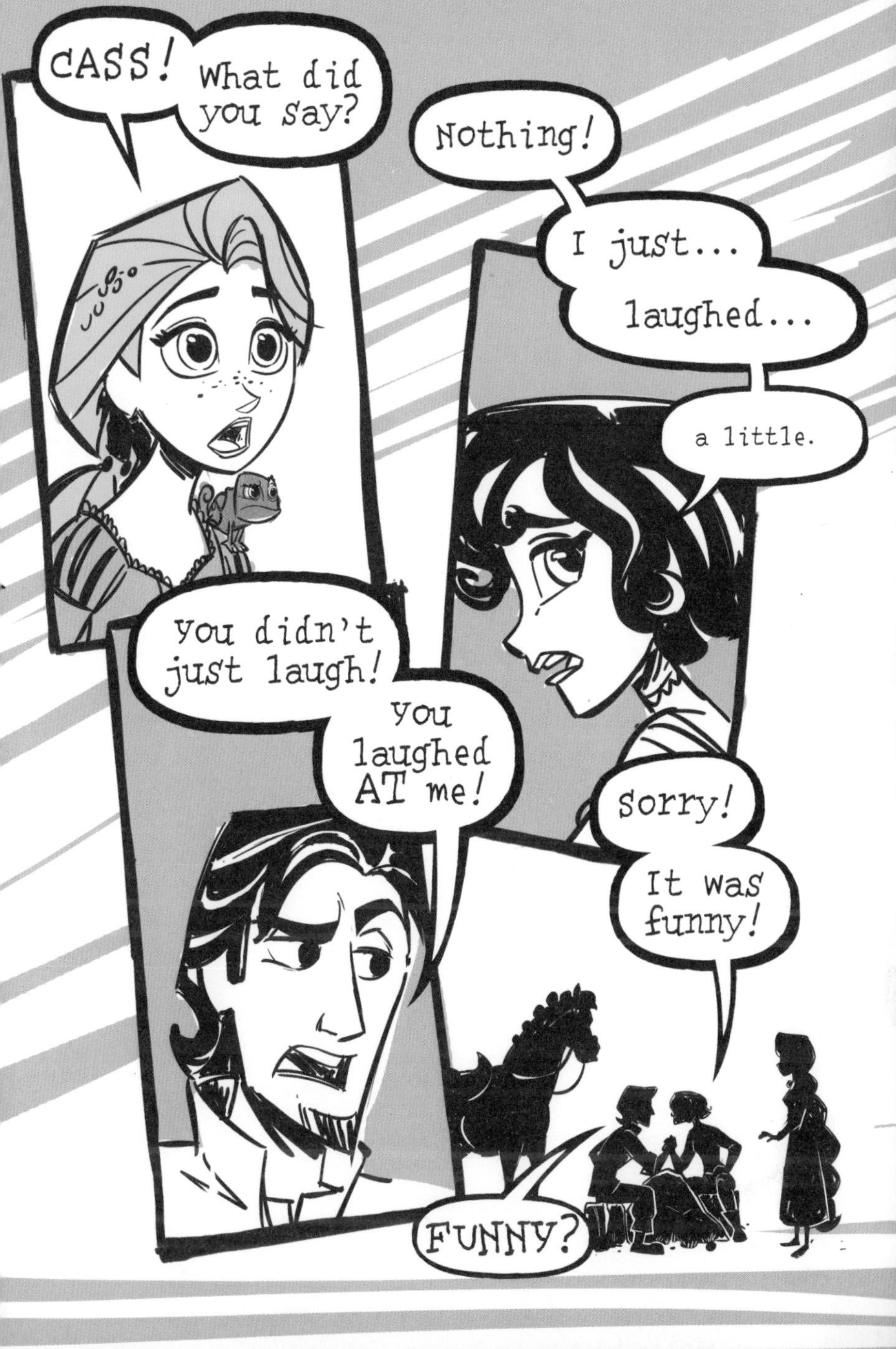
CASS!
What did you say?
Nothing!
I just...
laughed...
a little.
You didn't just laugh!
You laughed AT me!
Sorry!
It was funny!
FUNNY?

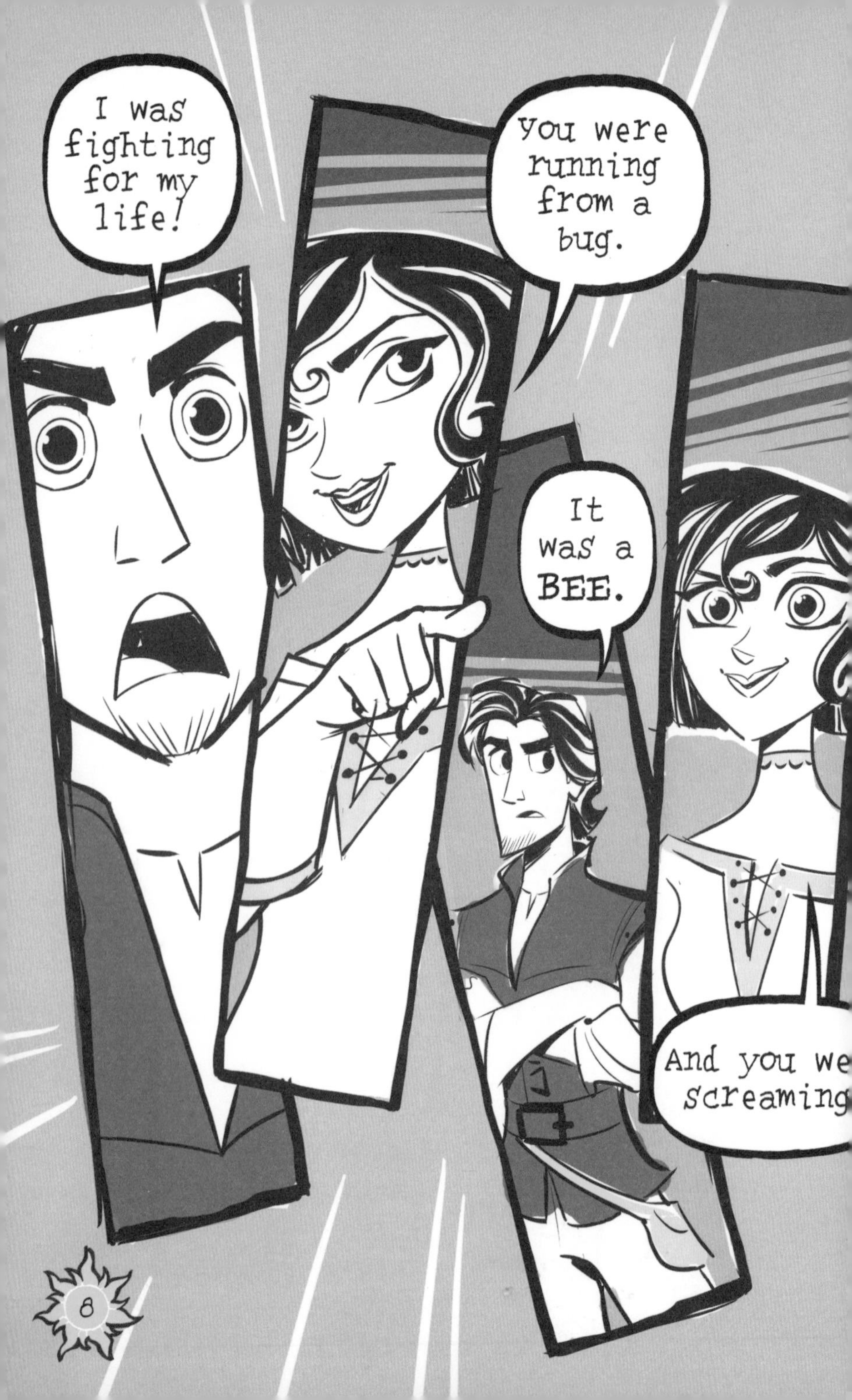
I was fighting for my life!
You were running from a bug.
It was a BEE.
And you we
screaming

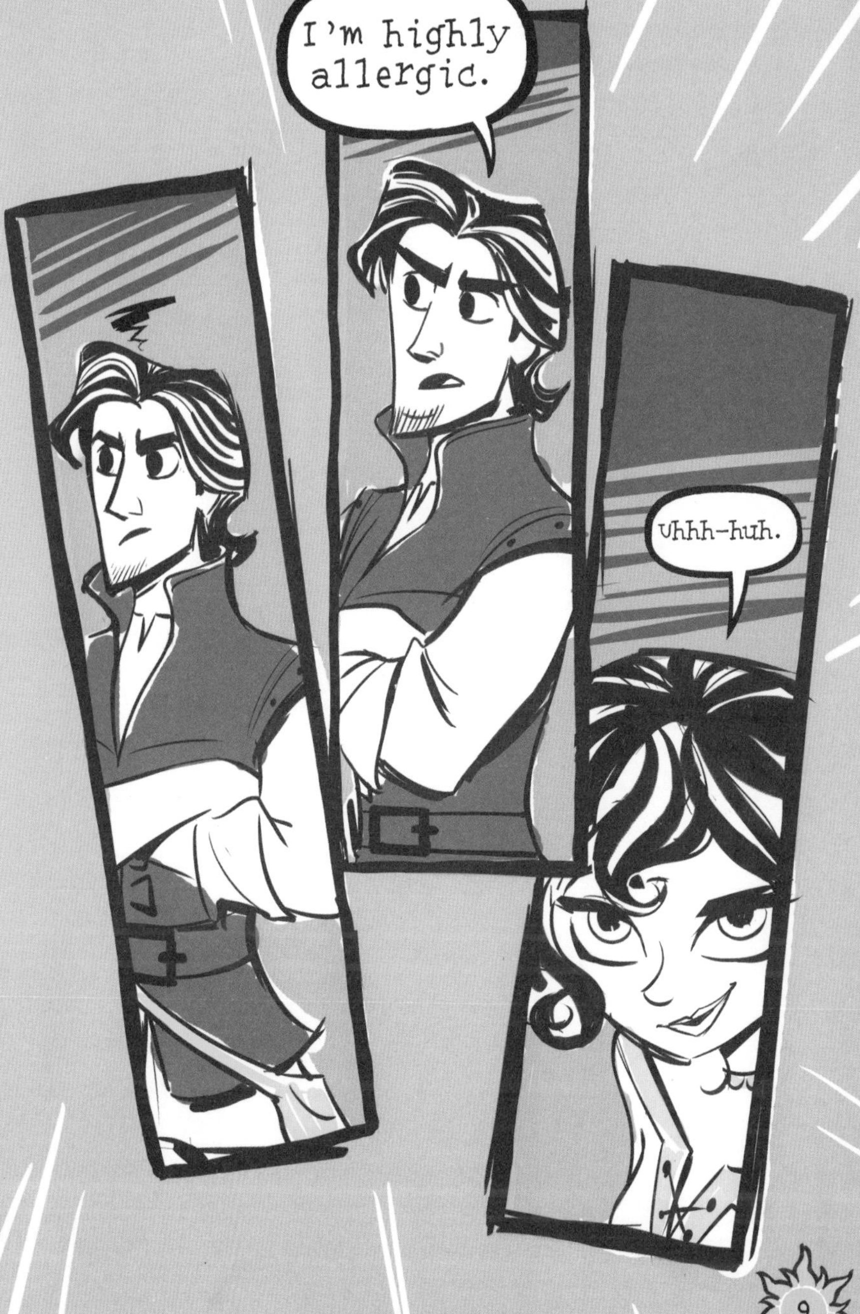
I'm highly allergic.
Uhhh-huh.

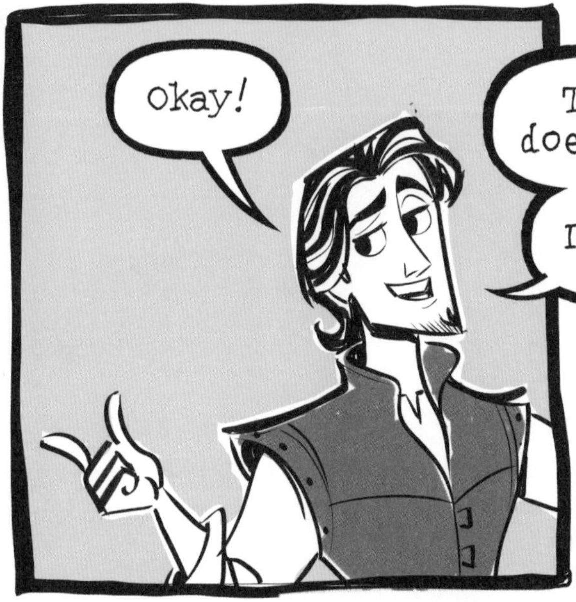
Okay!
That does it!
I am...

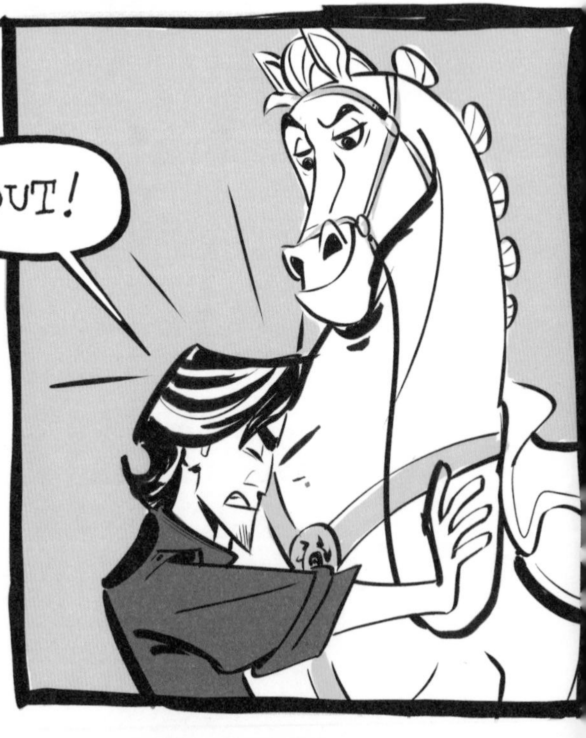
OUT!

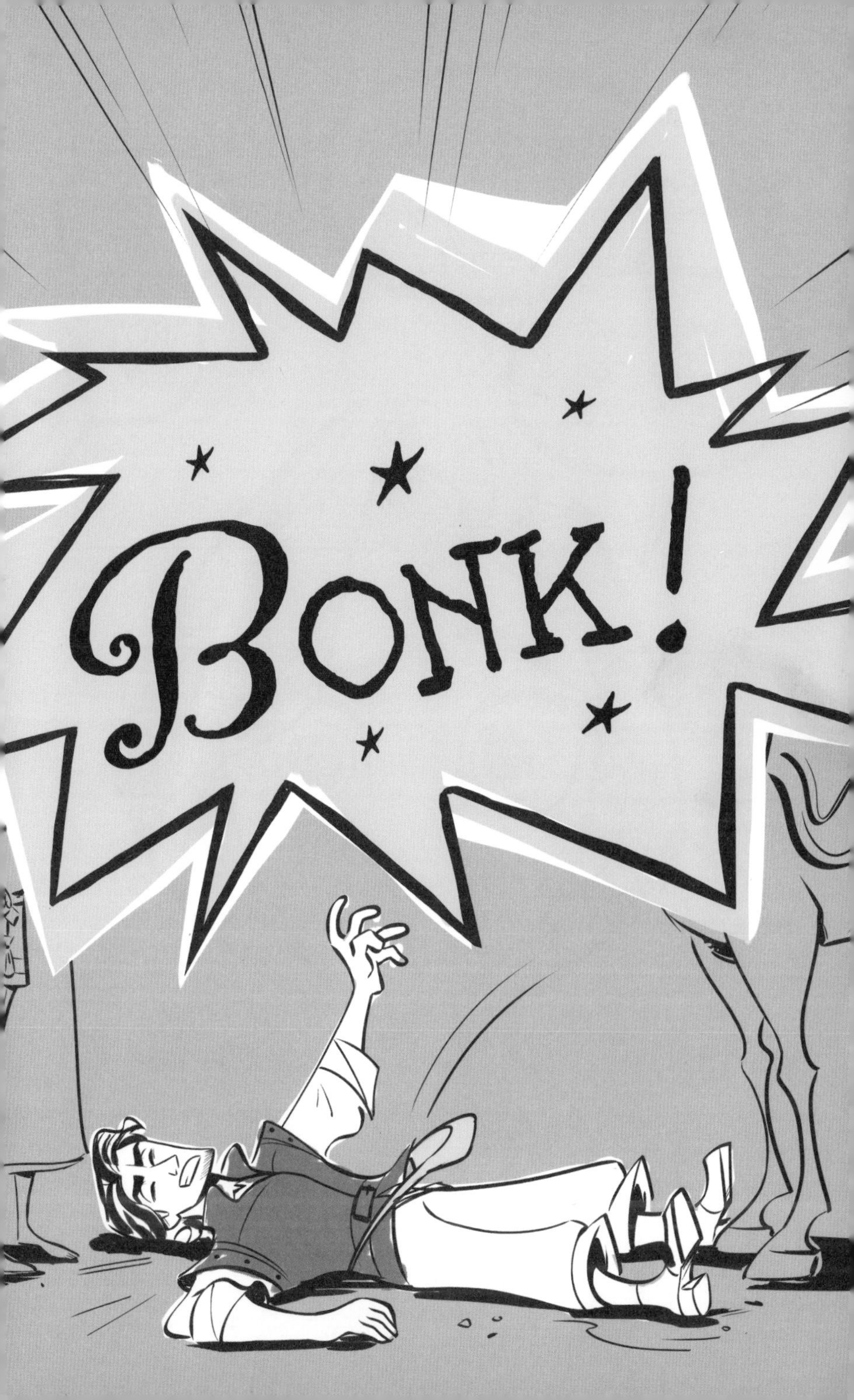
BONK!

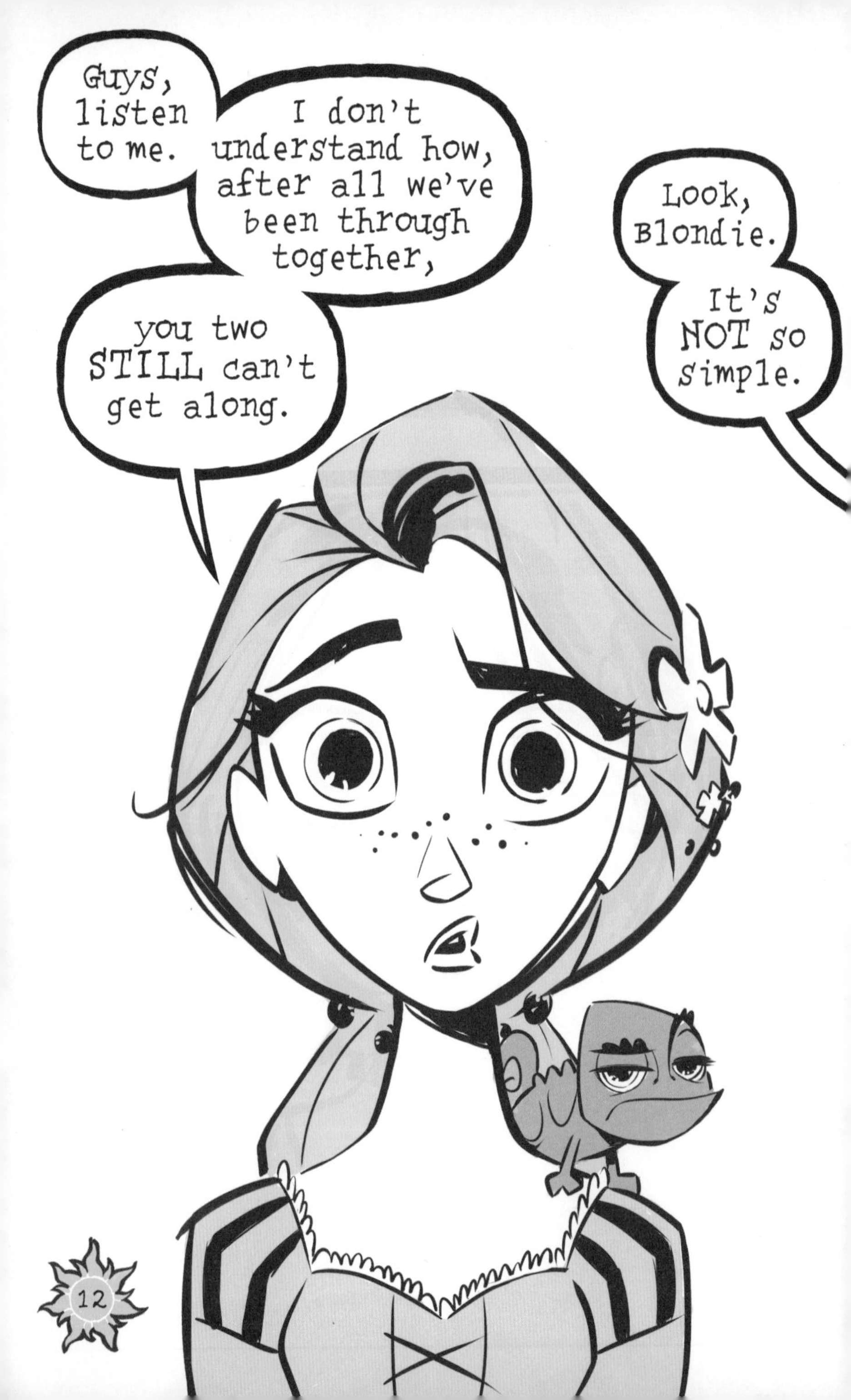
Guys, listen to me.
I don't understand how, after all we've been through together,
you two STILL can't get along.
Look, Blondie.
It's NOT so simple.

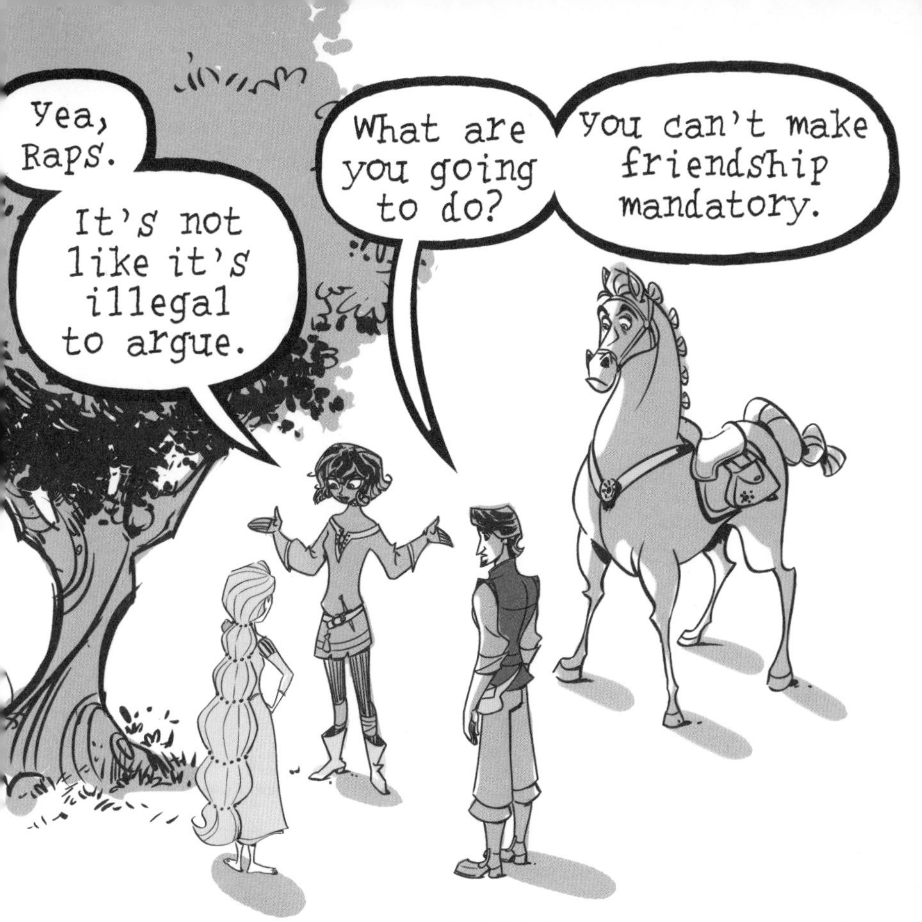
Yea, Raps.
It's not like it's illegal to argue.
What are you going to do?
You can't make friendship mandatory.

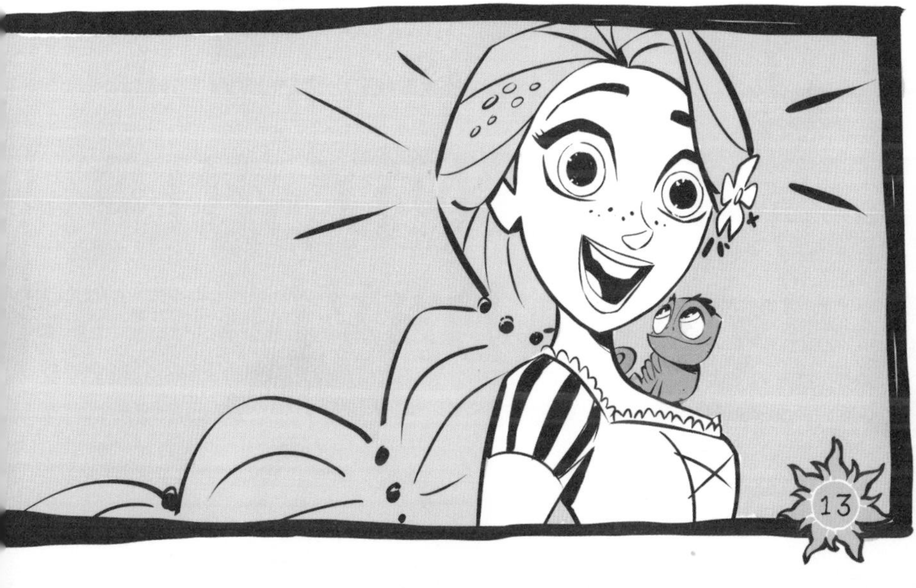

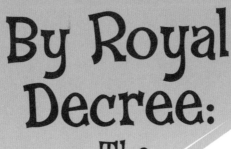

By Royal
Decree:
The
KINGDOM
of **CORONA**
hereby announces
that this Saturday will
be the first annual
**FRIENDSHIP
DAY!**

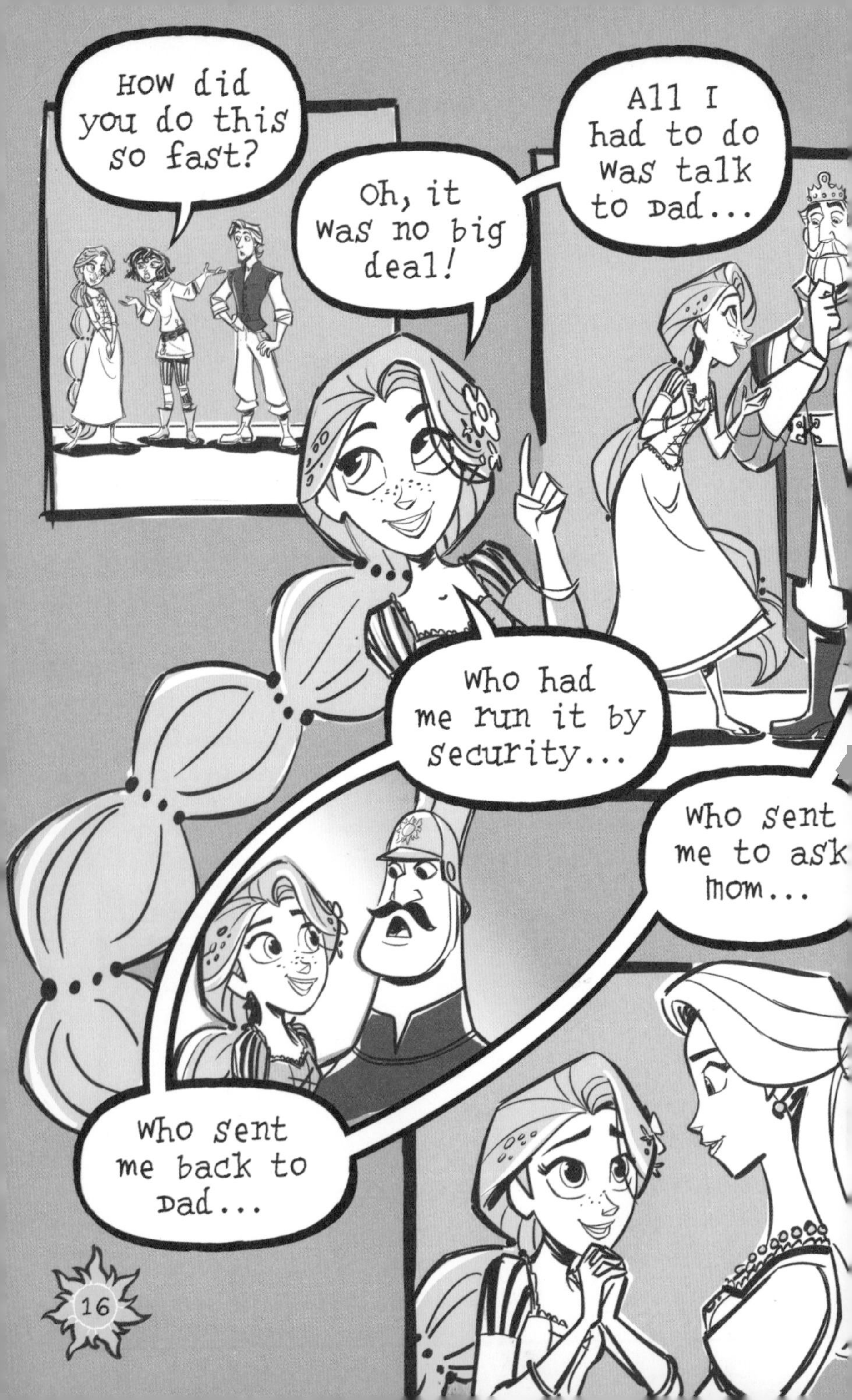
HOW did you do this so fast?
Oh, it was no big deal!
All I had to do was talk to Dad...
Who had me run it by security...
Who sent me to ask mom...
Who sent me back to Dad...

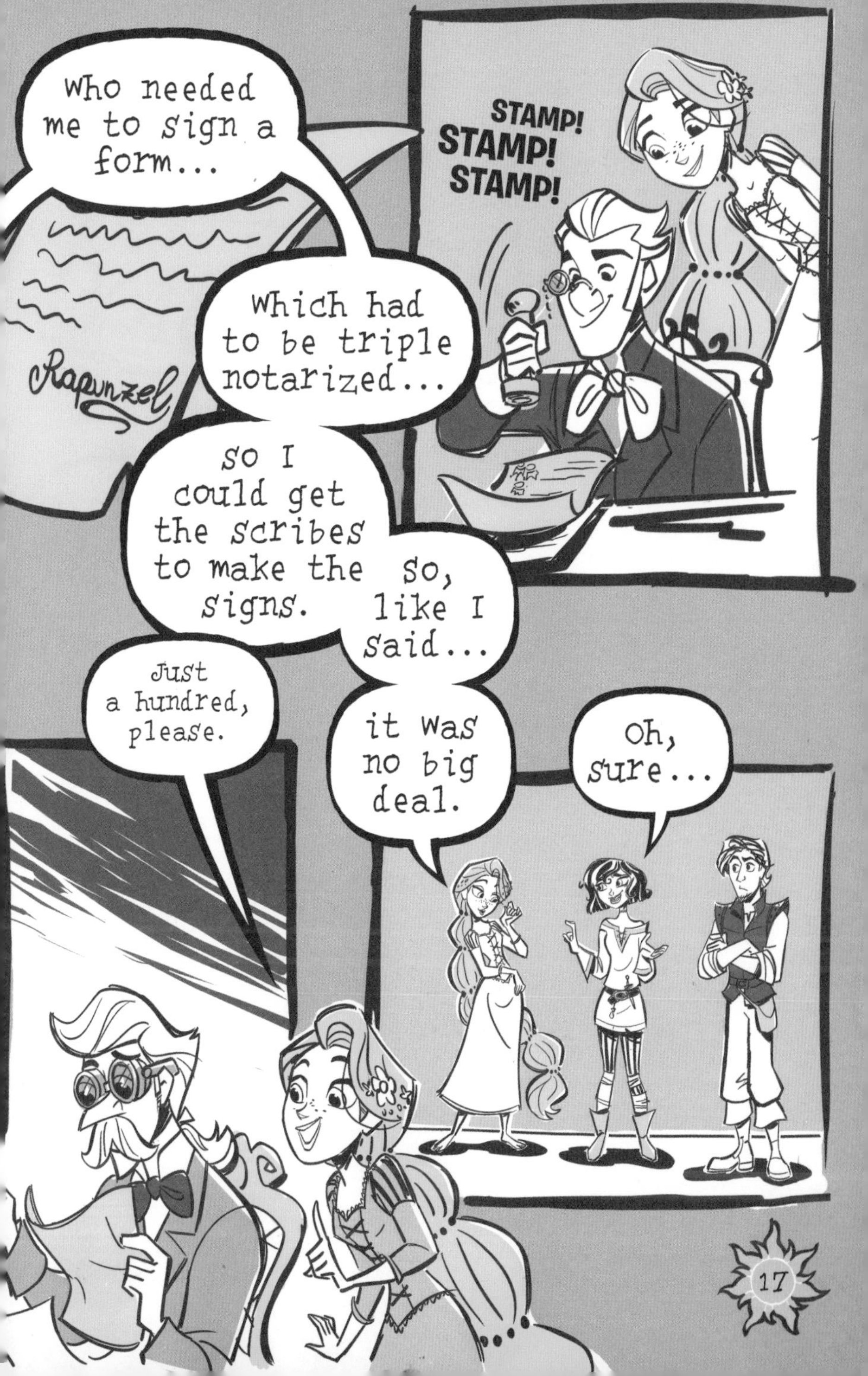
Who needed me to sign a form...
STAMP! STAMP! STAMP!
Rapunzel
Which had to be triple notarized...
so I could get the scribes to make the signs.
So, like I said...
Just a hundred, please.
it was no big deal.
Oh, sure...

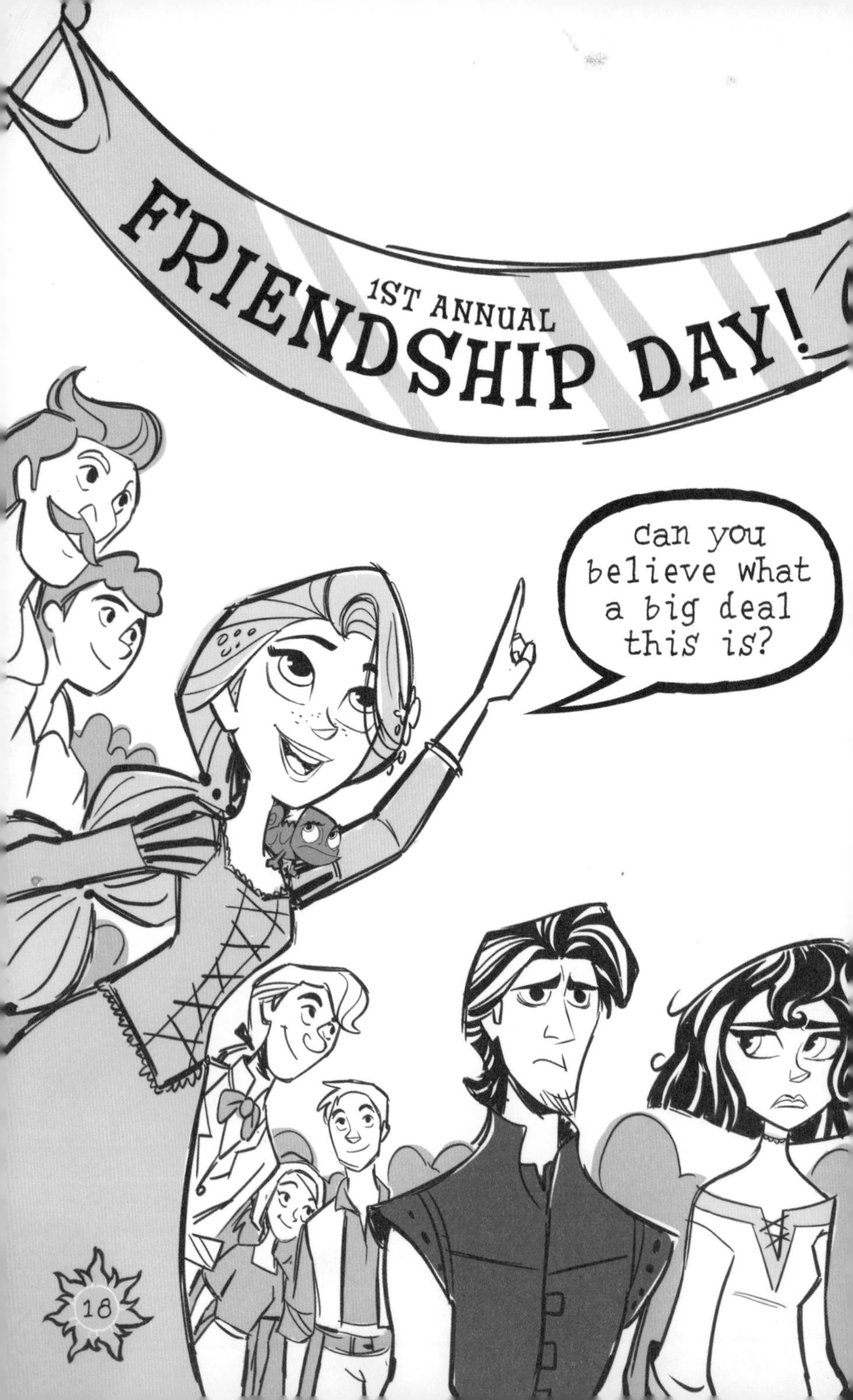
1ST ANNUAL
FRIENDSHIP DAY!
can you believe what a big deal this is?

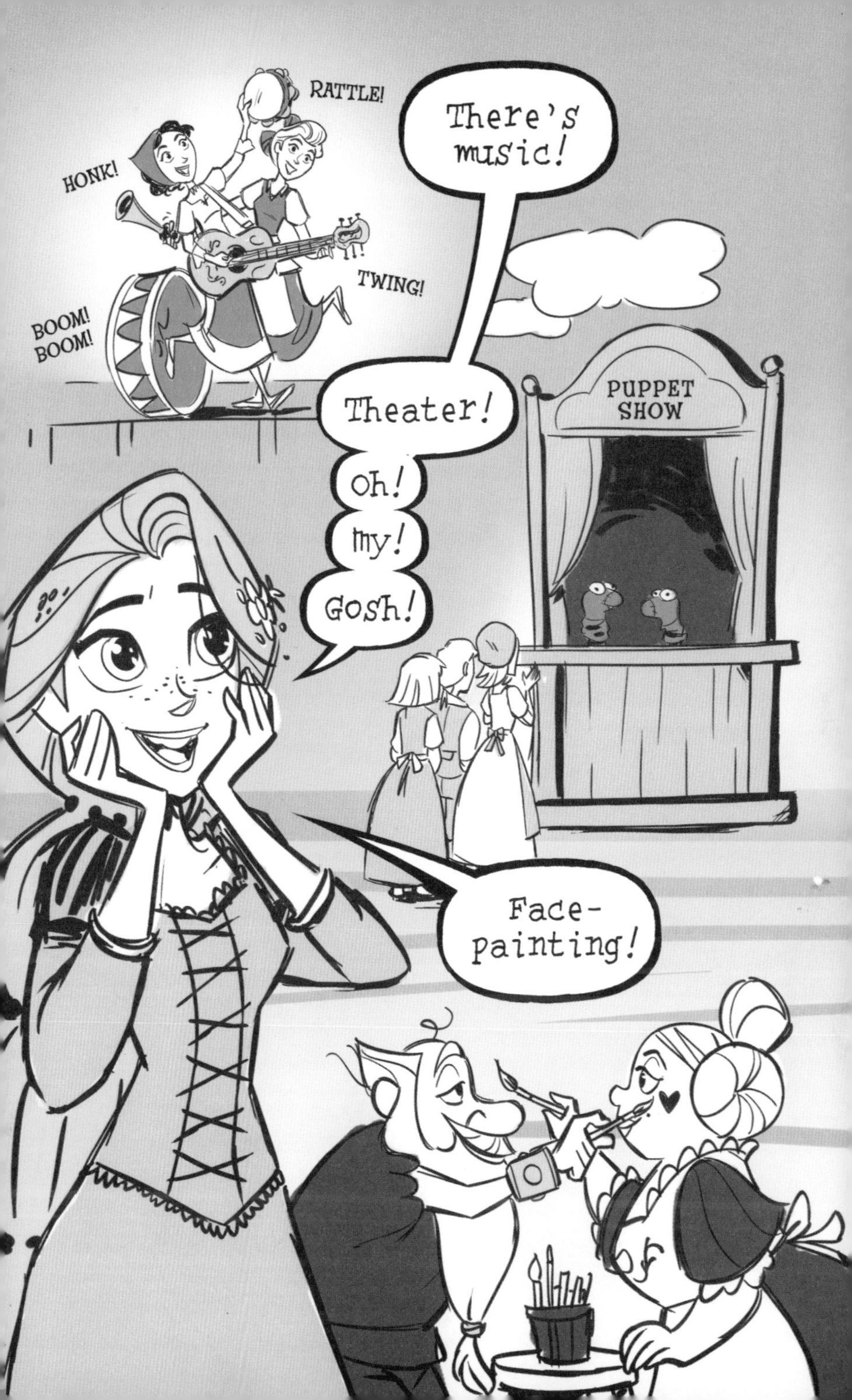
RATTLE!
HONK!
TWING!
BOOM! BOOM!
There's music!
Theater!
Oh!
my!
Gosh!
PUPPET SHOW
Face-painting!

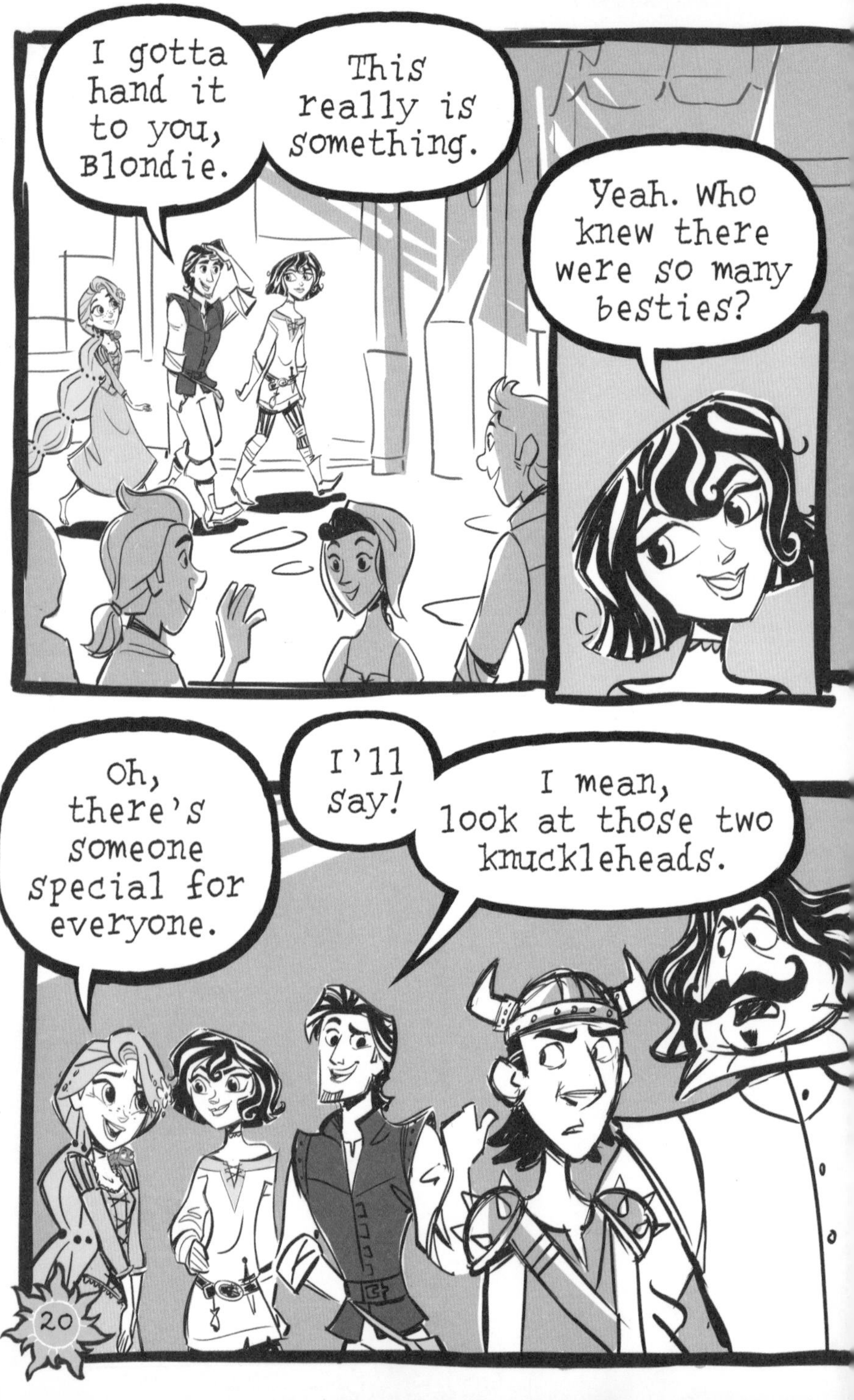
I gotta hand it to you, Blondie.
This really is something.
Yeah. Who knew there were so many besties?
Oh, there's someone special for everyone.
I'll say!
I mean, look at those two knuckleheads.

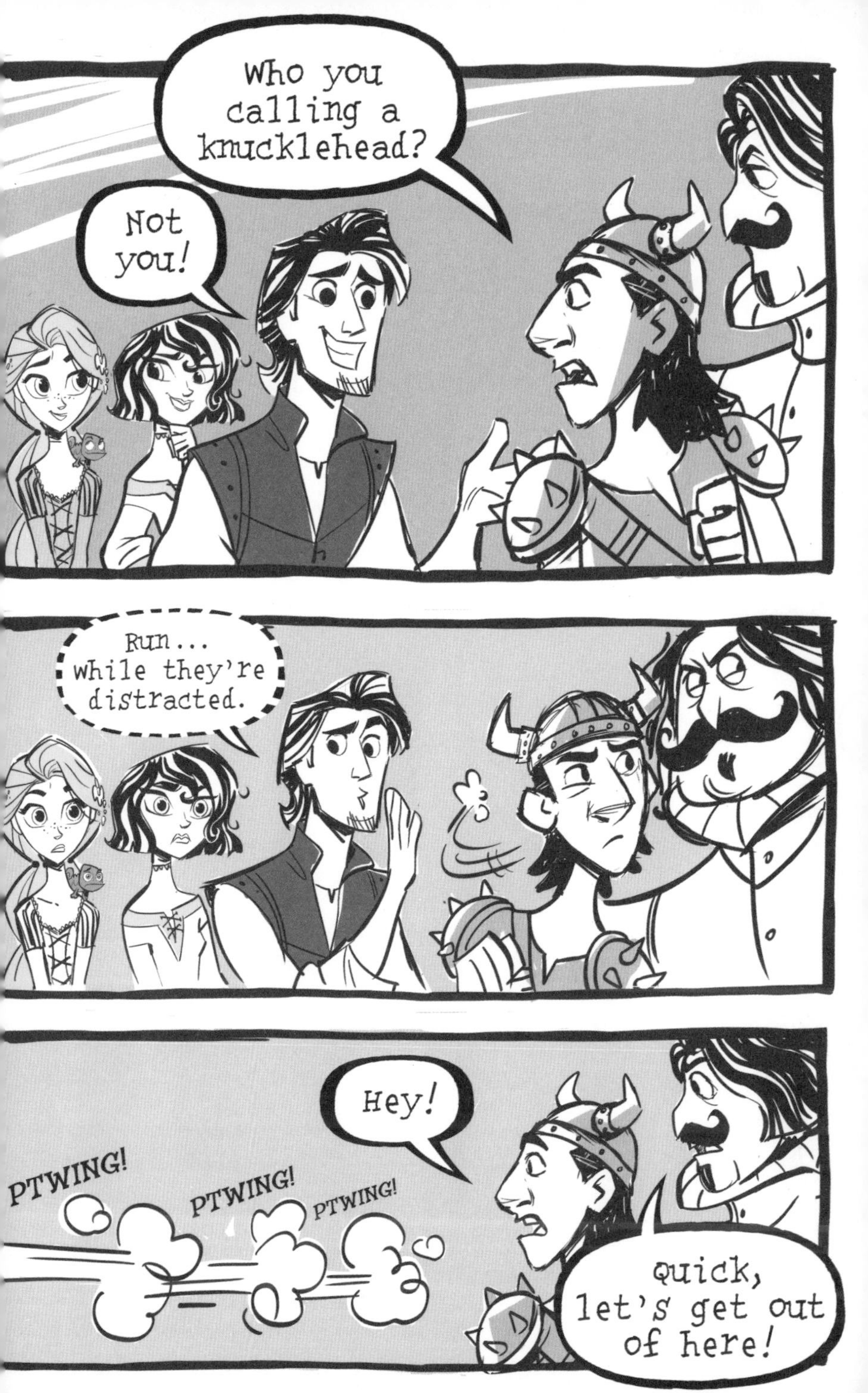
Who you calling a knucklehead?
Not you!
Run... while they're distracted.
PTWING!
PTWING!
PTWING!
Hey!
Quick, let's get out of here!

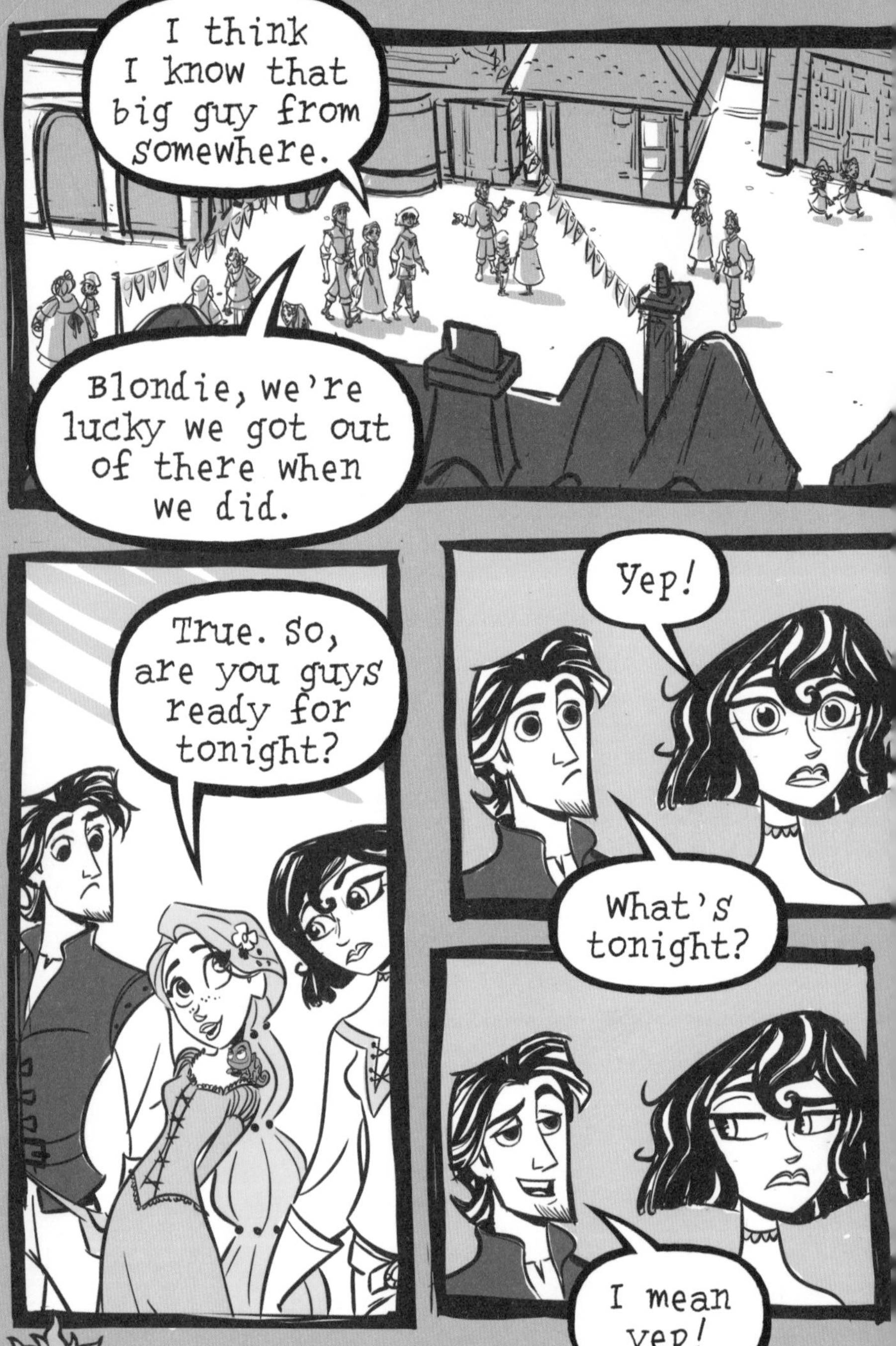
I think I know that big guy from somewhere.
Blondie, we're lucky we got out of there when we did.
True. So, are you guys ready for tonight?
Yep!
What's tonight?
I mean yep!

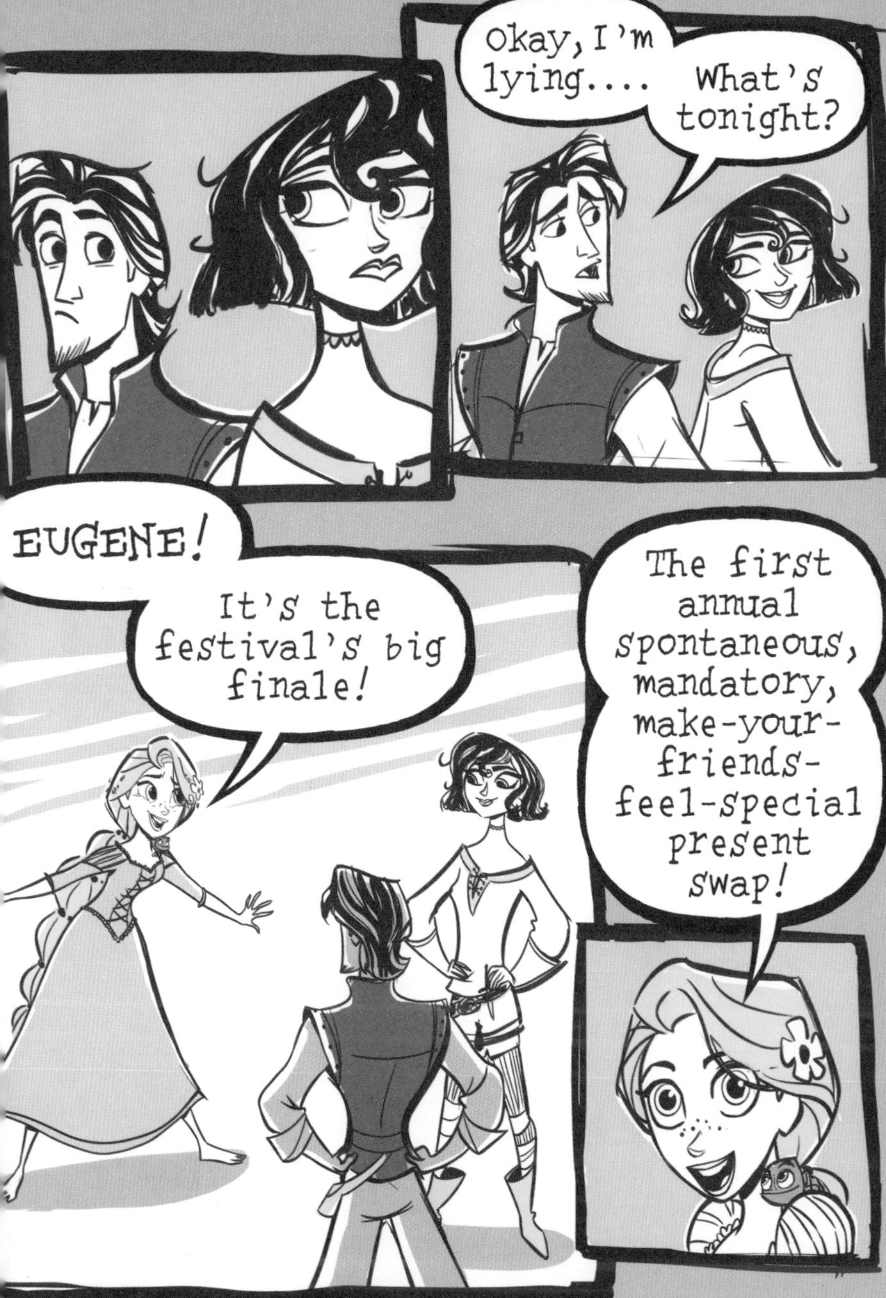
Okay, I'm lying....
What's tonight?
EUGENE!
It's the festival's big finale!
The first annual spontaneous, mandatory, make-your-friends-feel-special present swap!

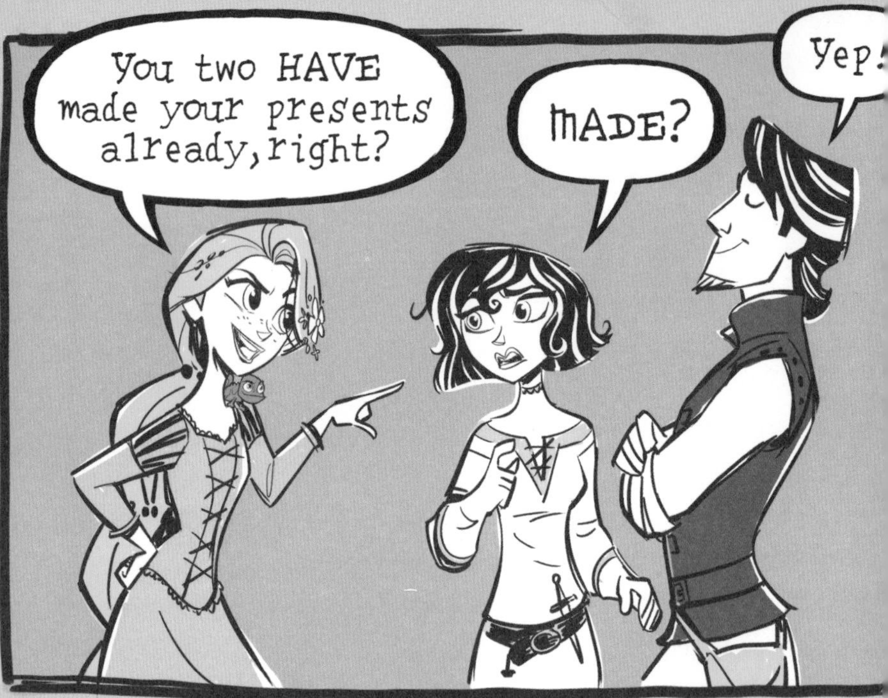
You two HAVE made your presents already, right?
MADE?
Yep!

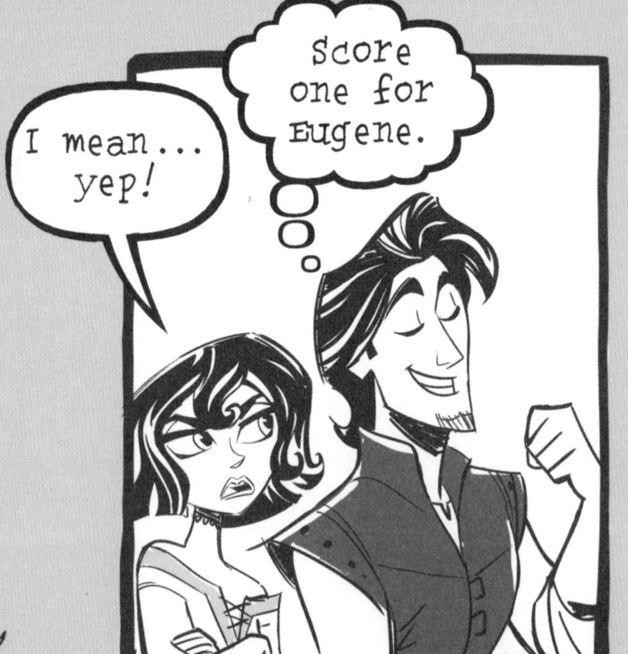
I mean... yep!
Score one for Eugene.

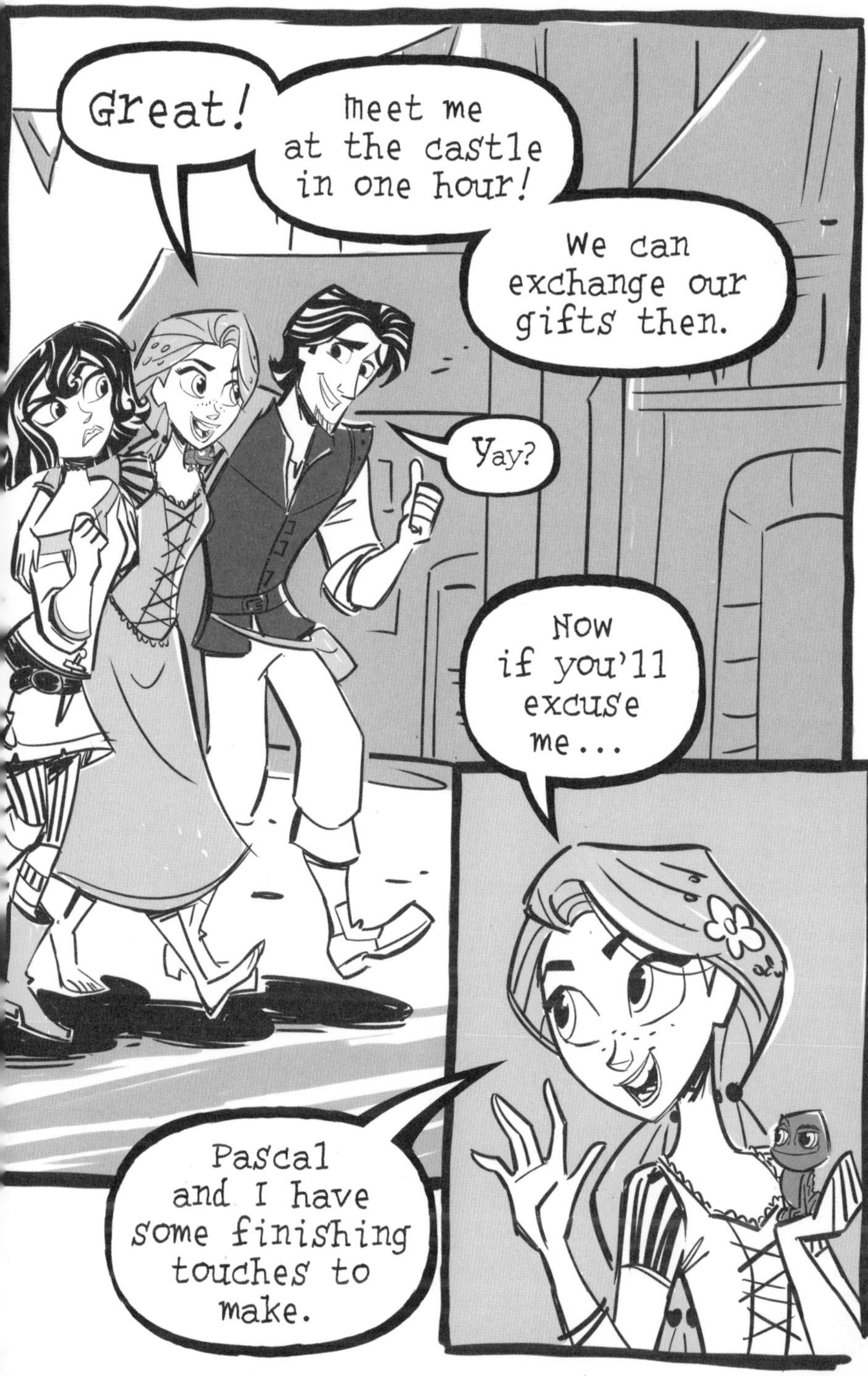
Great!
Meet me at the castle in one hour!
We can exchange our gifts then.
Yay?
Now if you'll excuse me...
Pascal and I have some finishing touches to make.

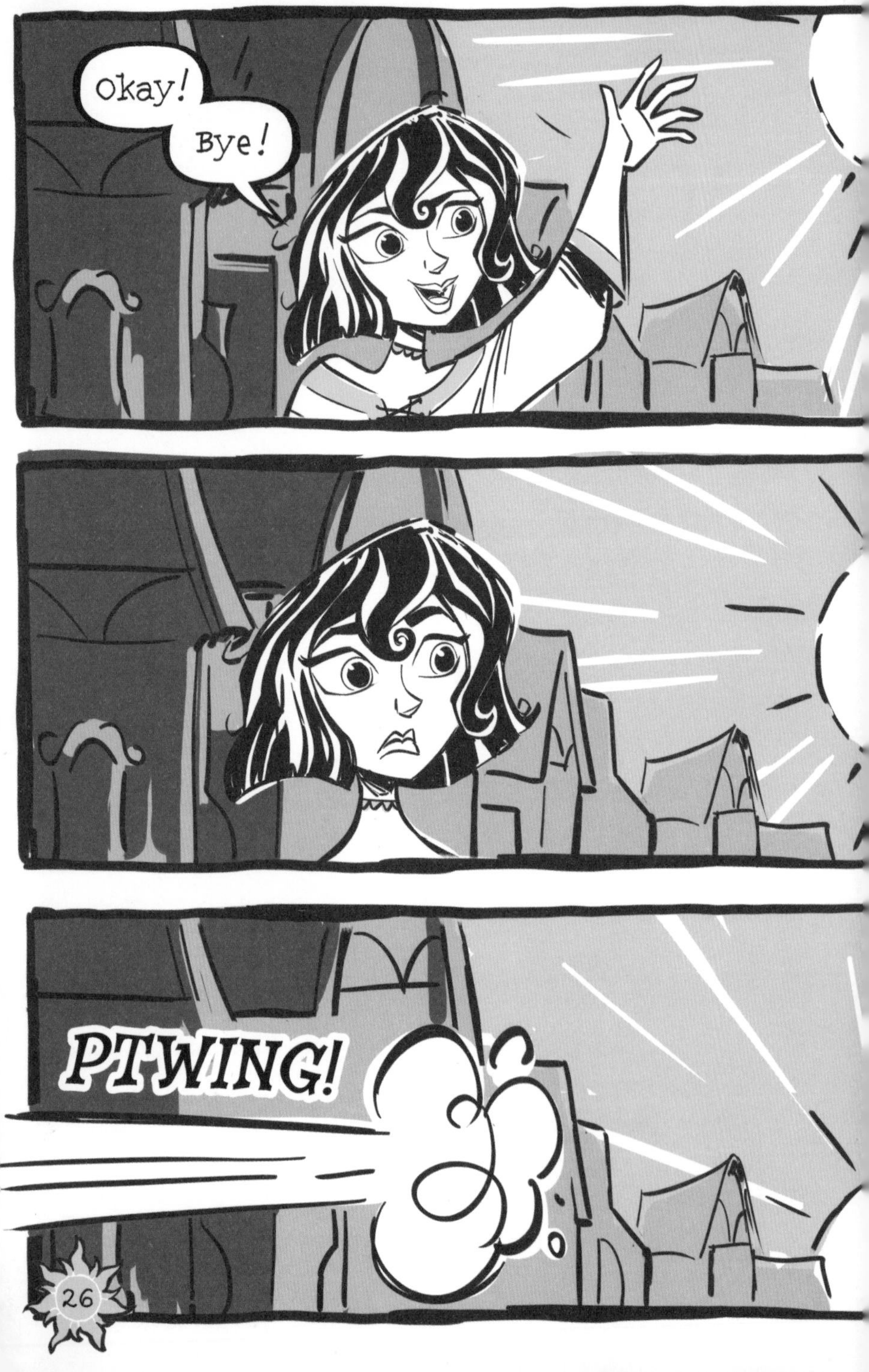
Okay!
Bye!
PTWING!

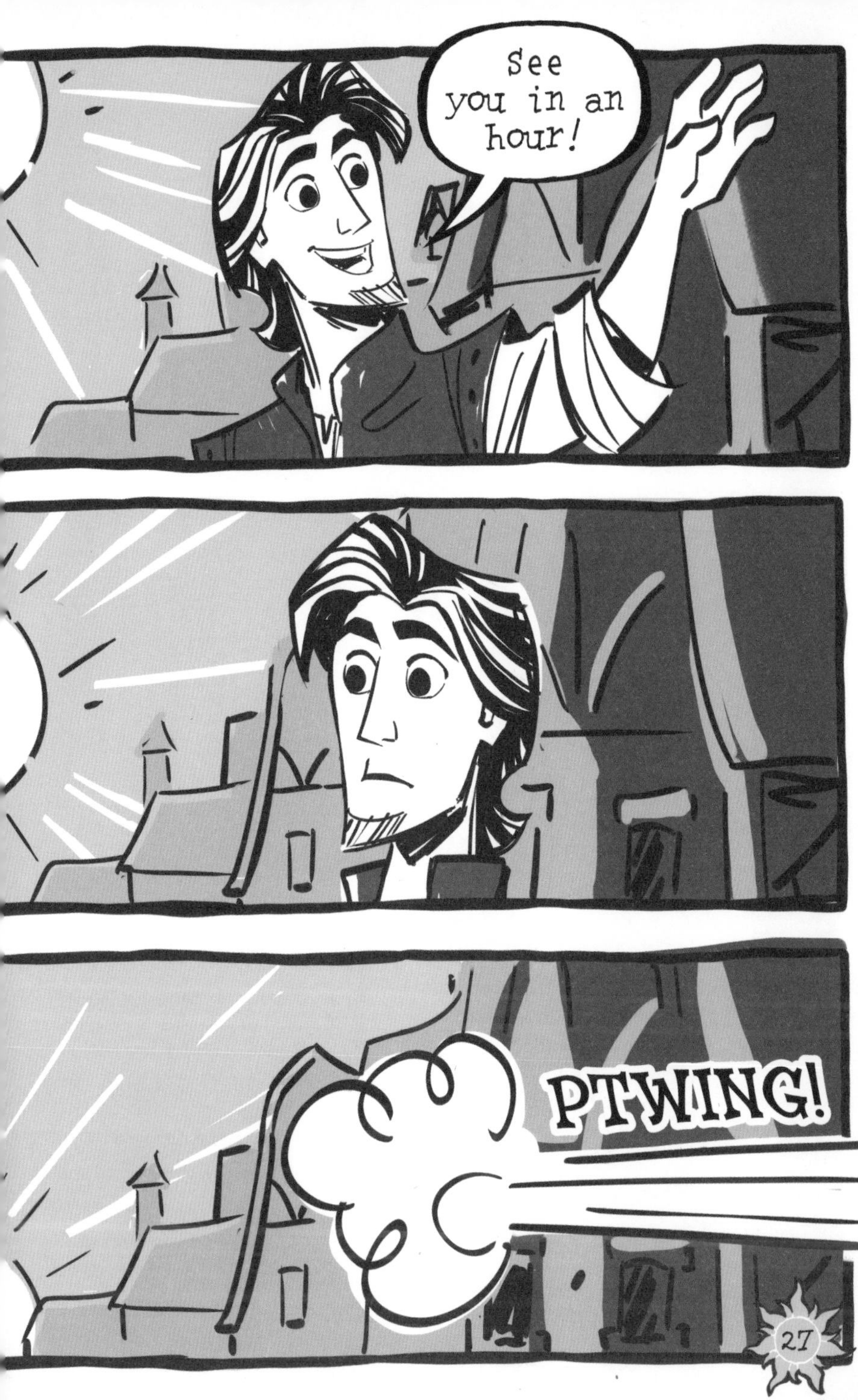
See you in an hour!
PTWING!

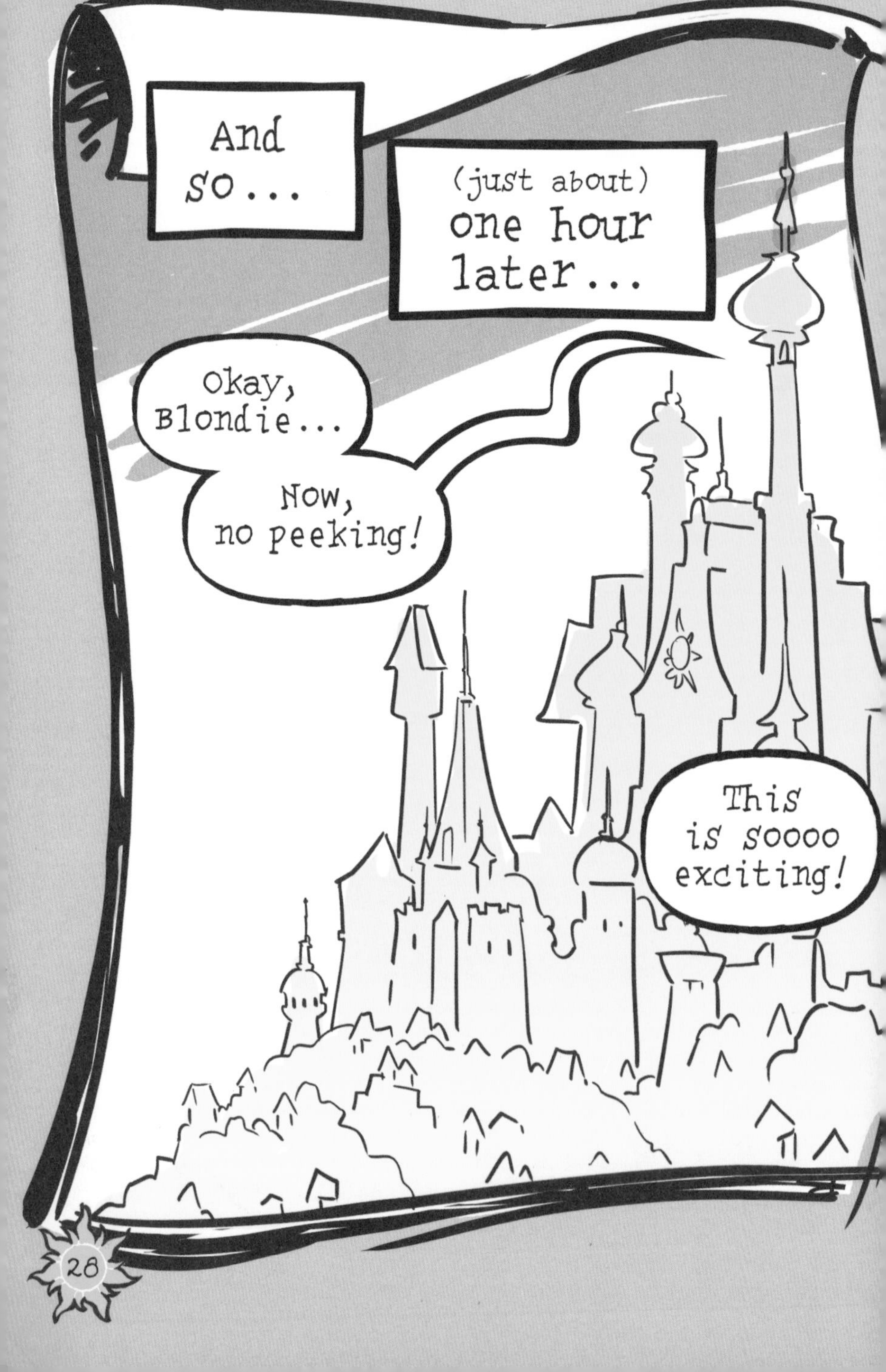
And so...
(just about) one hour later...
Okay, Blondie...
Now, no peeking!
This is soooo exciting!

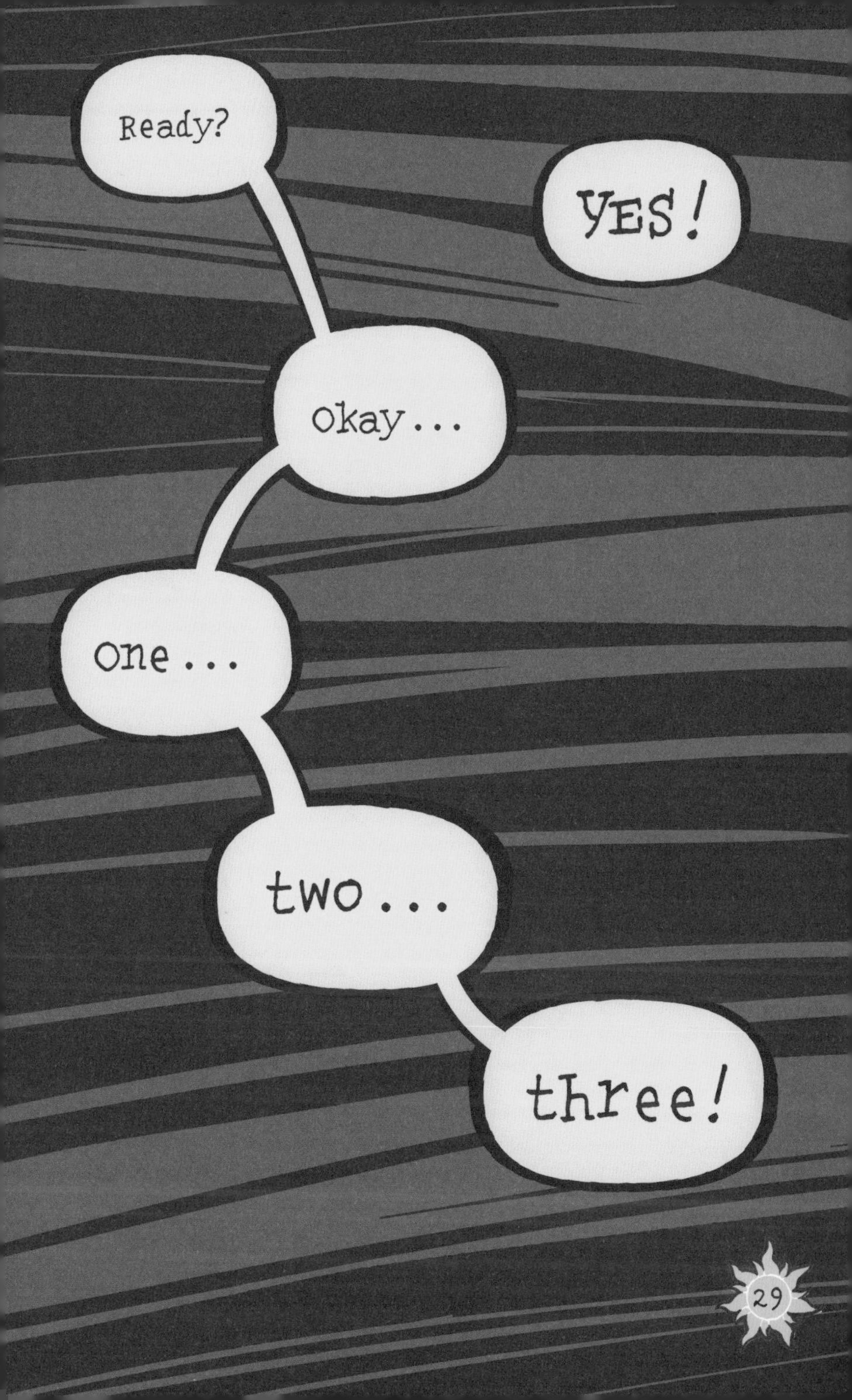
Ready?
YES!
Okay...
one...
two...
three!

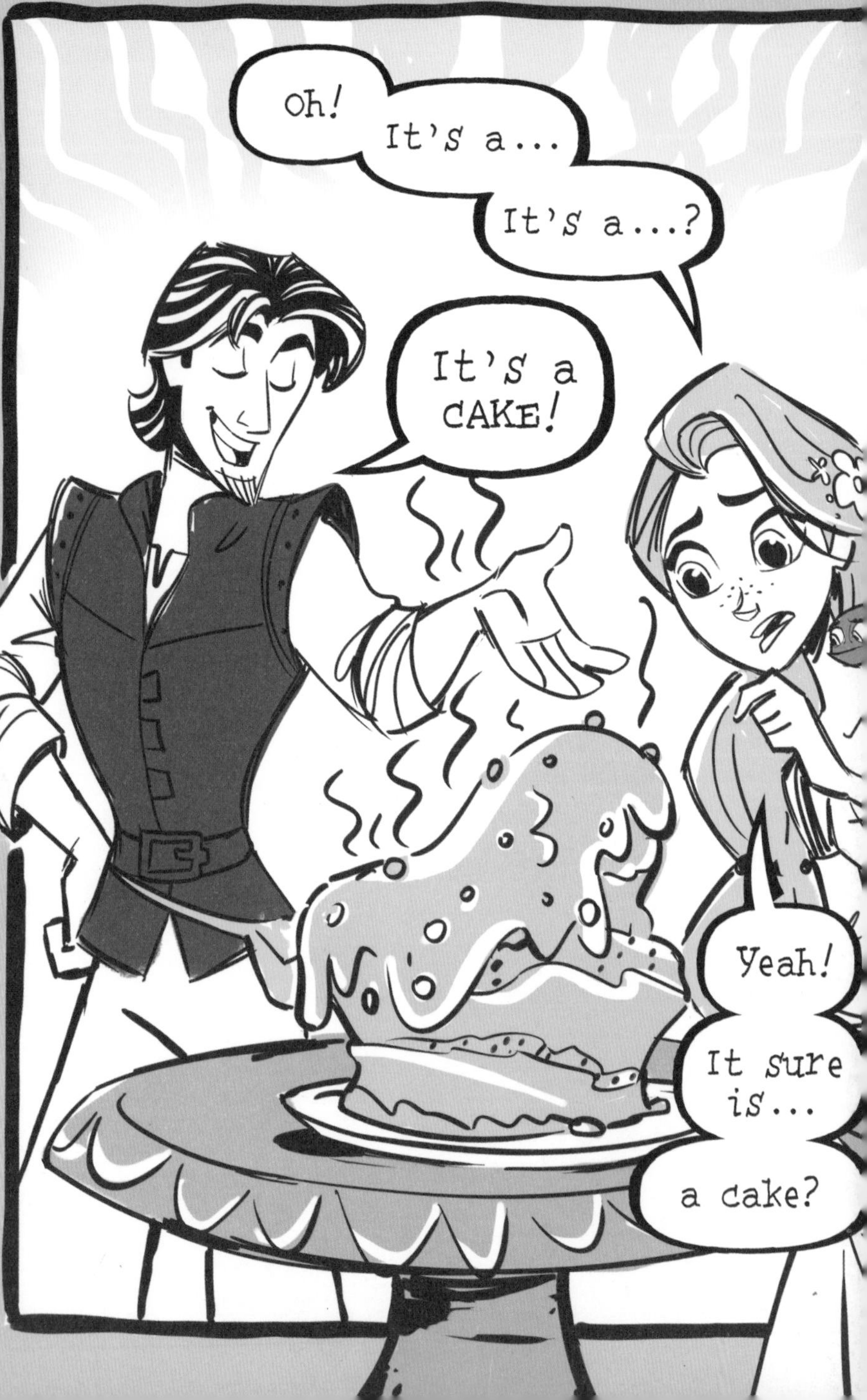
Oh!
It's a...
It's a...?
It's a CAKE!
Yeah!
It sure is...
a cake?

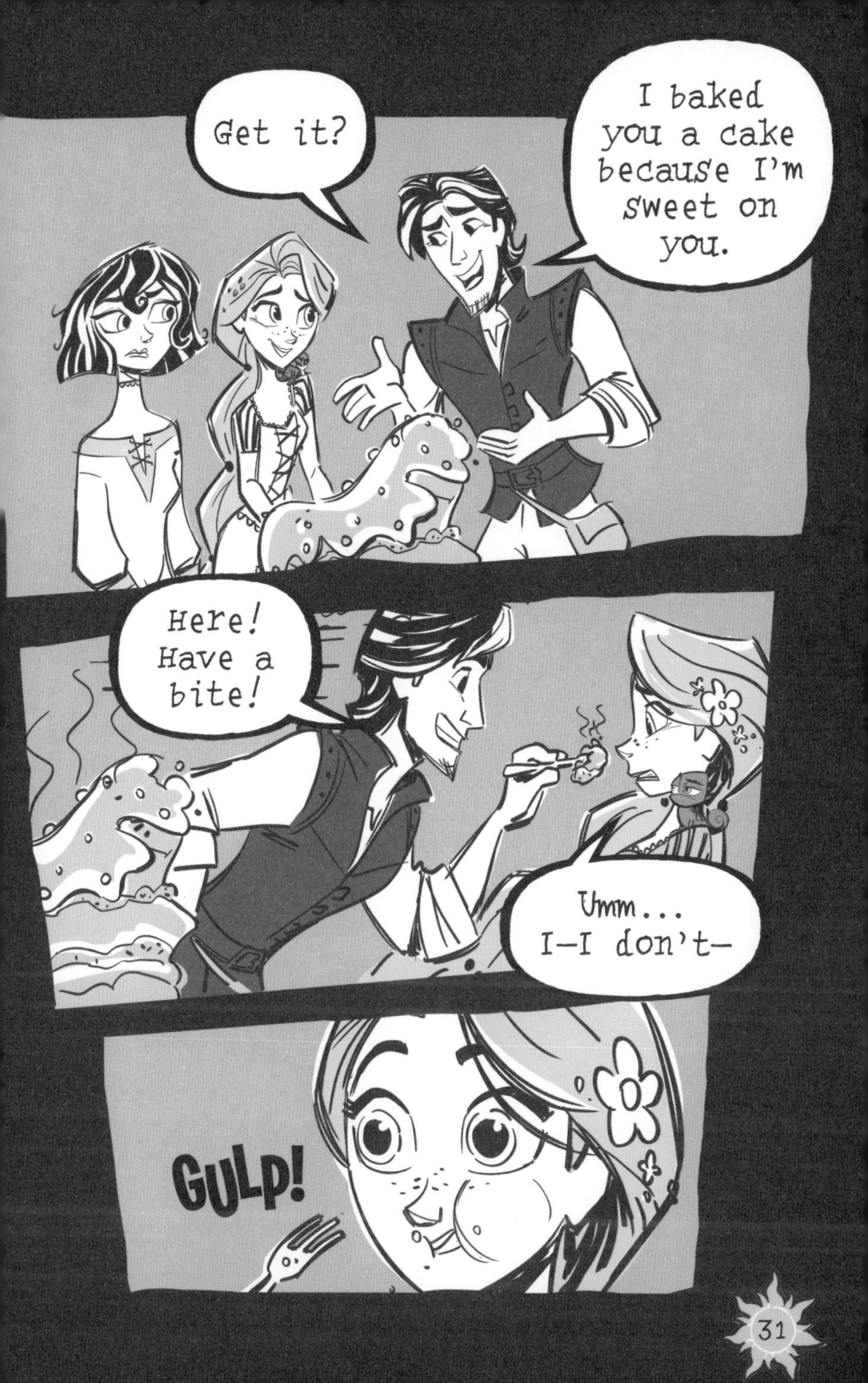

Get it?
I baked you a cake because I'm sweet on you.
Here! Have a bite!
Umm... I—I don't—
GULP!

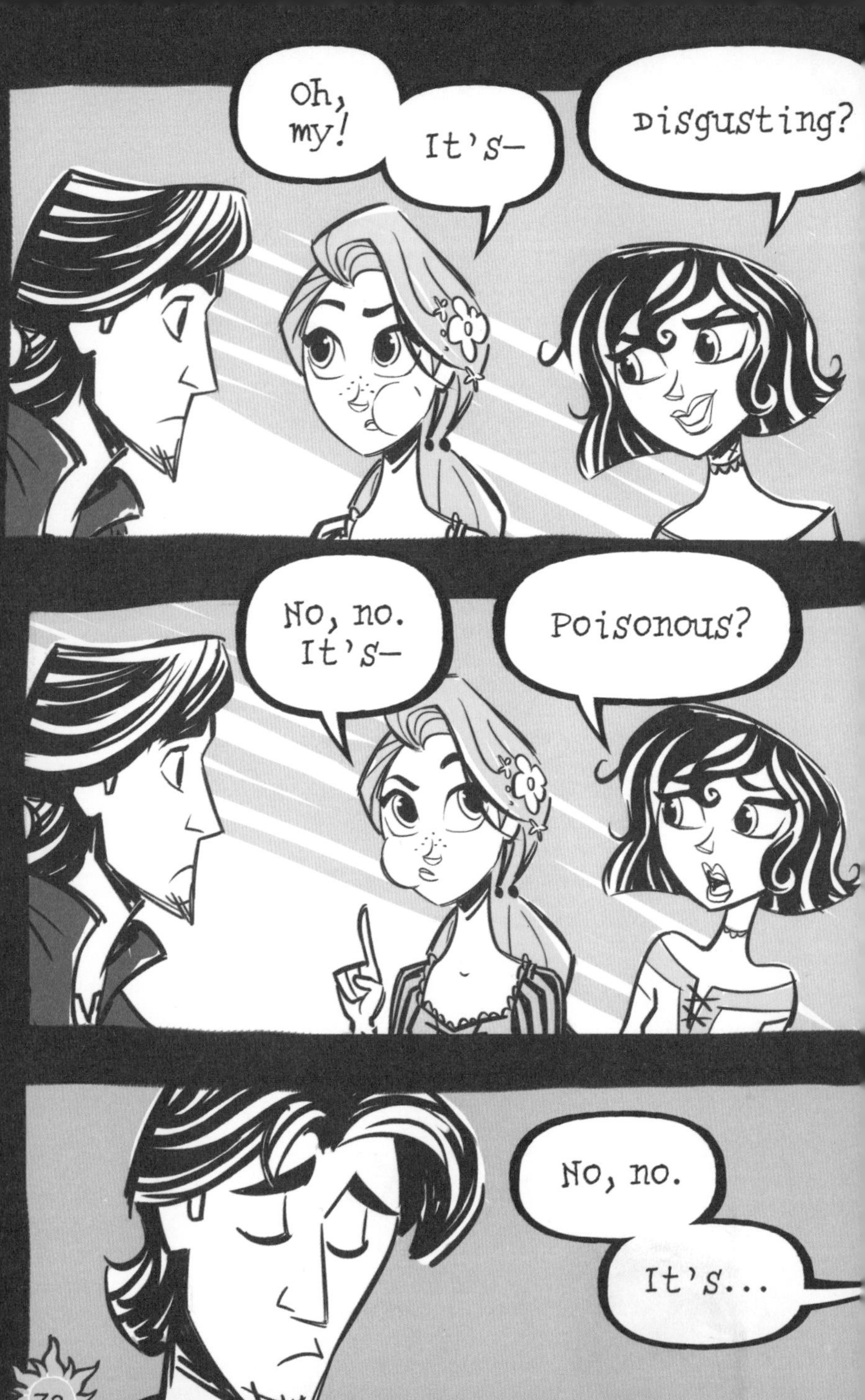
Oh, my!
It's—
Disgusting?
No, no. It's—
Poisonous?
No, no.
It's...

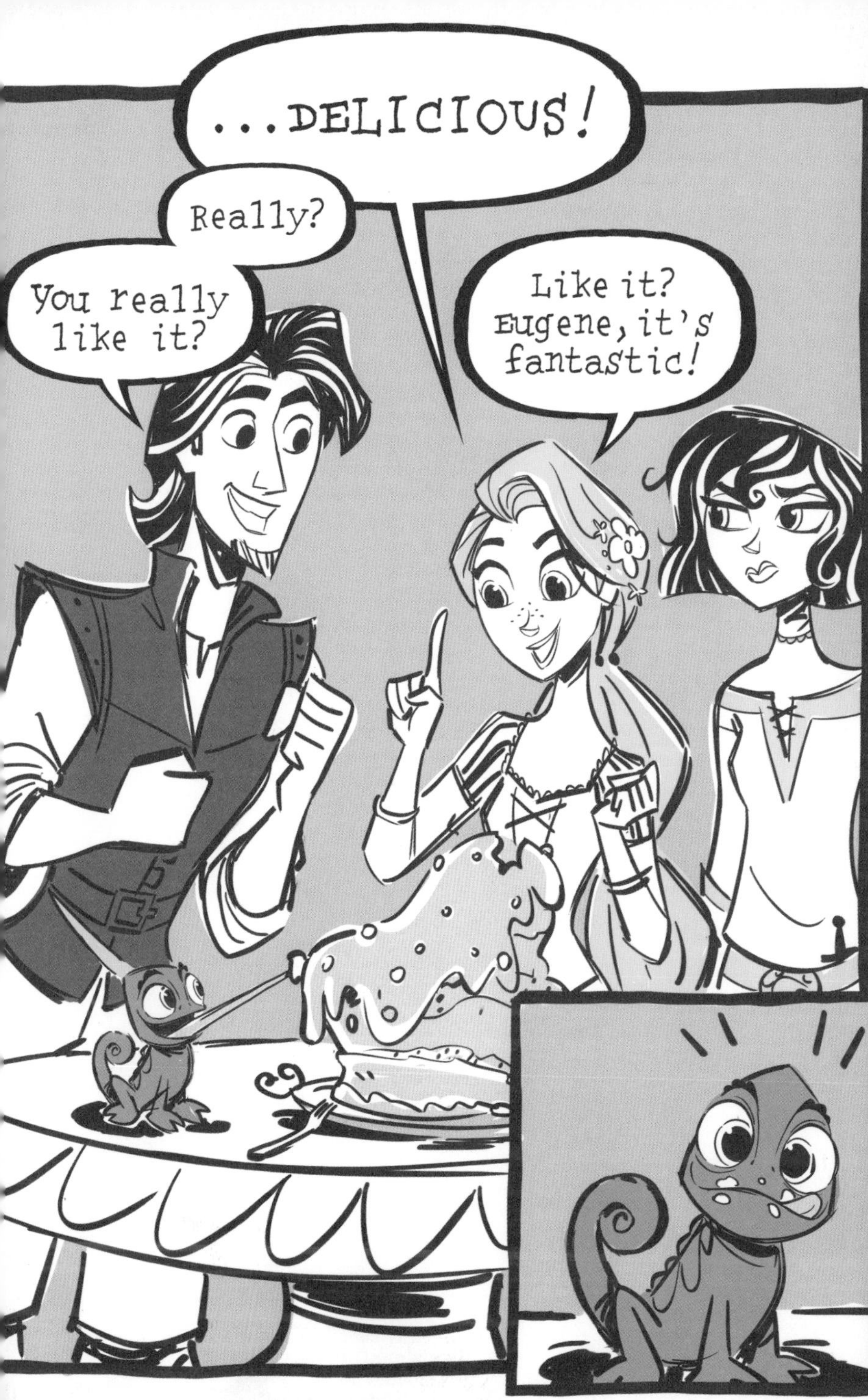
...DELICIOUS!
Really?
You really like it?
Like it? Eugene, it's fantastic!

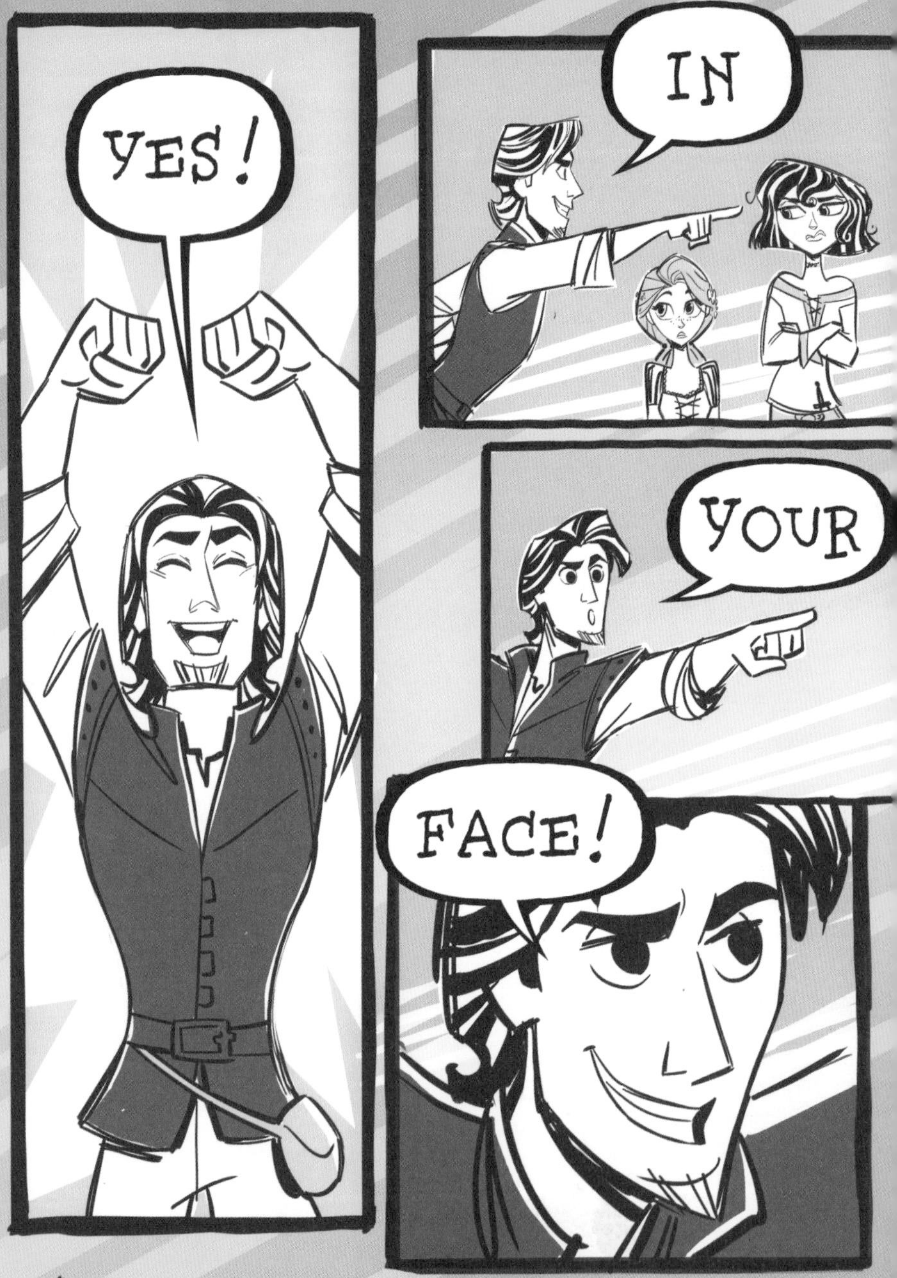
YES!
IN
YOUR
FACE!

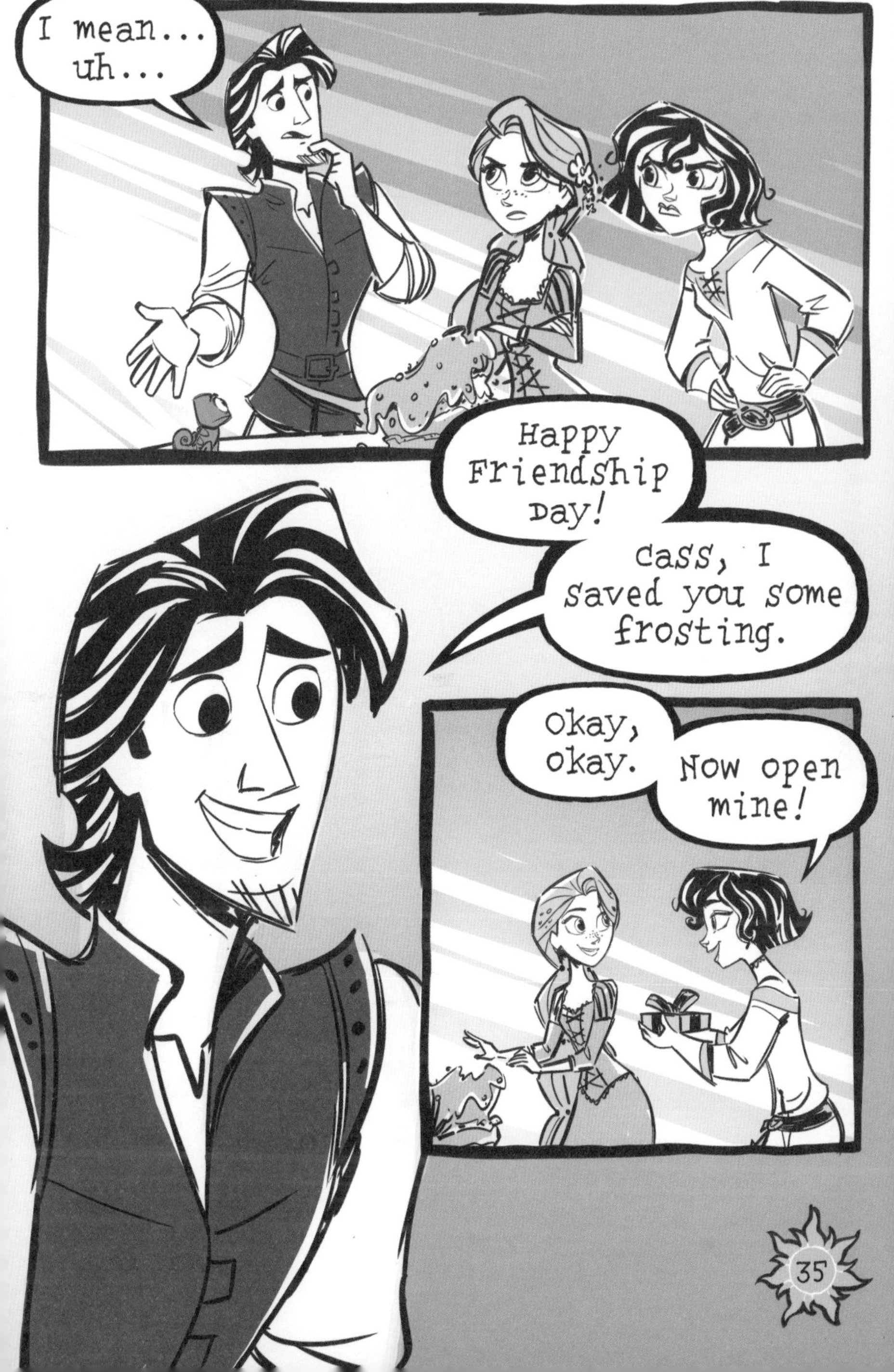
I mean... uh...
Happy Friendship Day!
Cass, I saved you some frosting.
Okay, okay.
Now open mine!

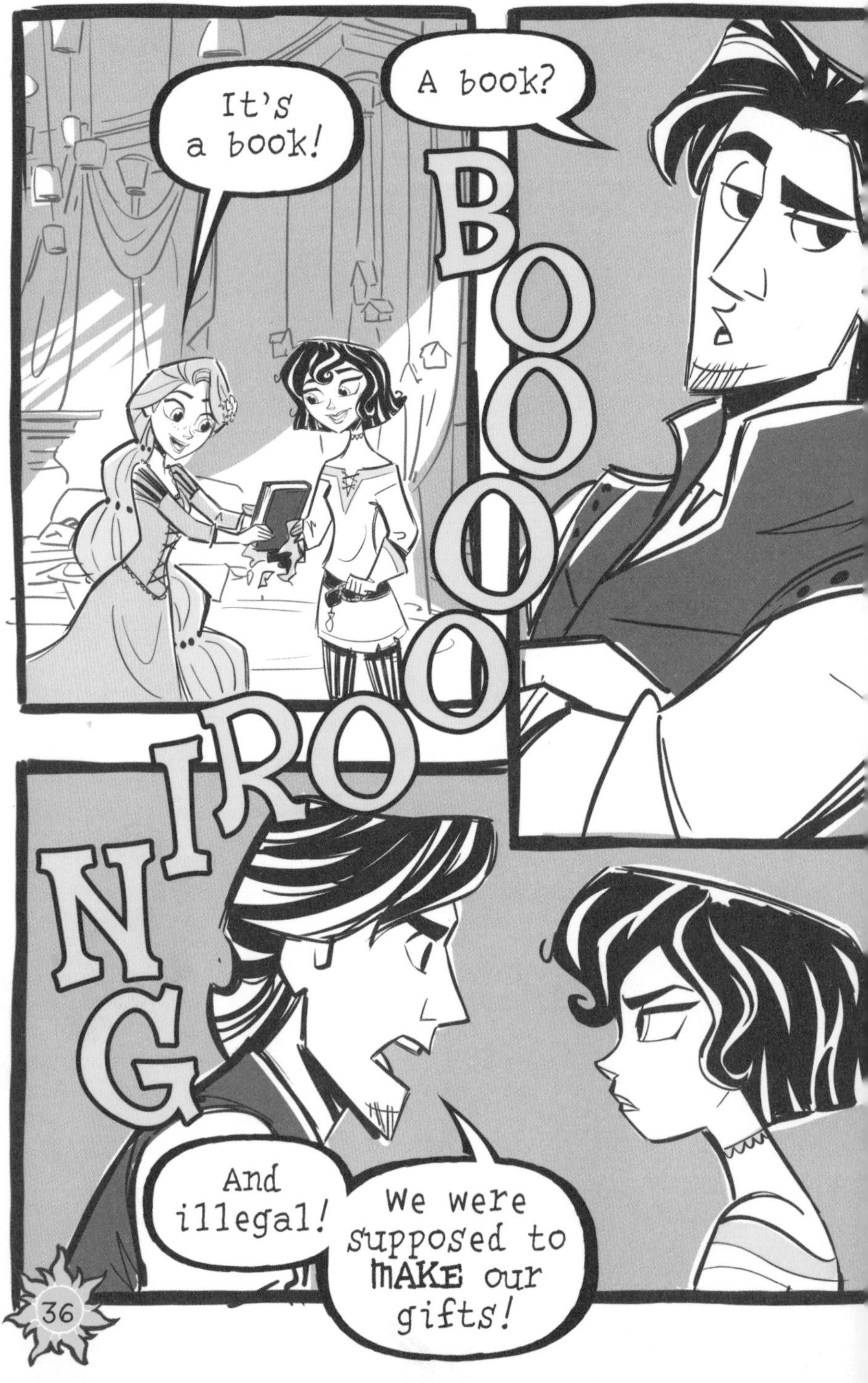
It's a book!
A book?
BOOOOORING
And illegal!
We were supposed to MAKE our gifts!

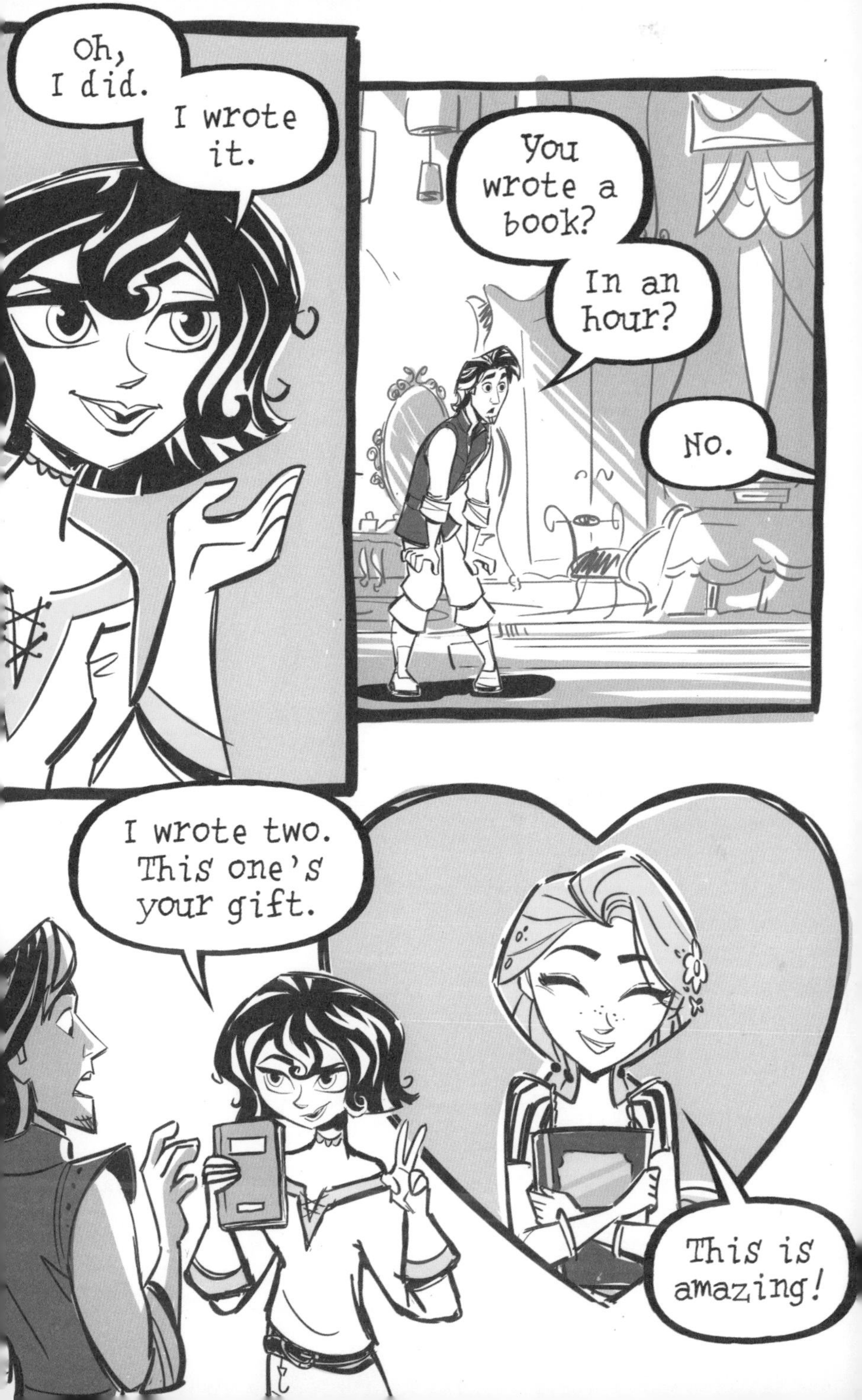
Oh, I did.
I wrote it.
You wrote a book?
In an hour?
No.
I wrote two. This one's your gift.
This is amazing!

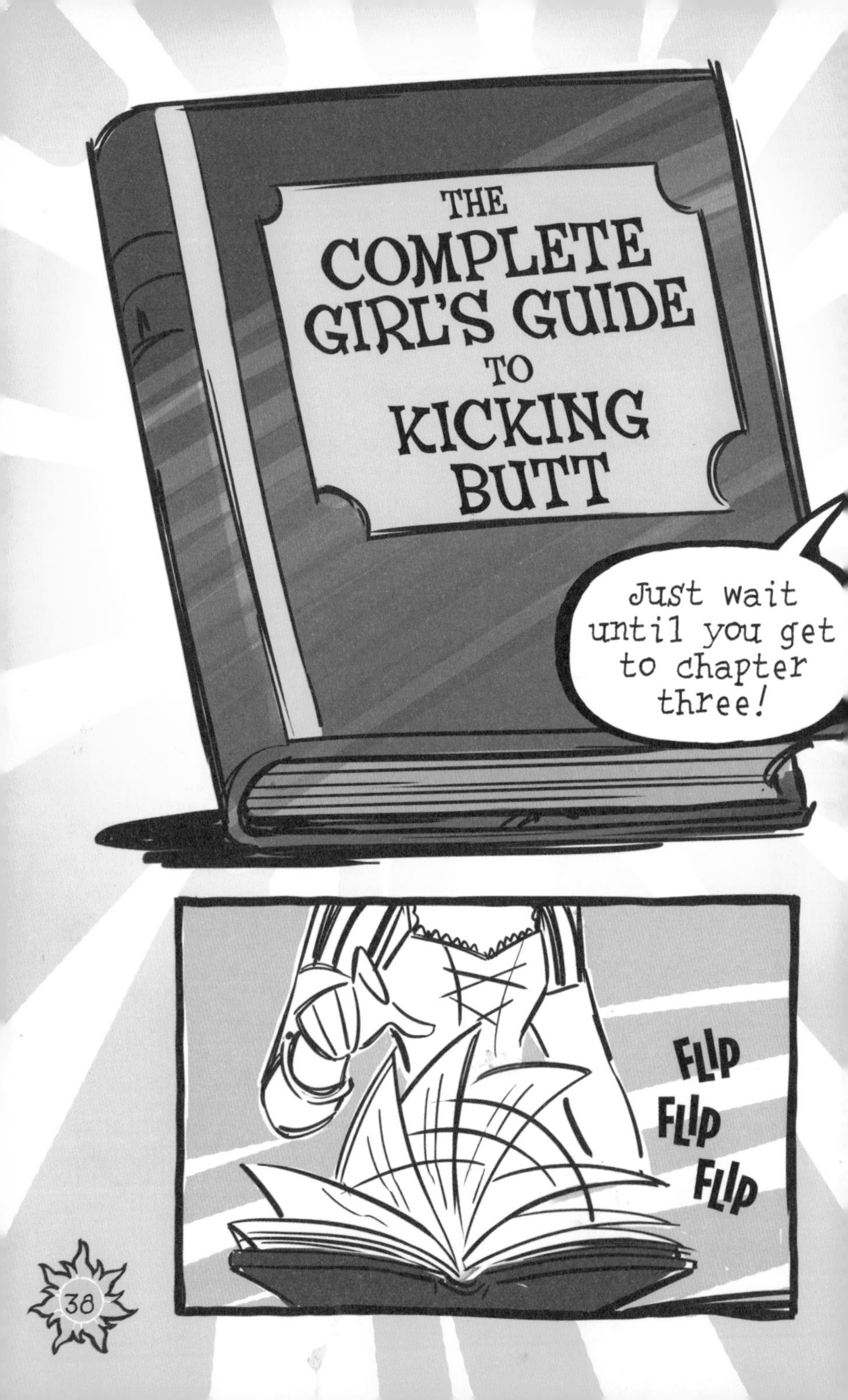
THE COMPLETE GIRL'S GUIDE TO KICKING BUTT
Just wait until you get to chapter three!
FLIP
FLIP
FLIP

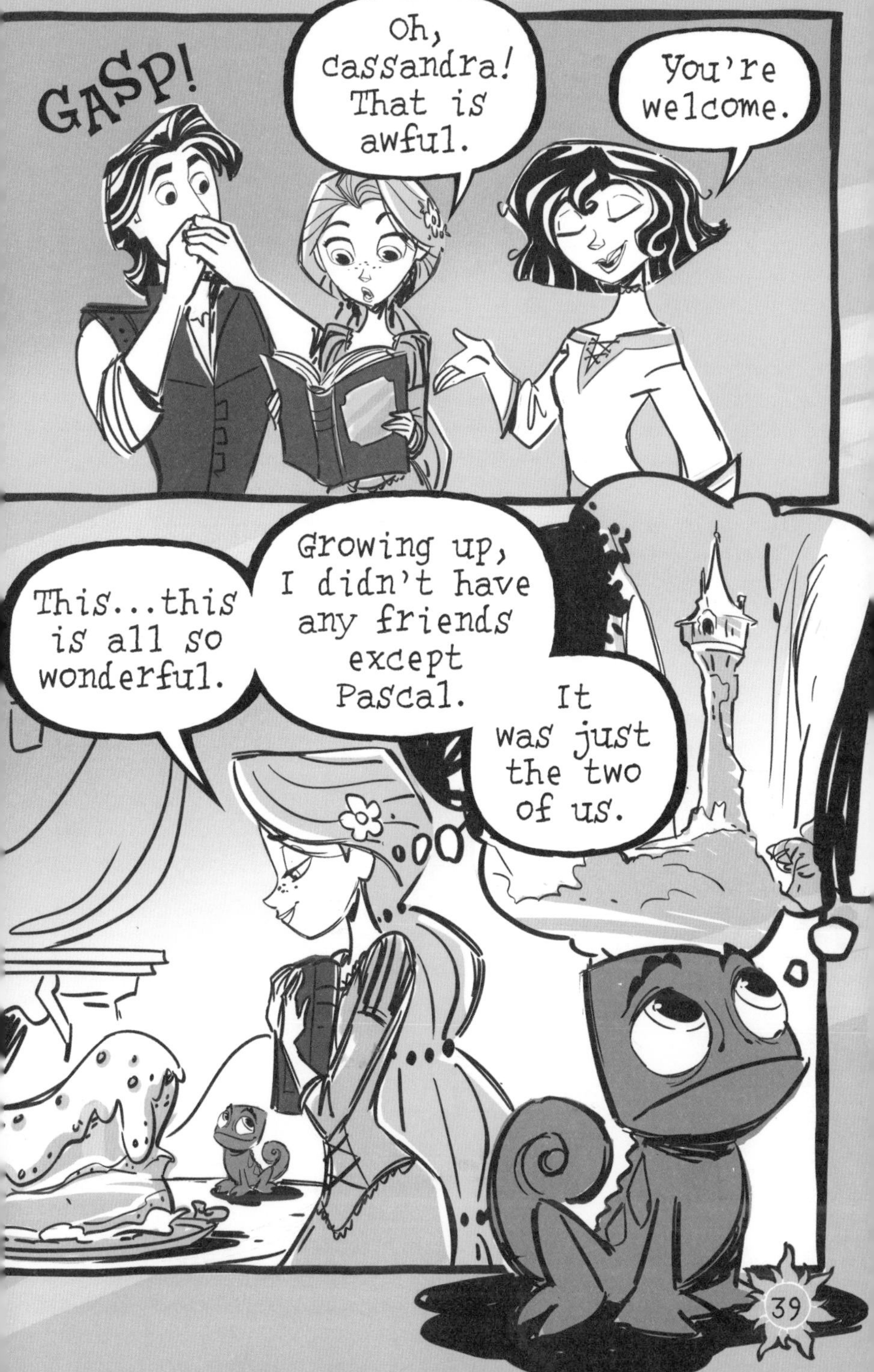
GASP!
Oh, cassandra! That is awful.
You're welcome.
This...this is all so wonderful.
Growing up, I didn't have any friends except Pascal.
It was just the two of us.

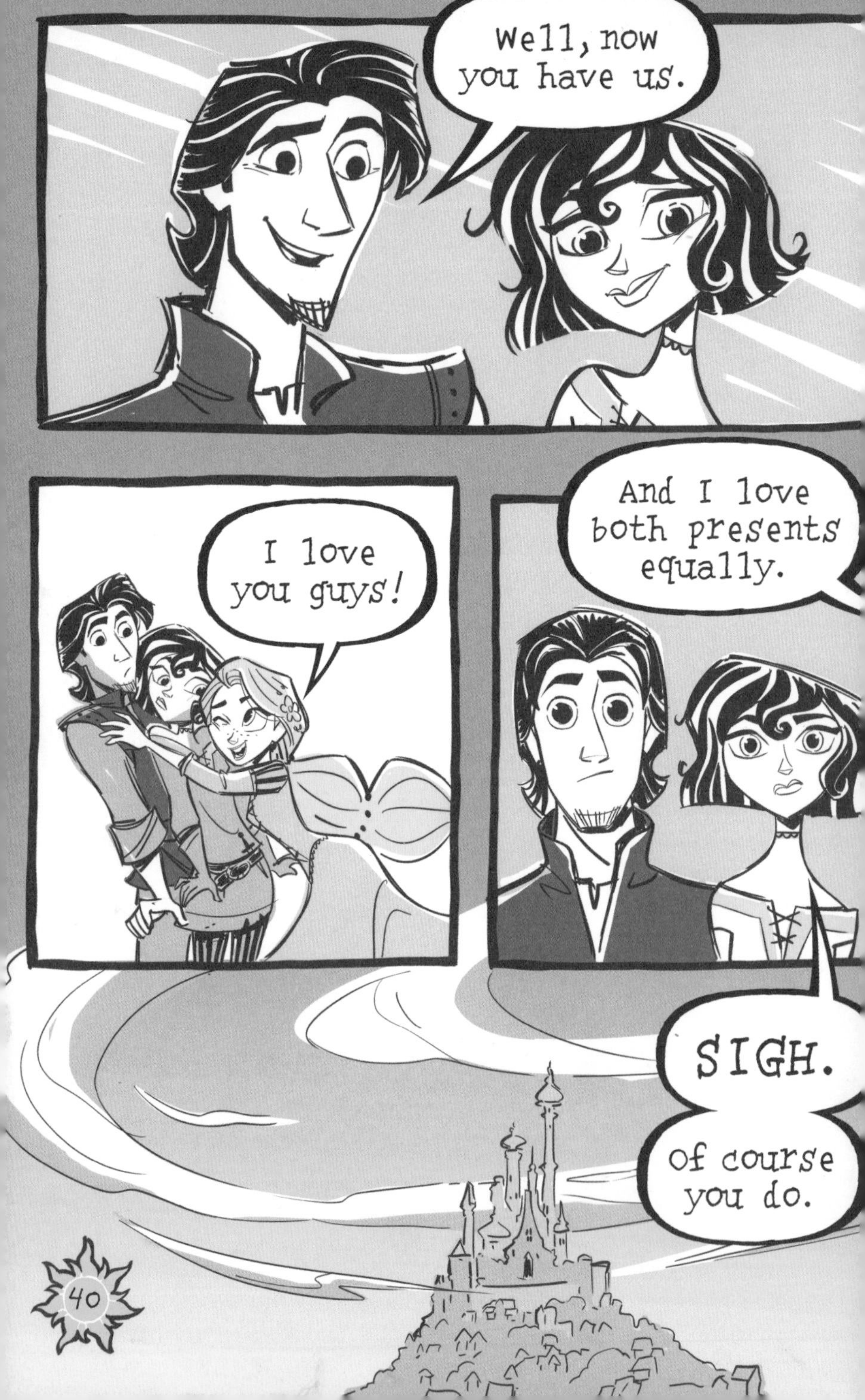
Well, now you have us.
I love you guys!
And I love both presents equally.
SIGH.
Of course you do.

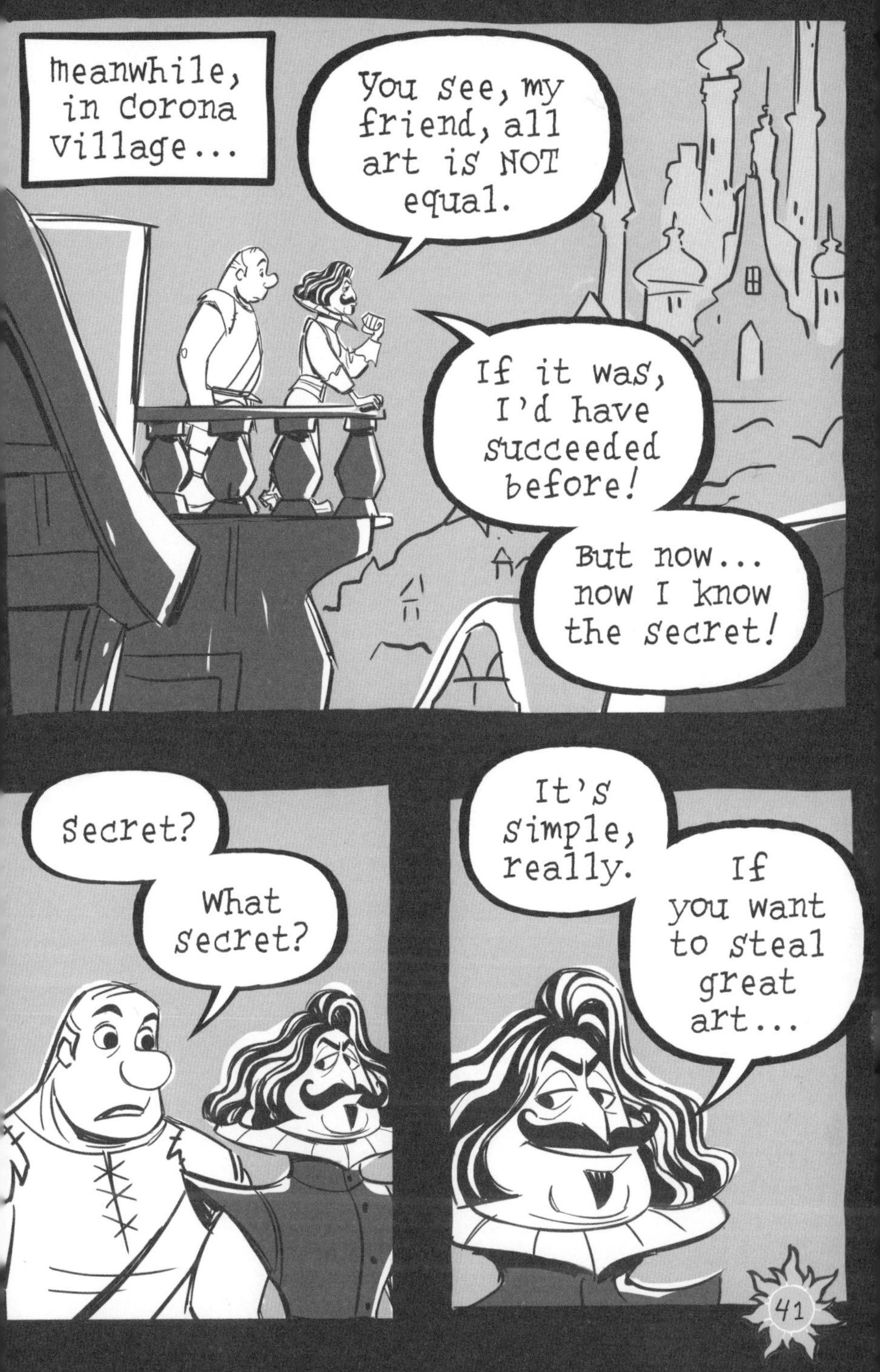
Meanwhile, in Corona village...
You see, my friend, all art is NOT equal.
If it was, I'd have succeeded before!
But now... now I know the secret!
Secret?
What secret?
It's simple, really.
If you want to steal great art...

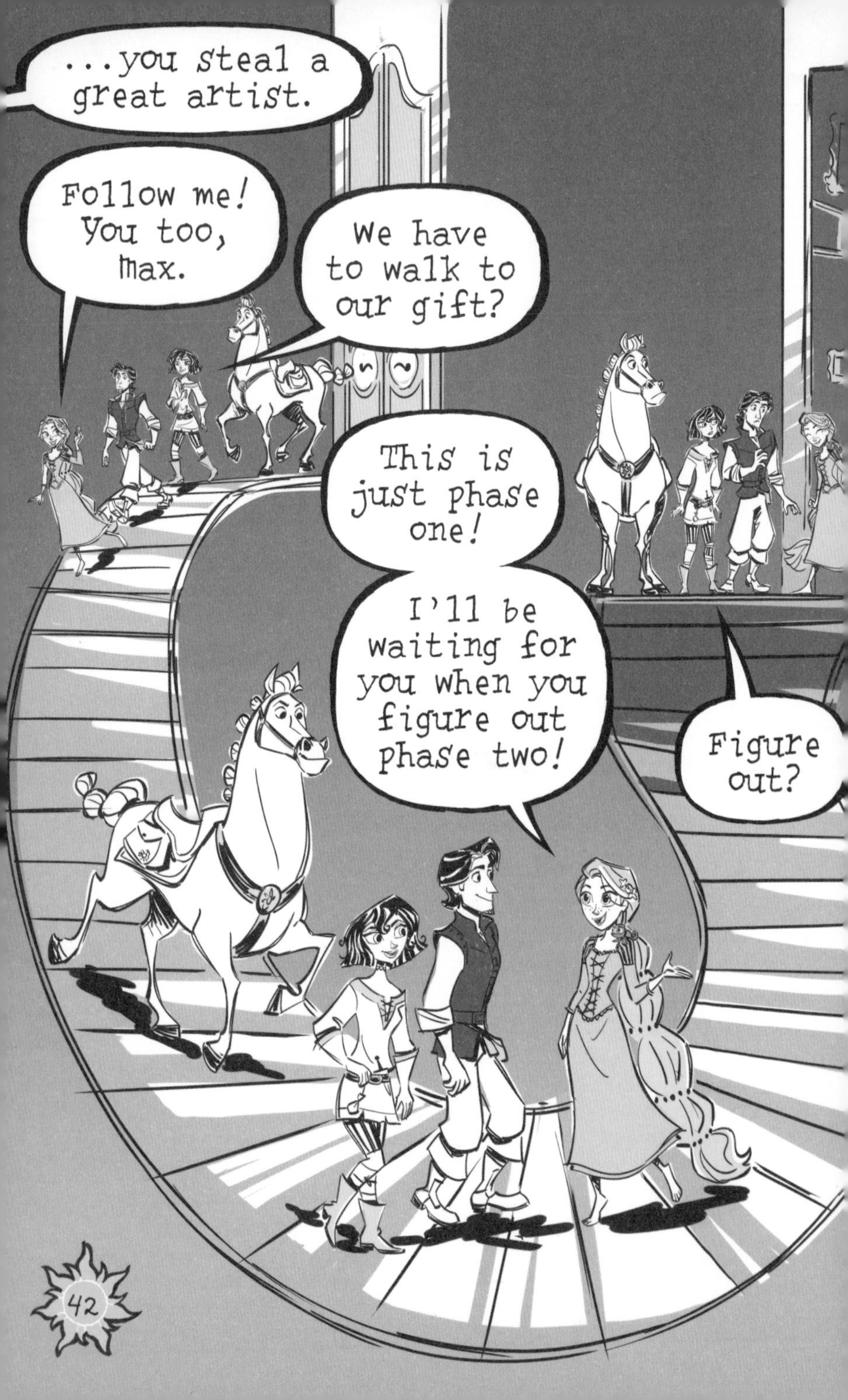
...you steal a great artist.
Follow me! You too, Max.
We have to walk to our gift?
This is just phase one!
I'll be waiting for you when you figure out phase two!
Figure out?

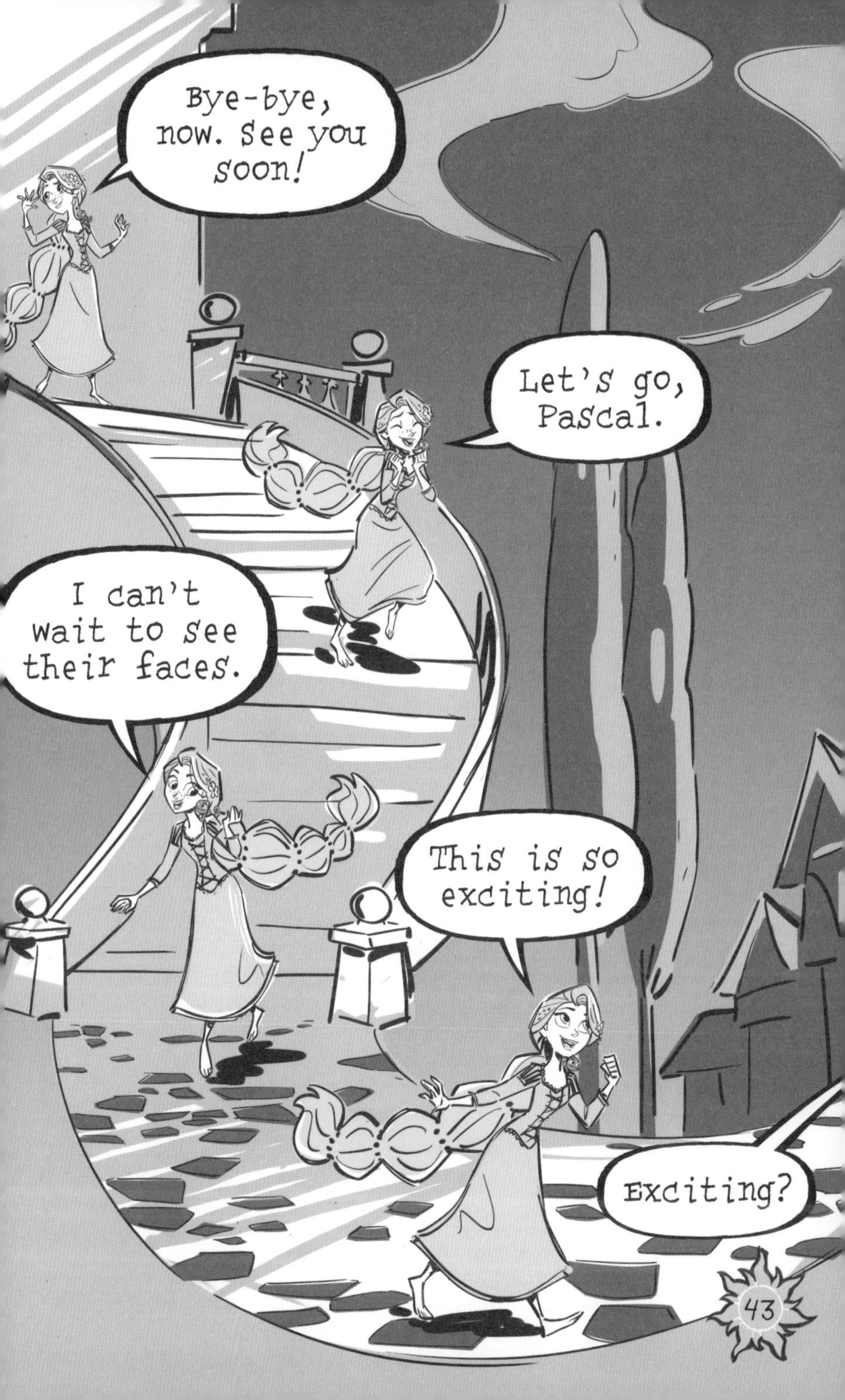
Bye-bye, now. See you soon!
Let's go, Pascal.
I can't wait to see their faces.
This is so exciting!
Exciting?

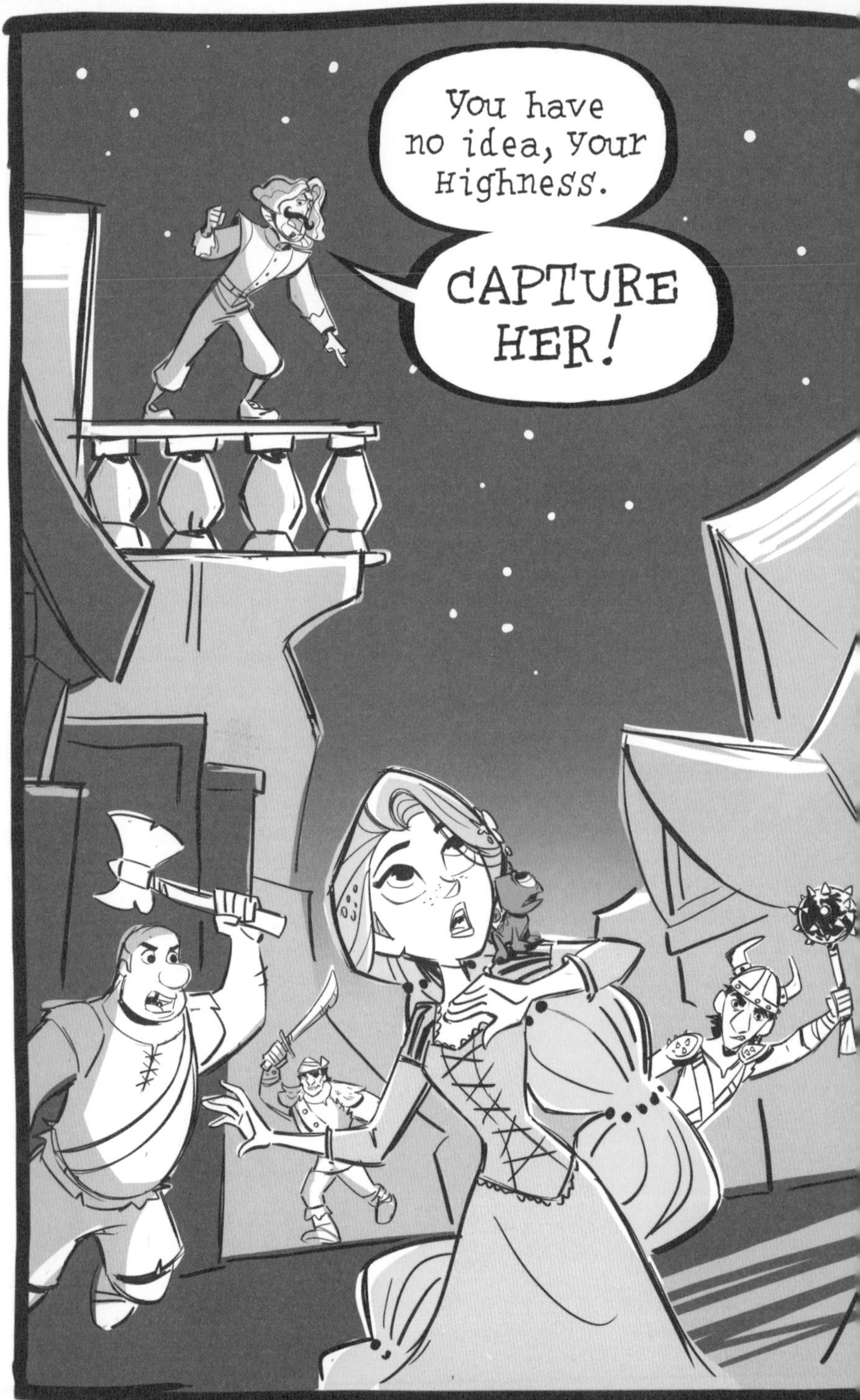
You have no idea, your Highness.
CAPTURE HER!

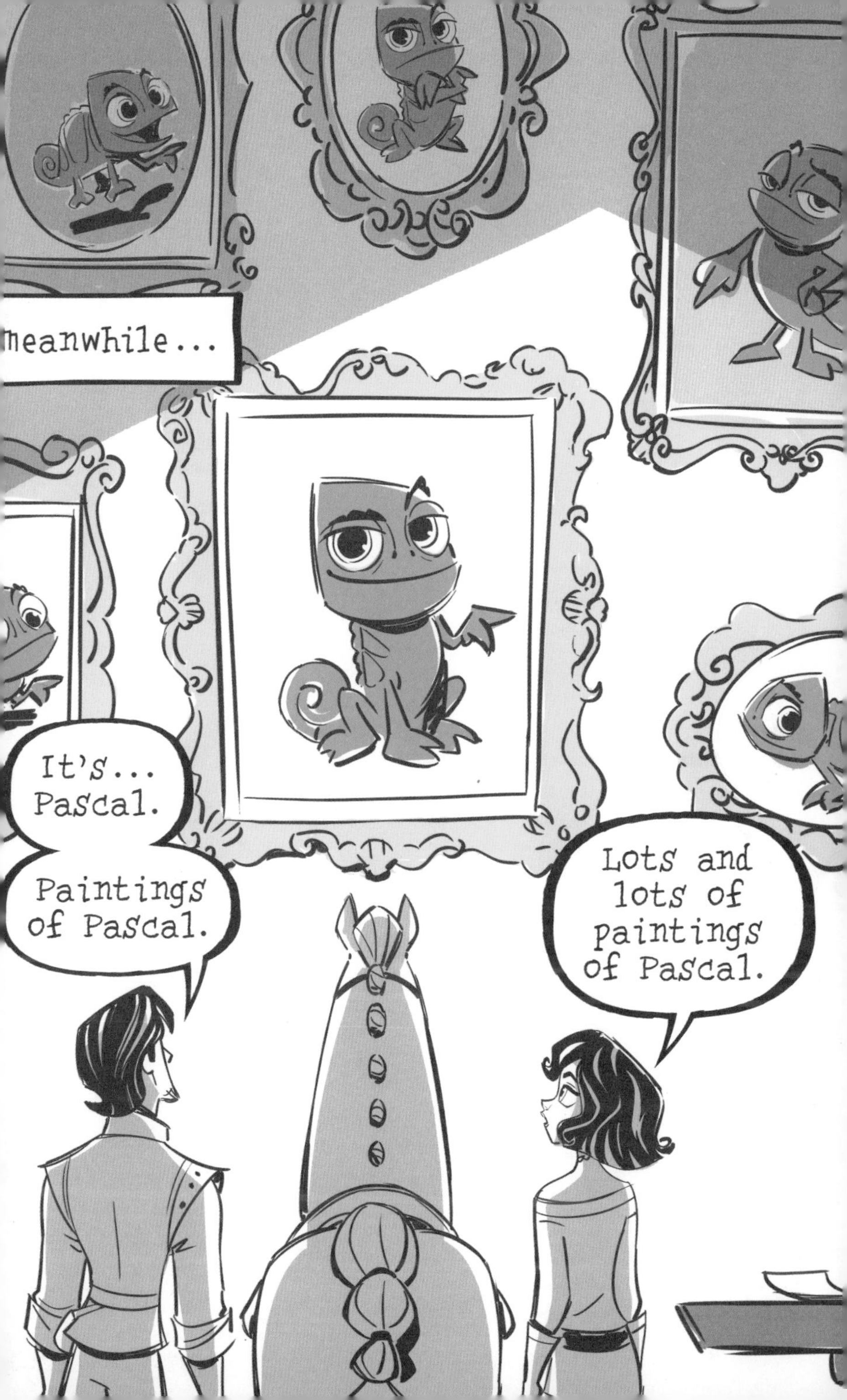
meanwhile...
It's... Pascal.
Paintings of Pascal.
Lots and lots of paintings of Pascal.

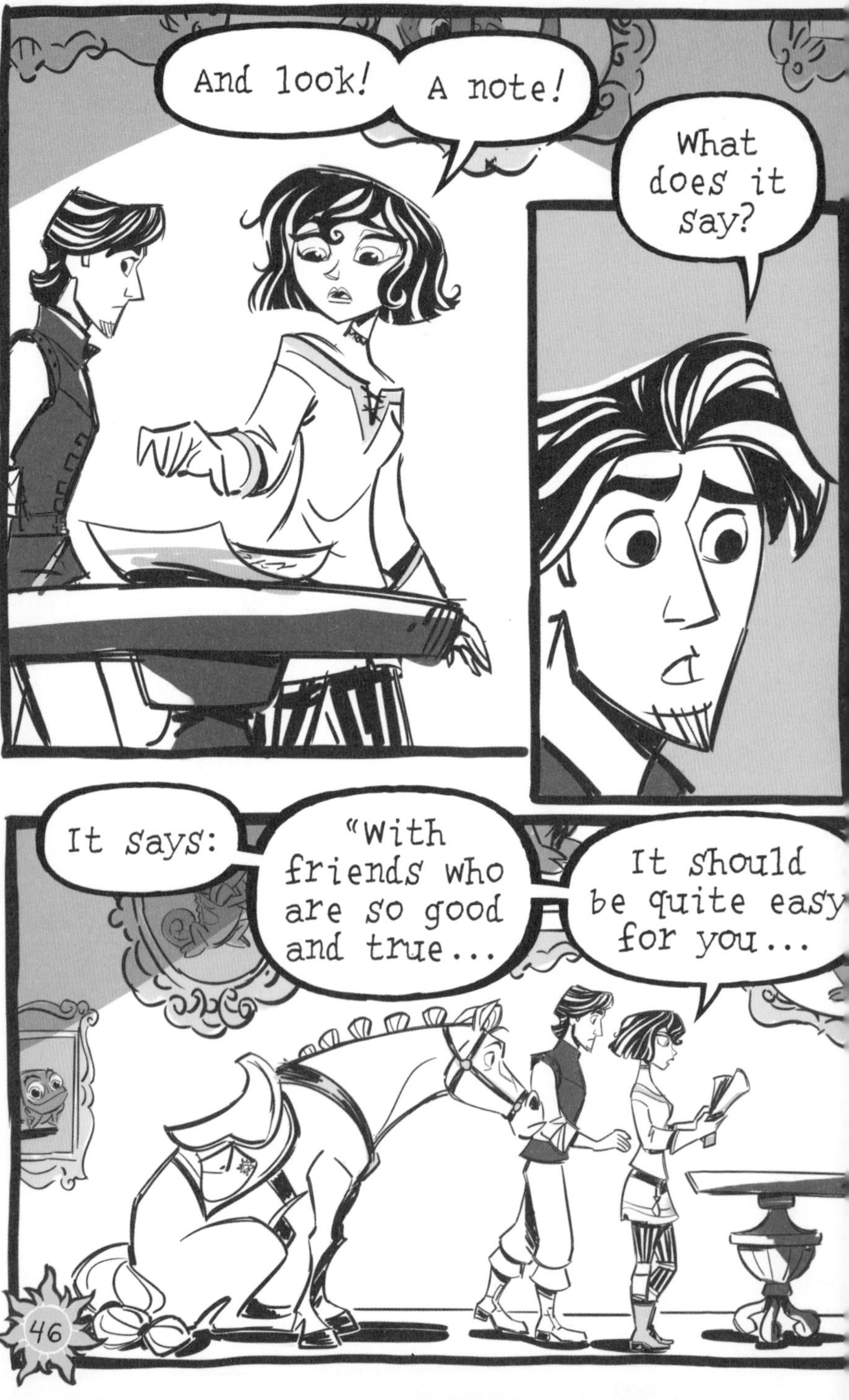
And look!
A note!
What does it say?
It says:
"With friends who are so good and true...
It should be quite easy for you...

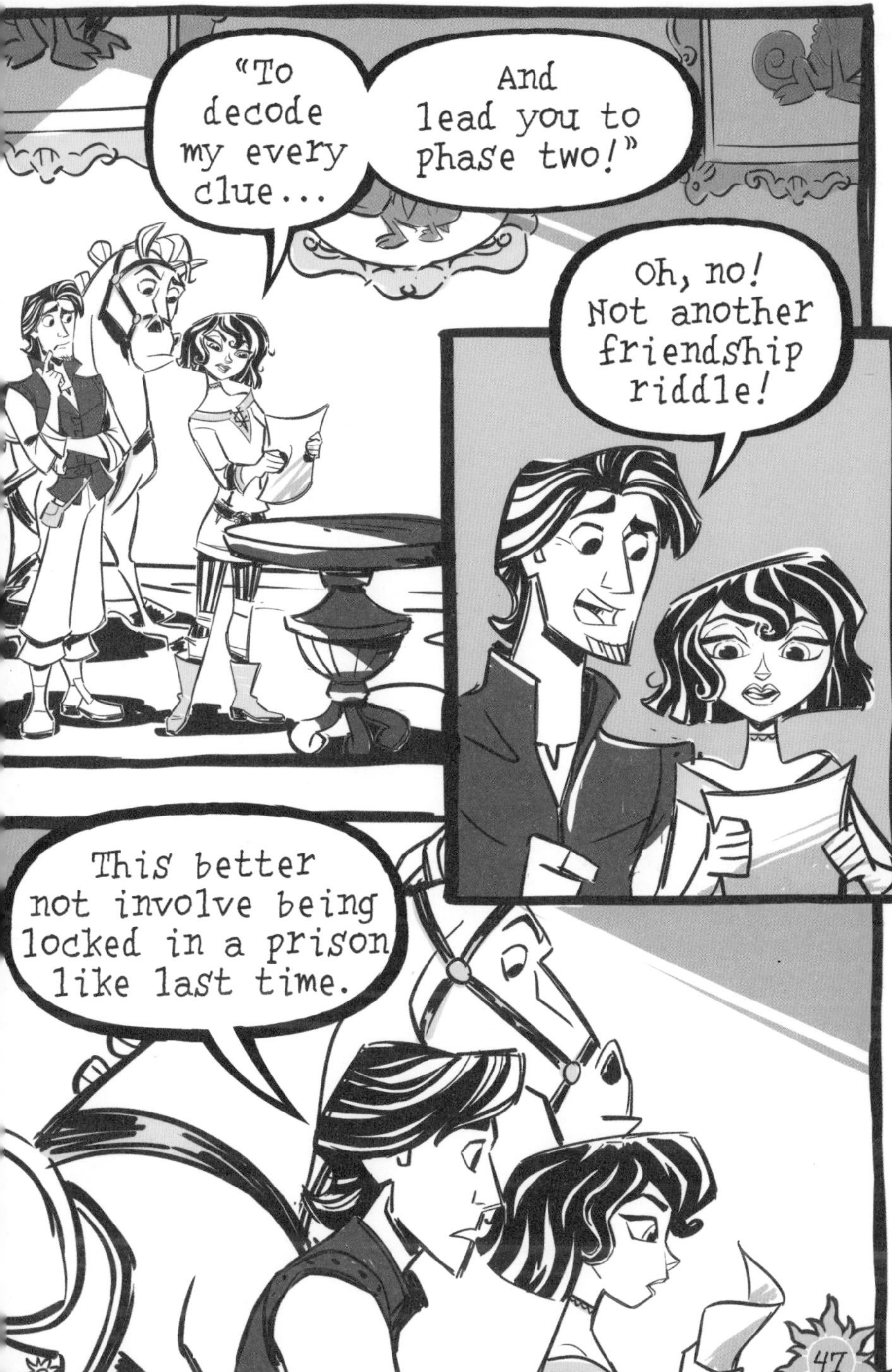
"To decode my every clue...
And lead you to phase two!"
Oh, no! Not another friendship riddle!
This better not involve being locked in a prison like last time.

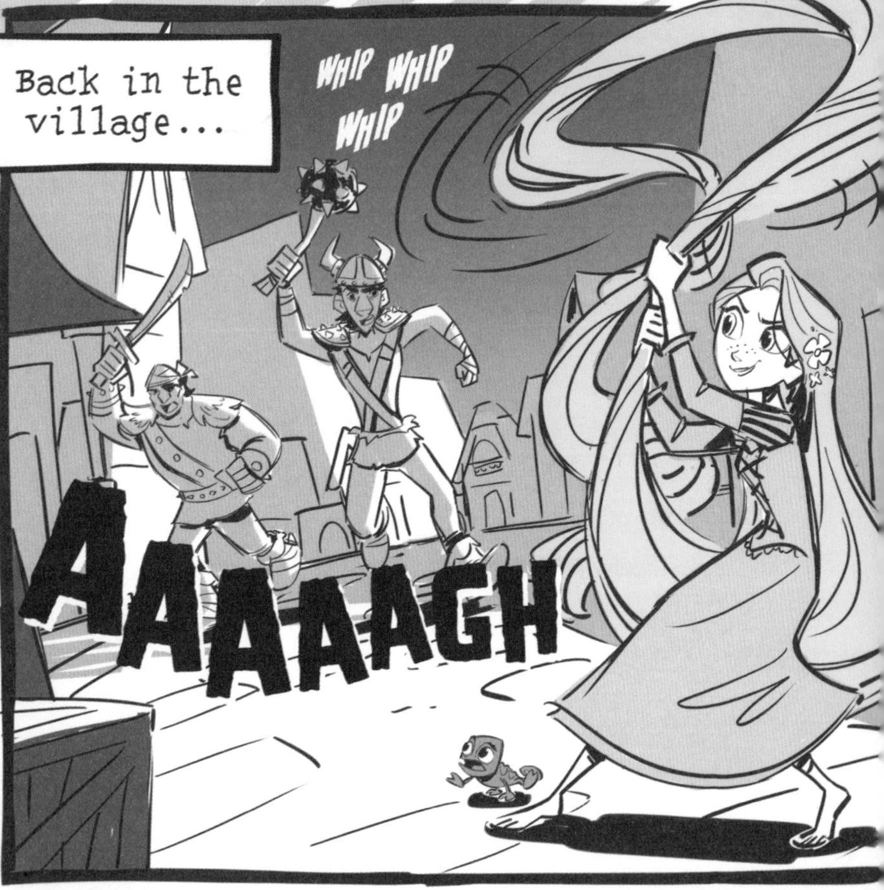
Back in the village...
WHIP WHIP
WHIP
AAAAAGH

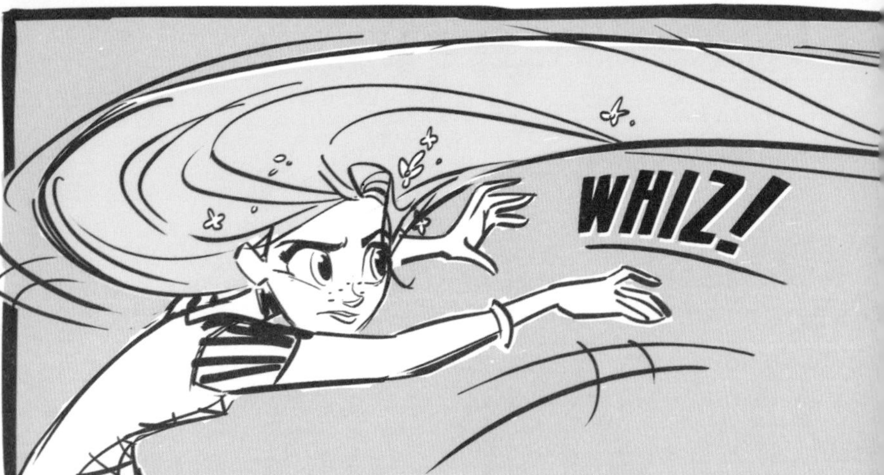
WHIZ!

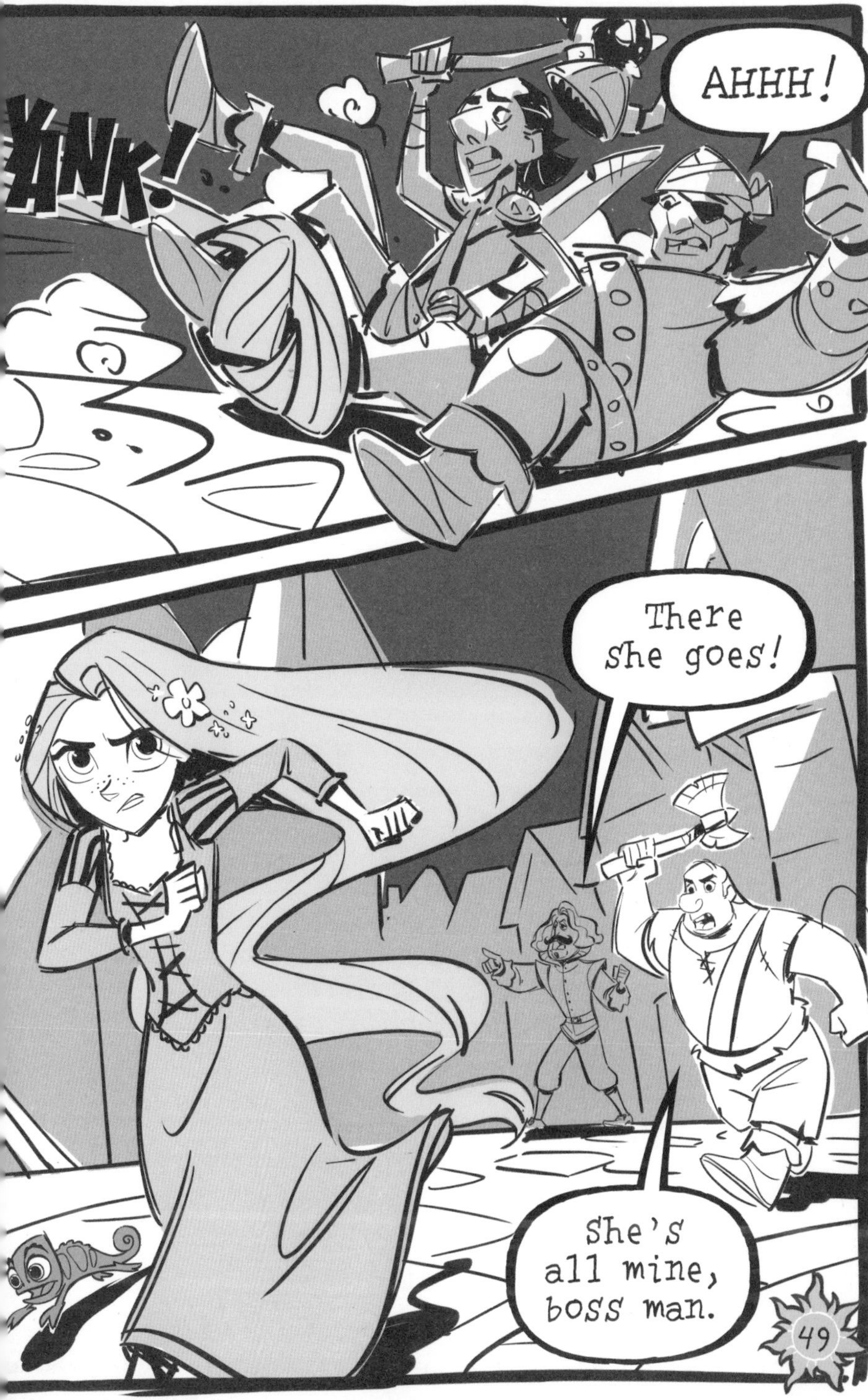
YANK!
AHHH!
There she goes!
She's all mine, boss man.

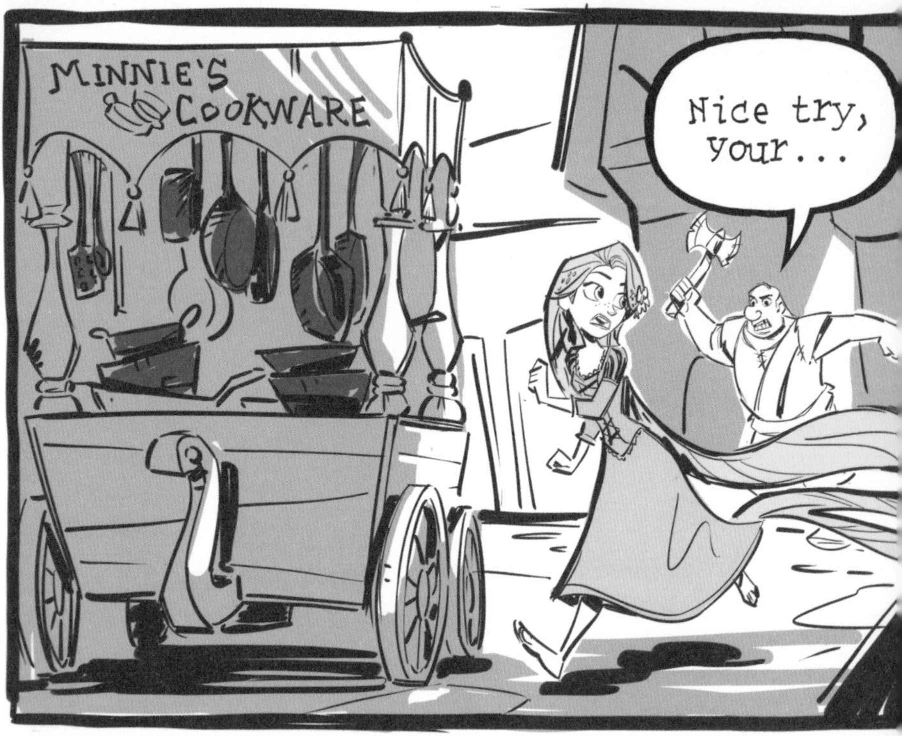
MINNIE'S COOKWARE
Nice try, your...

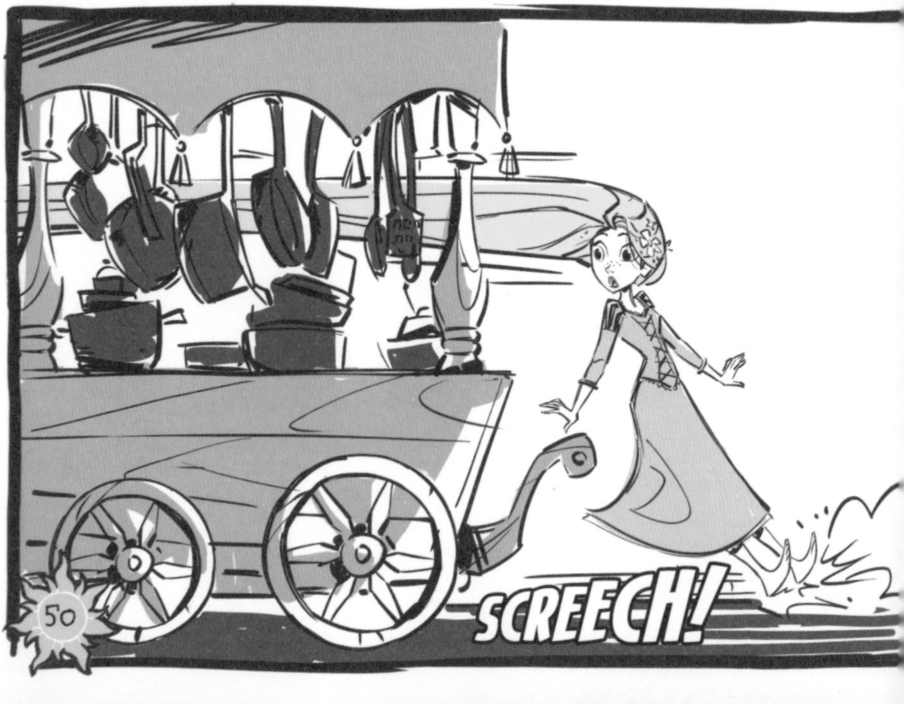
SCREECH!

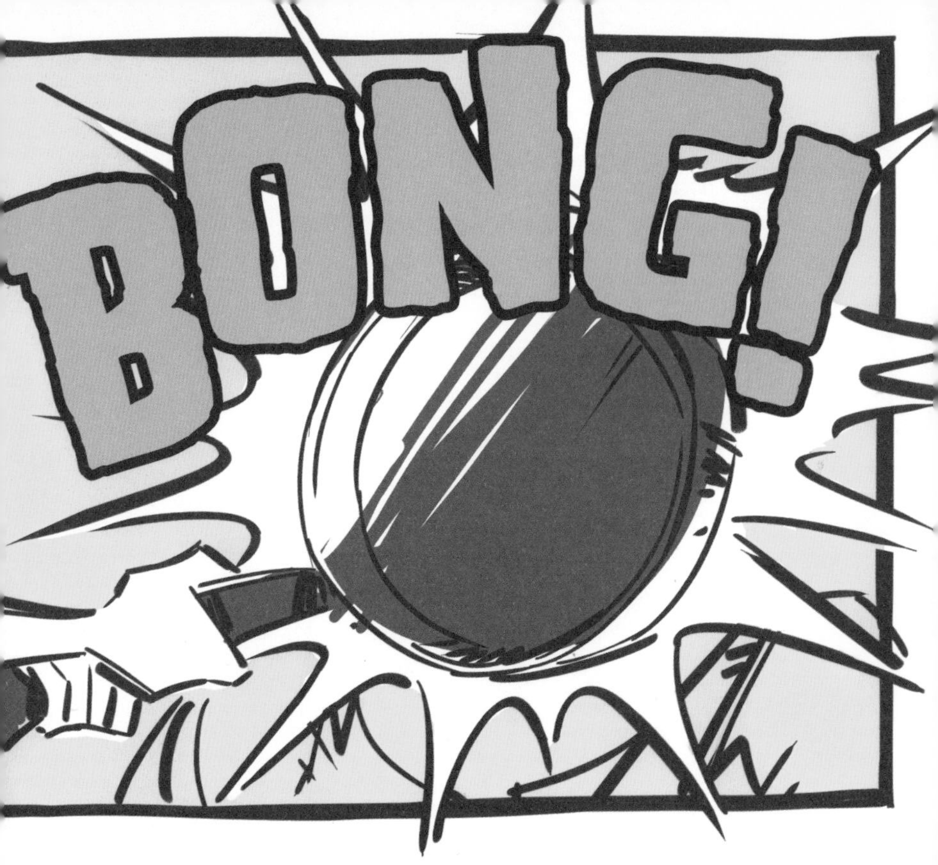
BONG!

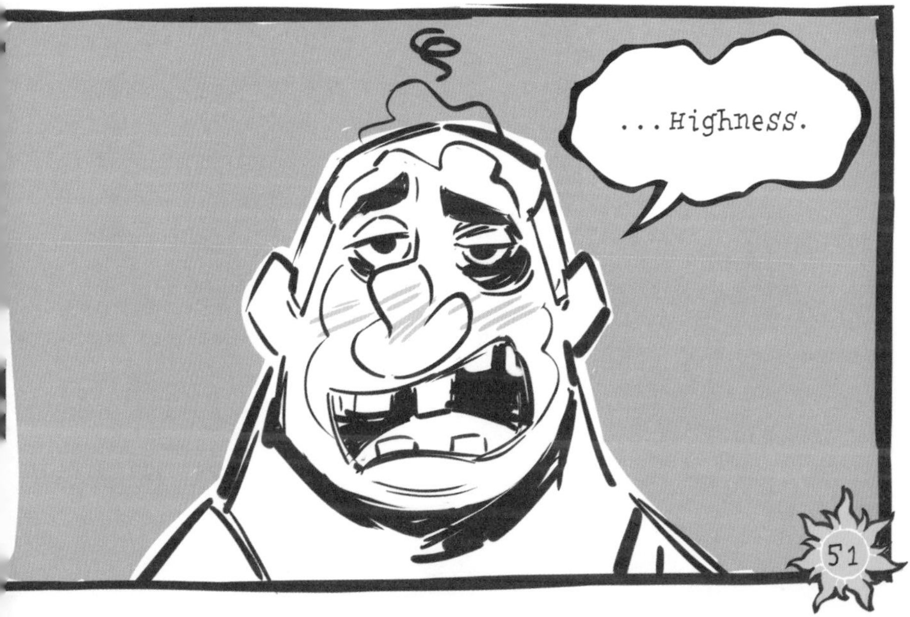
...Highness.

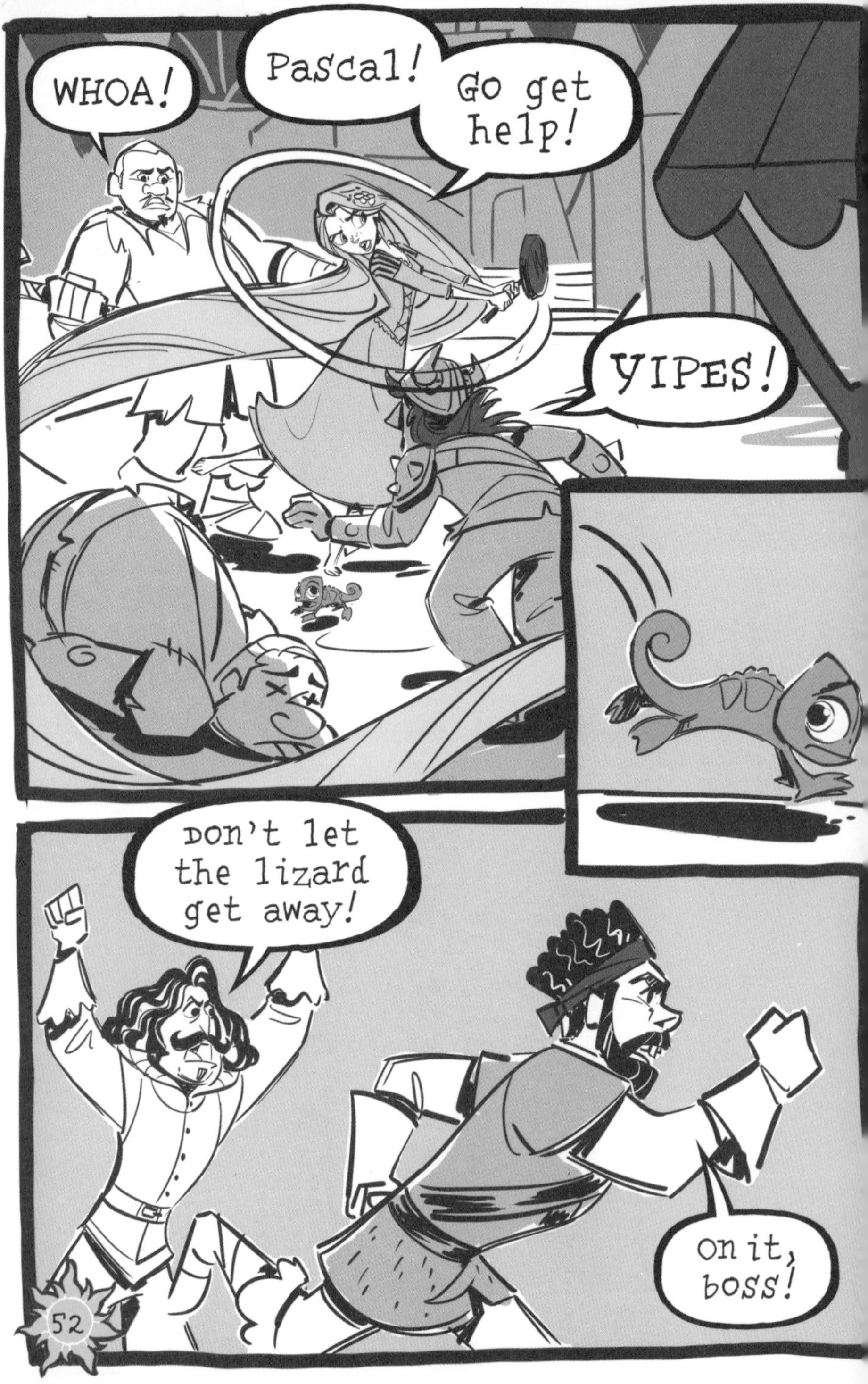
WHOA!
Pascal!
Go get help!
YIPES!
Don't let the lizard get away!
On it, boss!

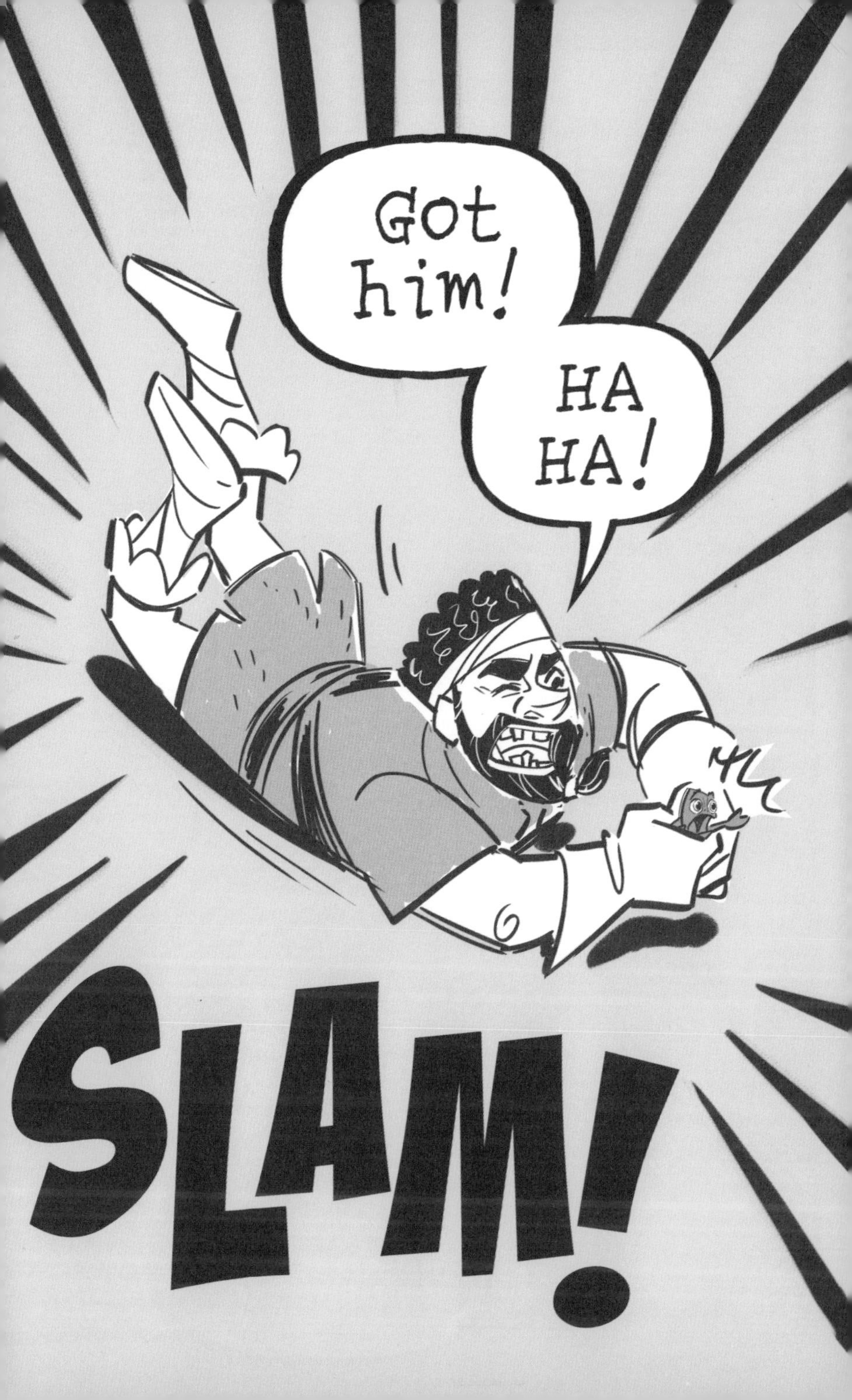
Got him!
HA HA!
SLAM!

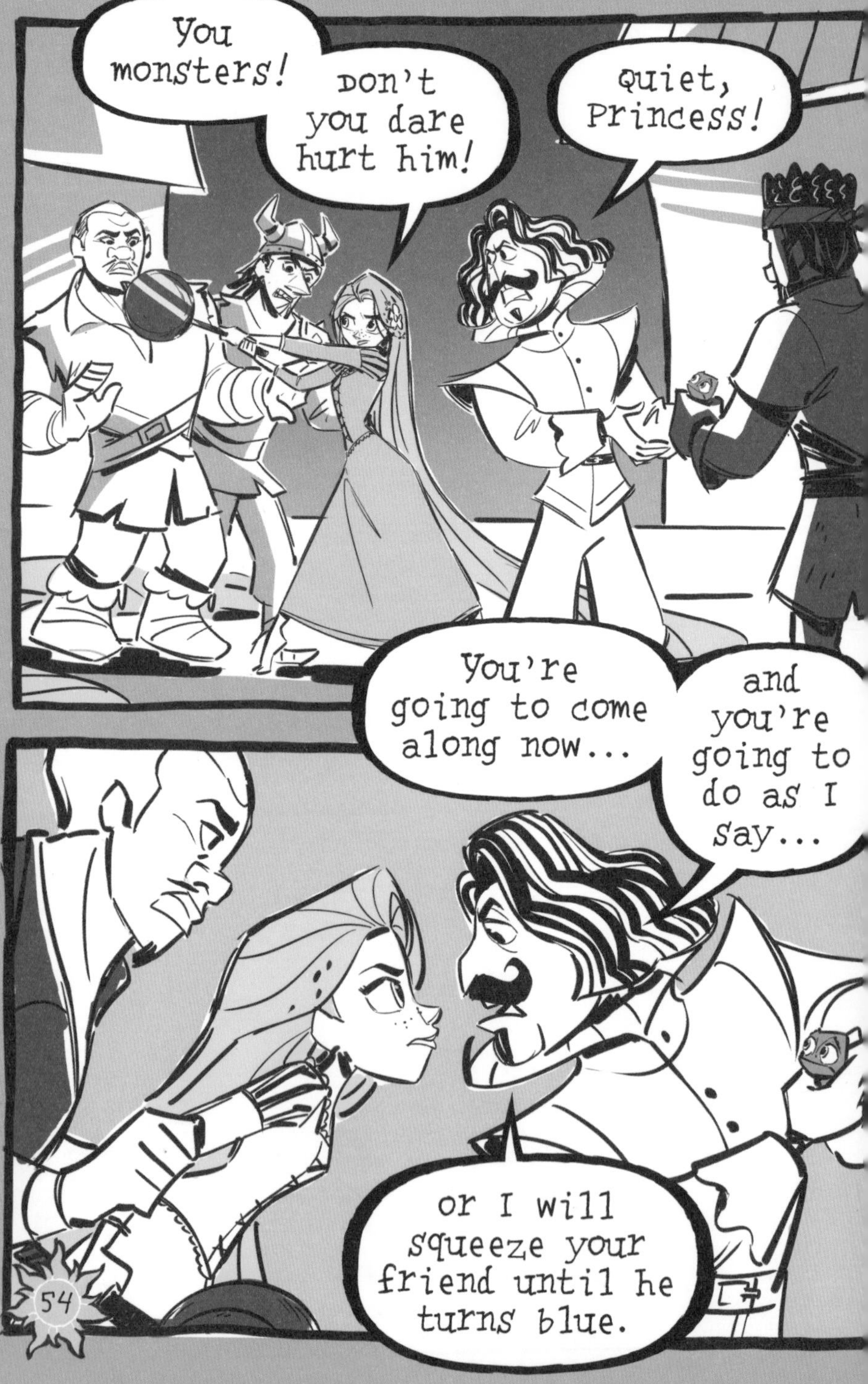
You monsters!
Don't you dare hurt him!
Quiet, Princess!
You're going to come along now...
and you're going to do as I say...
or I will squeeze your friend until he turns blue.

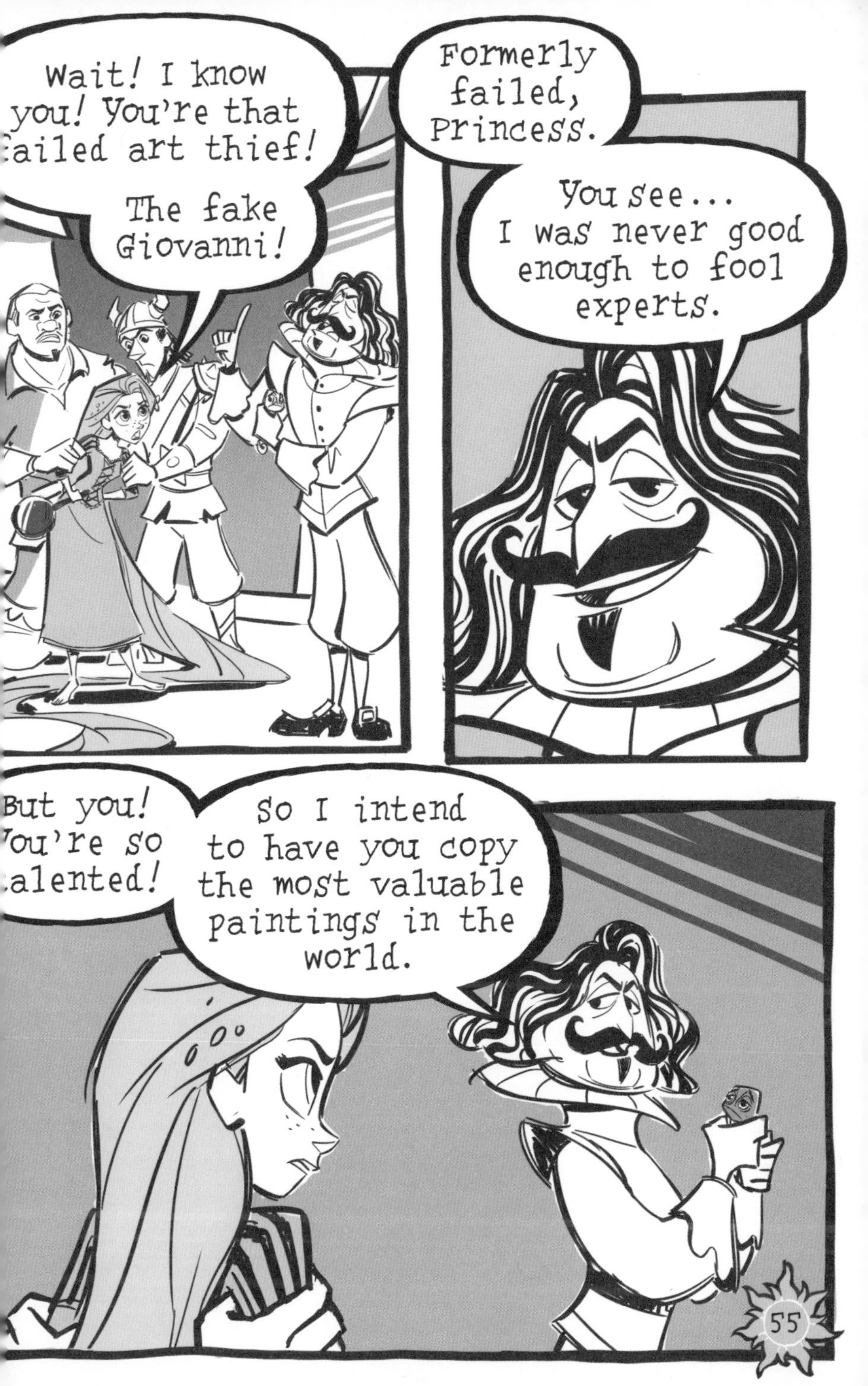
Wait! I know you! You're that ailed art thief!
The fake Giovanni!
Formerly failed, Princess.
You see... I was never good enough to fool experts.
But you! ou're so alented!
So I intend to have you copy the most valuable paintings in the world.

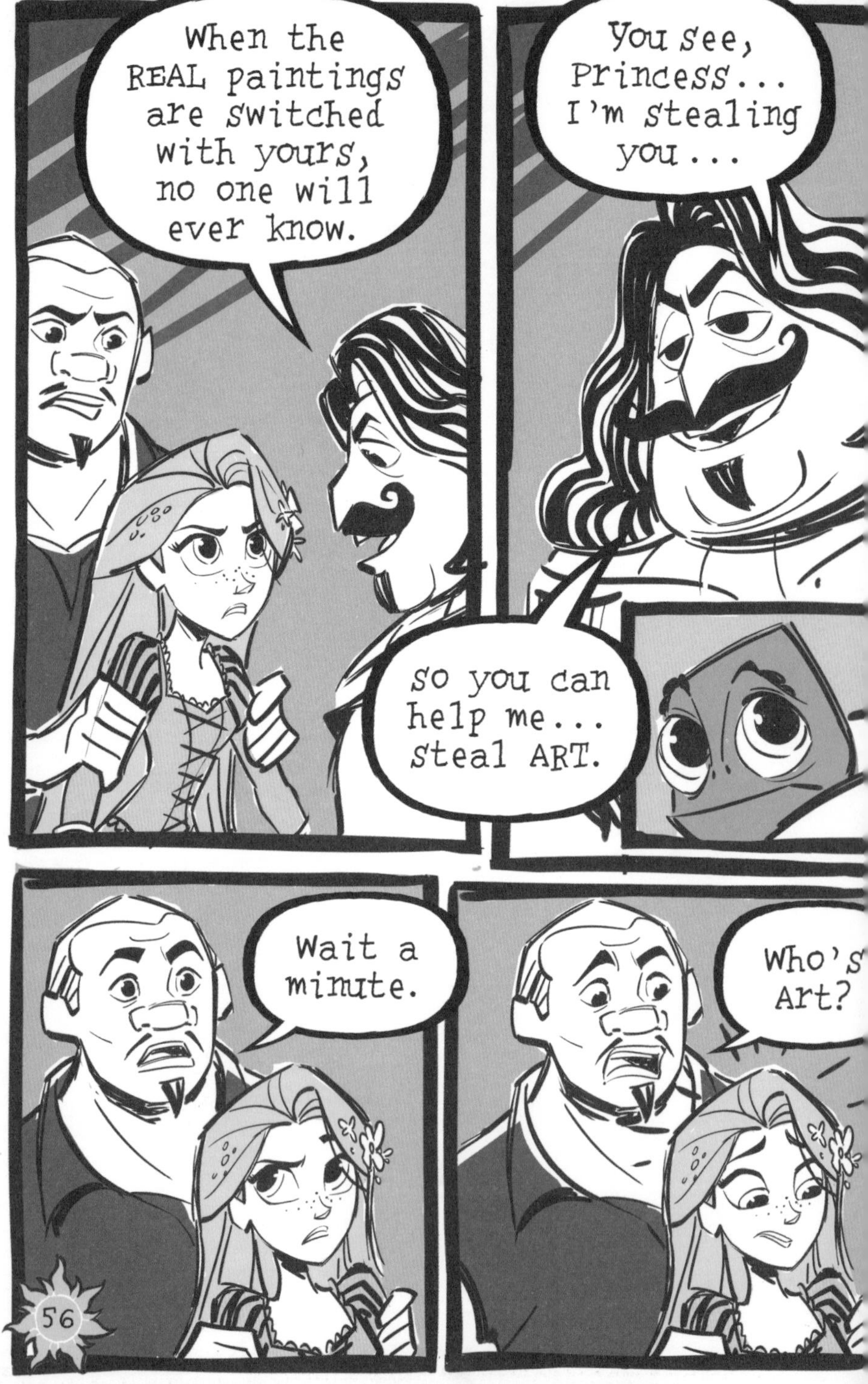
When the REAL paintings are switched with yours, no one will ever know.
You see, Princess... I'm stealing you...
so you can help me... steal ART.
Wait a minute.
Who's Art?

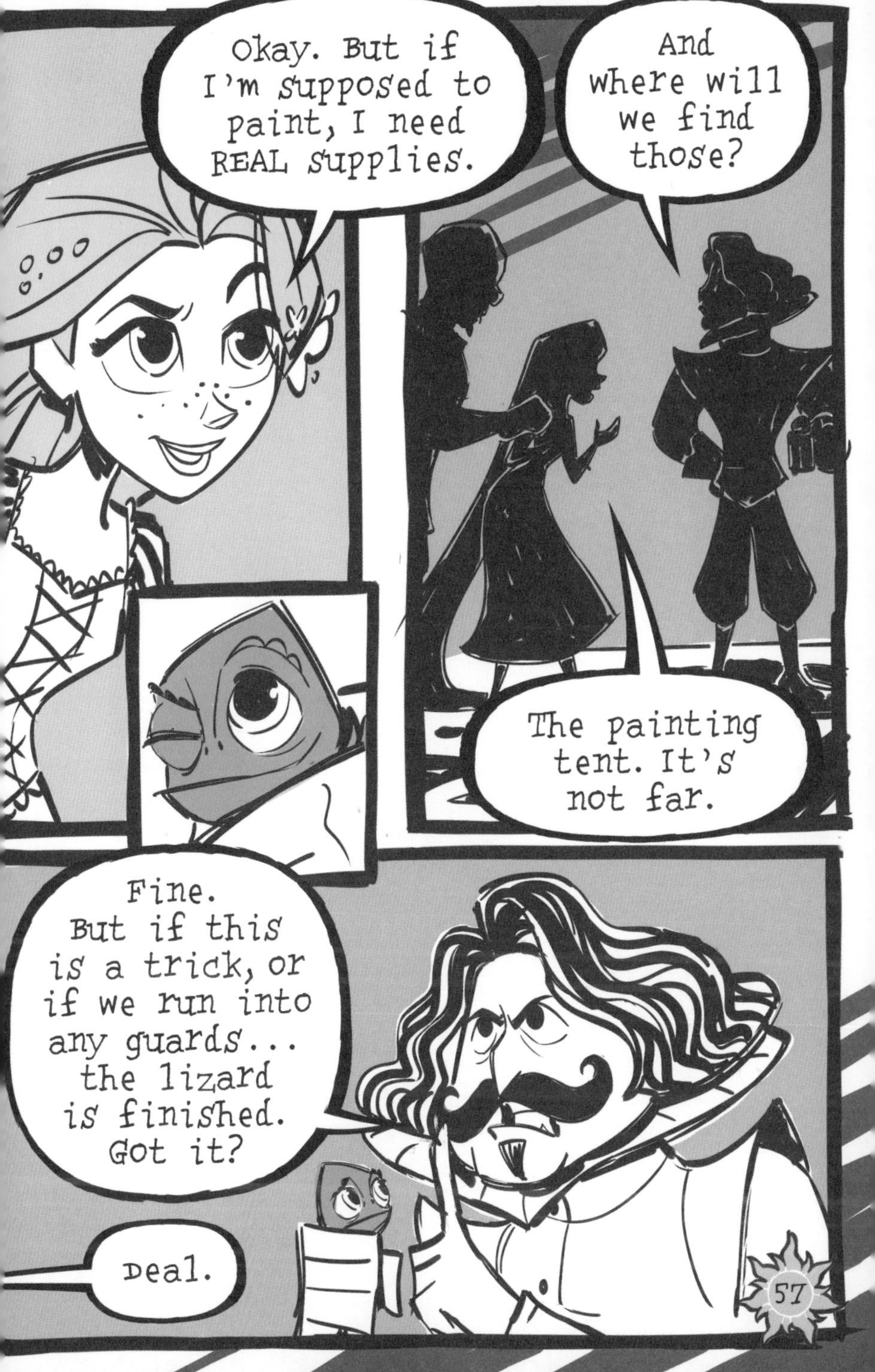
Okay. But if I'm supposed to paint, I need REAL supplies.
And where will we find those?
The painting tent. It's not far.
Fine. But if this is a trick, or if we run into any guards... the lizard is finished. Got it?
Deal.
57

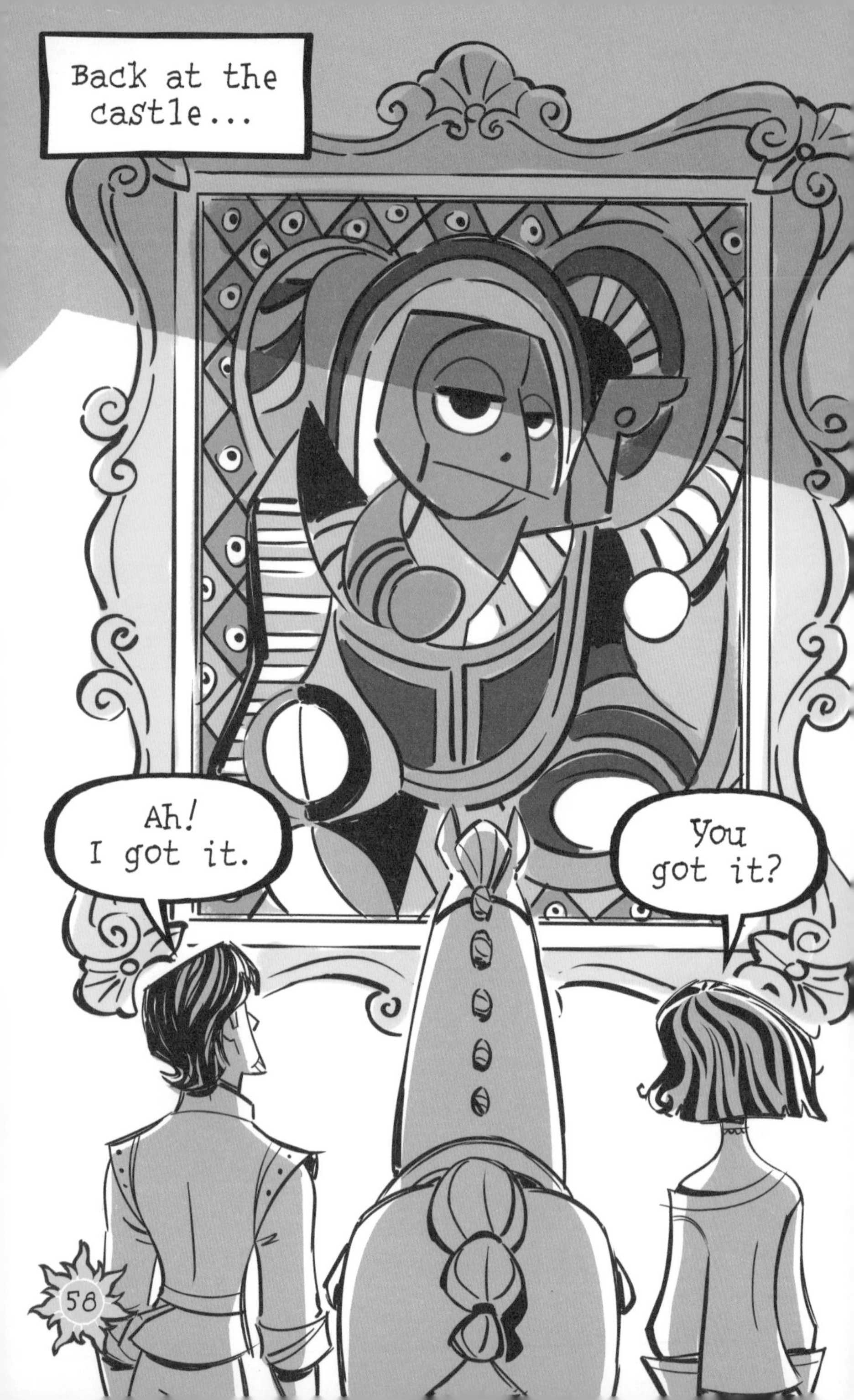

Back at the castle...
Ah! I got it.
You got it?

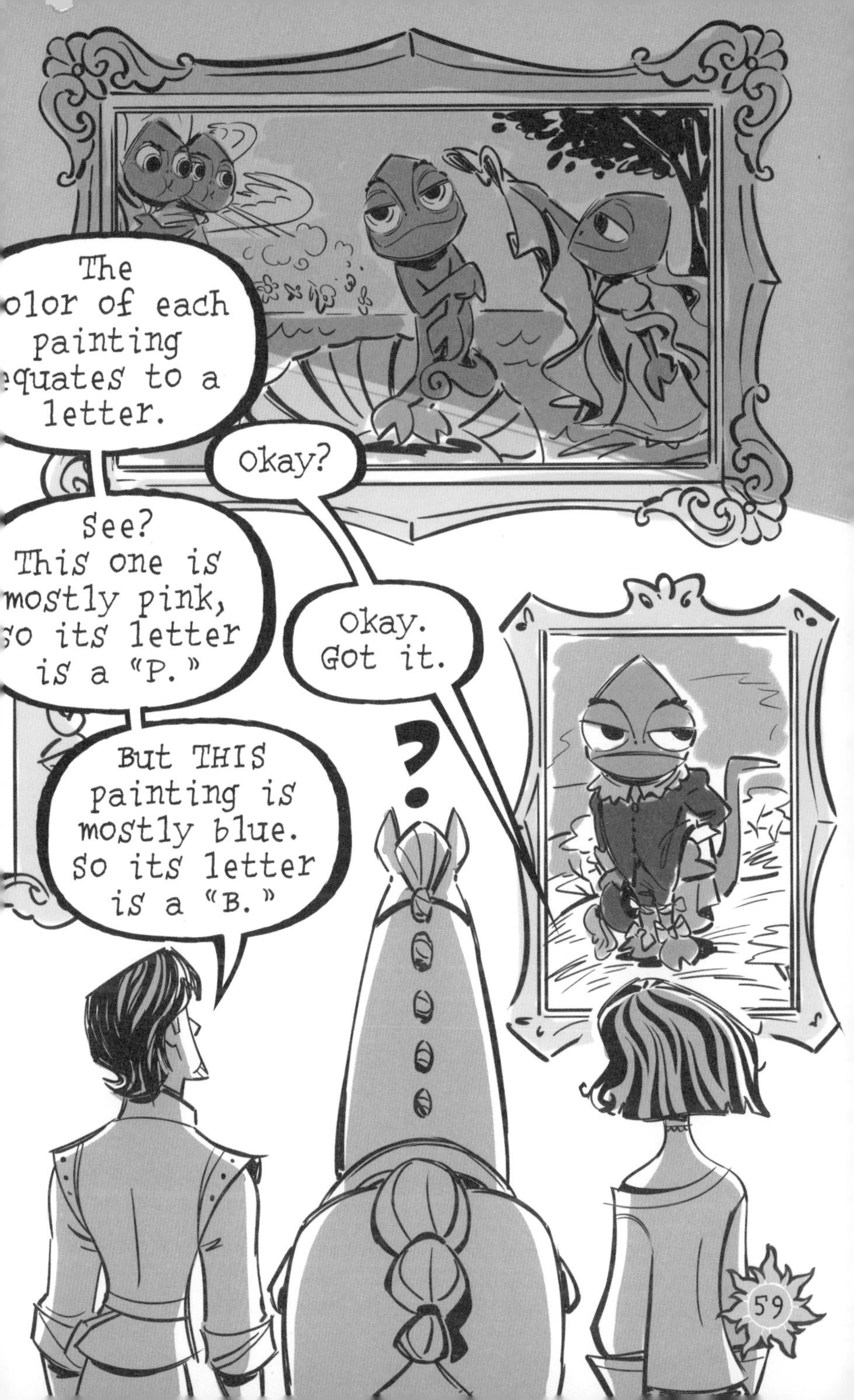
The olor of each painting quates to a letter.
Okay?
See? This one is mostly pink, o its letter is a "P."
Okay. Got it.
But THIS painting is mostly blue. So its letter is a "B."

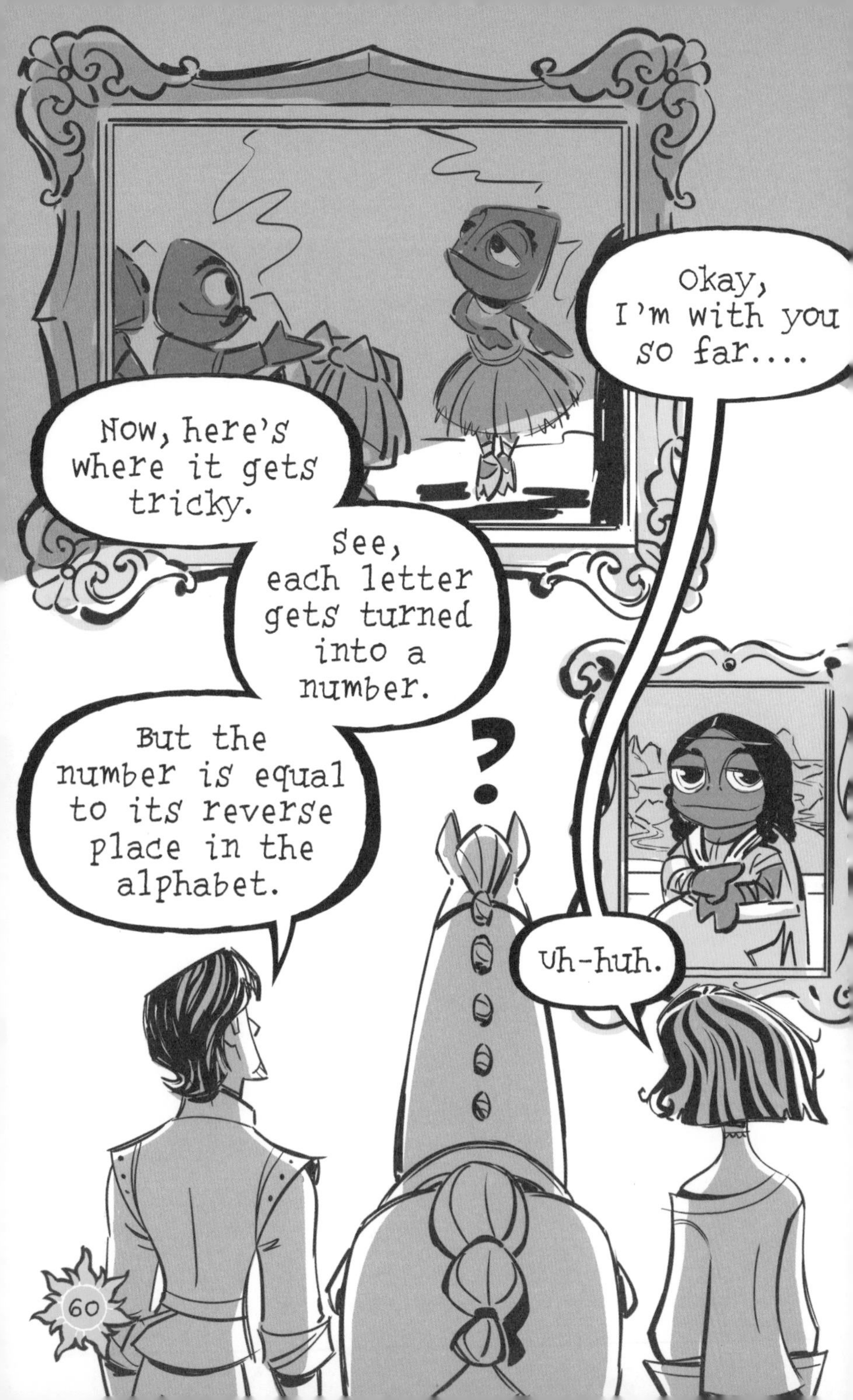
Now, here's where it gets tricky.
See, each letter gets turned into a number.
But the number is equal to its reverse place in the alphabet.
Okay, I'm with you so far....
Uh-huh.
?

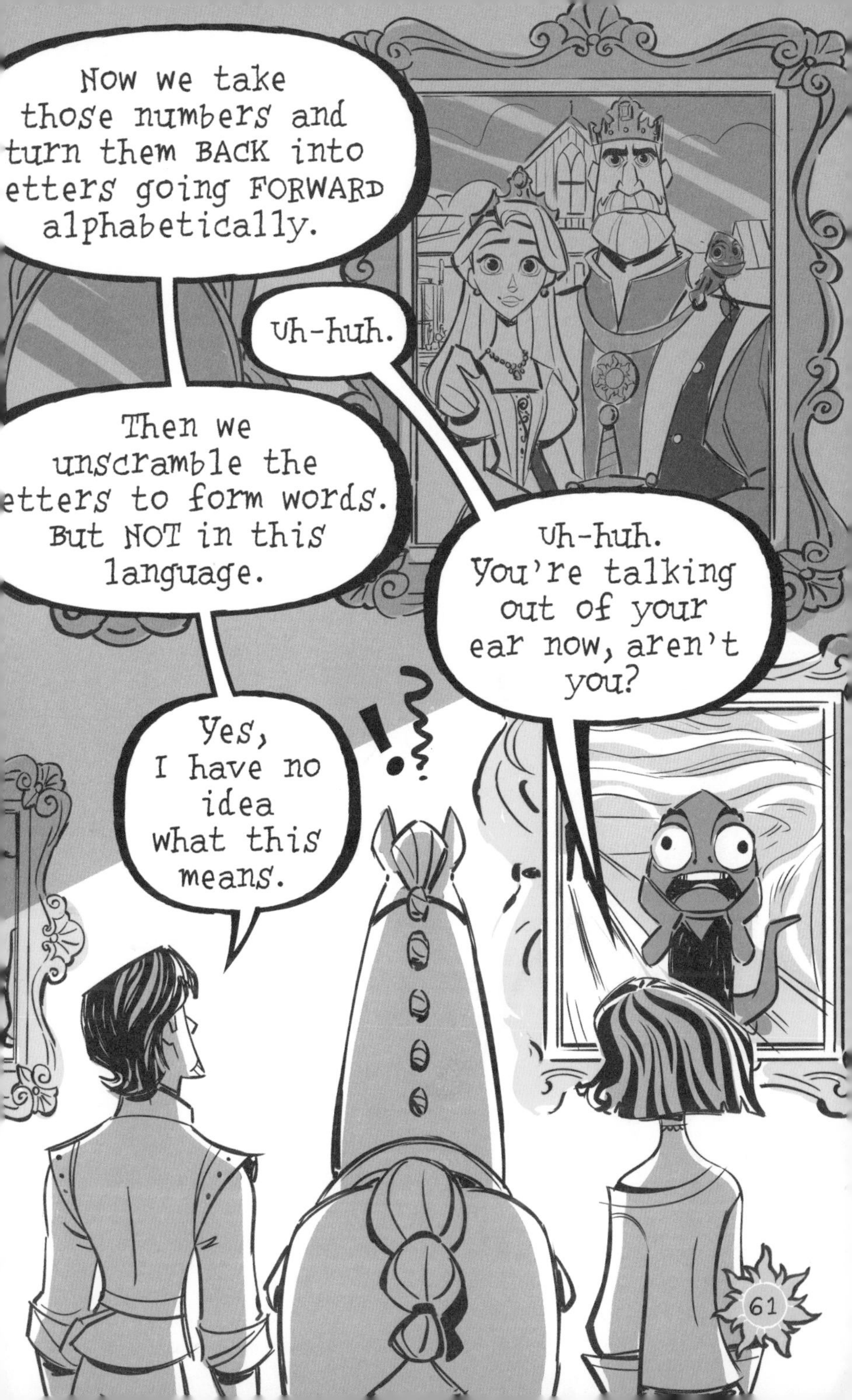
Now we take those numbers and turn them BACK into etters going FORWARD alphabetically.
Uh-huh.
Then we unscramble the etters to form words. But NOT in this language.
Uh-huh. You're talking out of your ear now, aren't you?
Yes, I have no idea what this means.

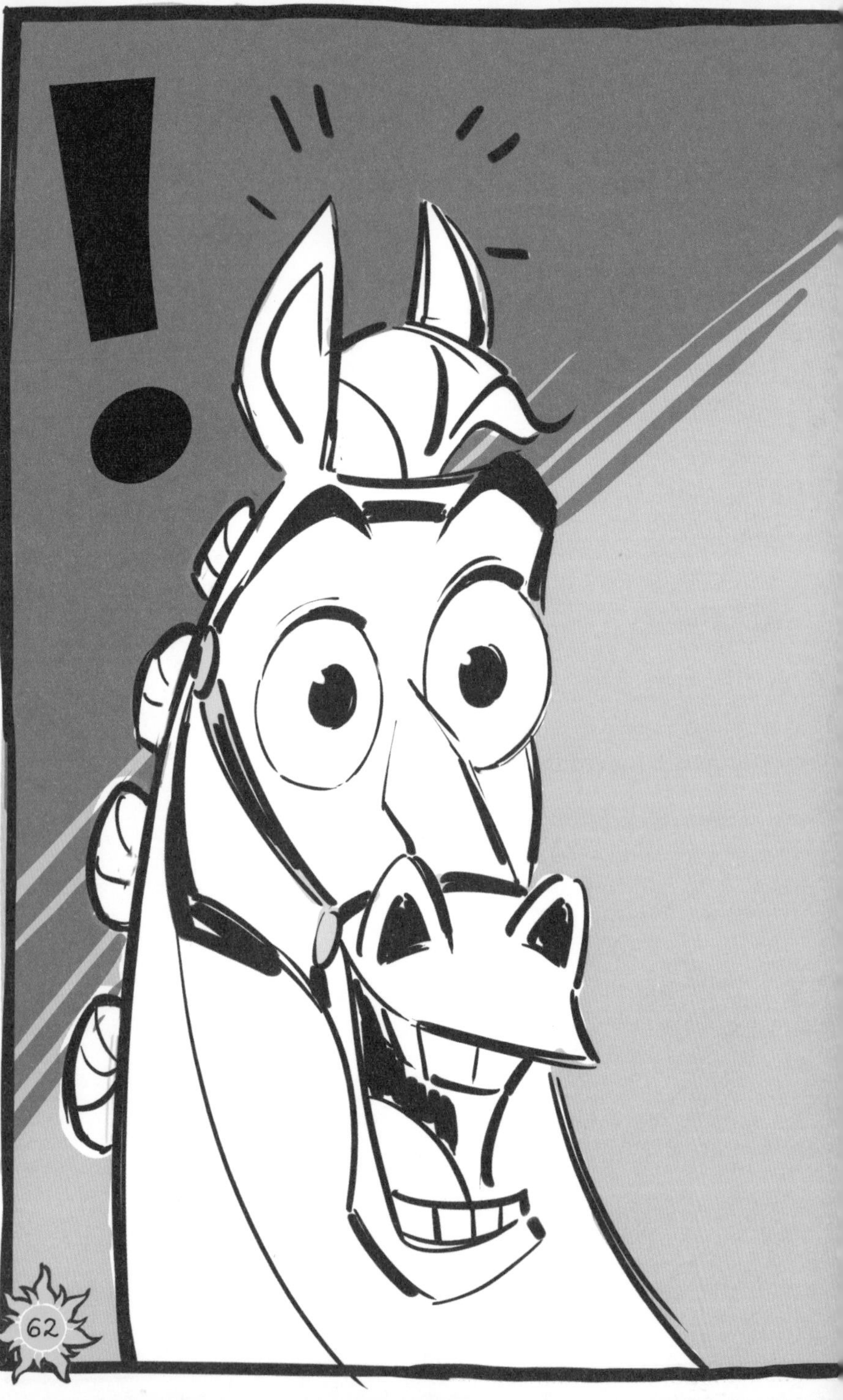
!

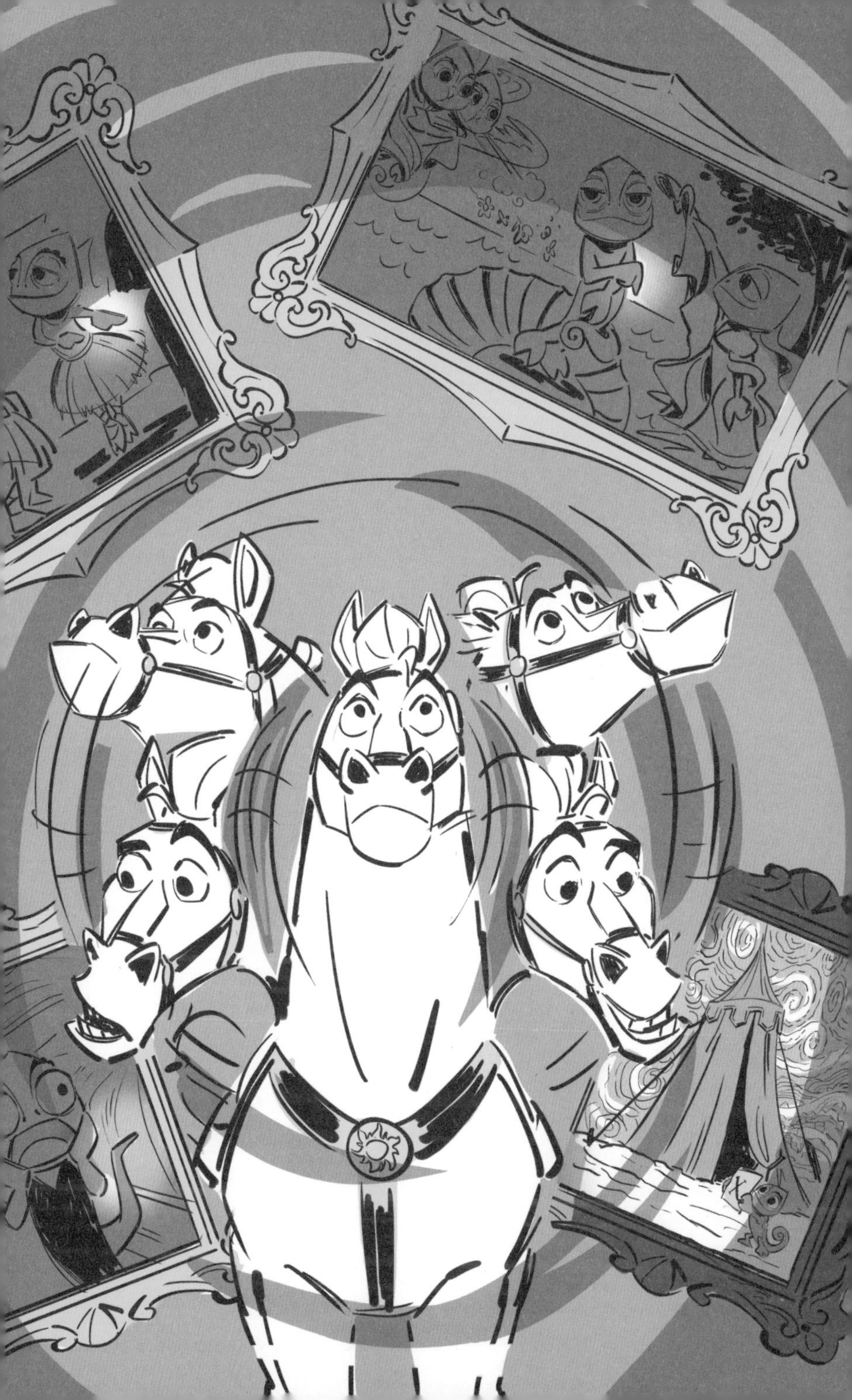

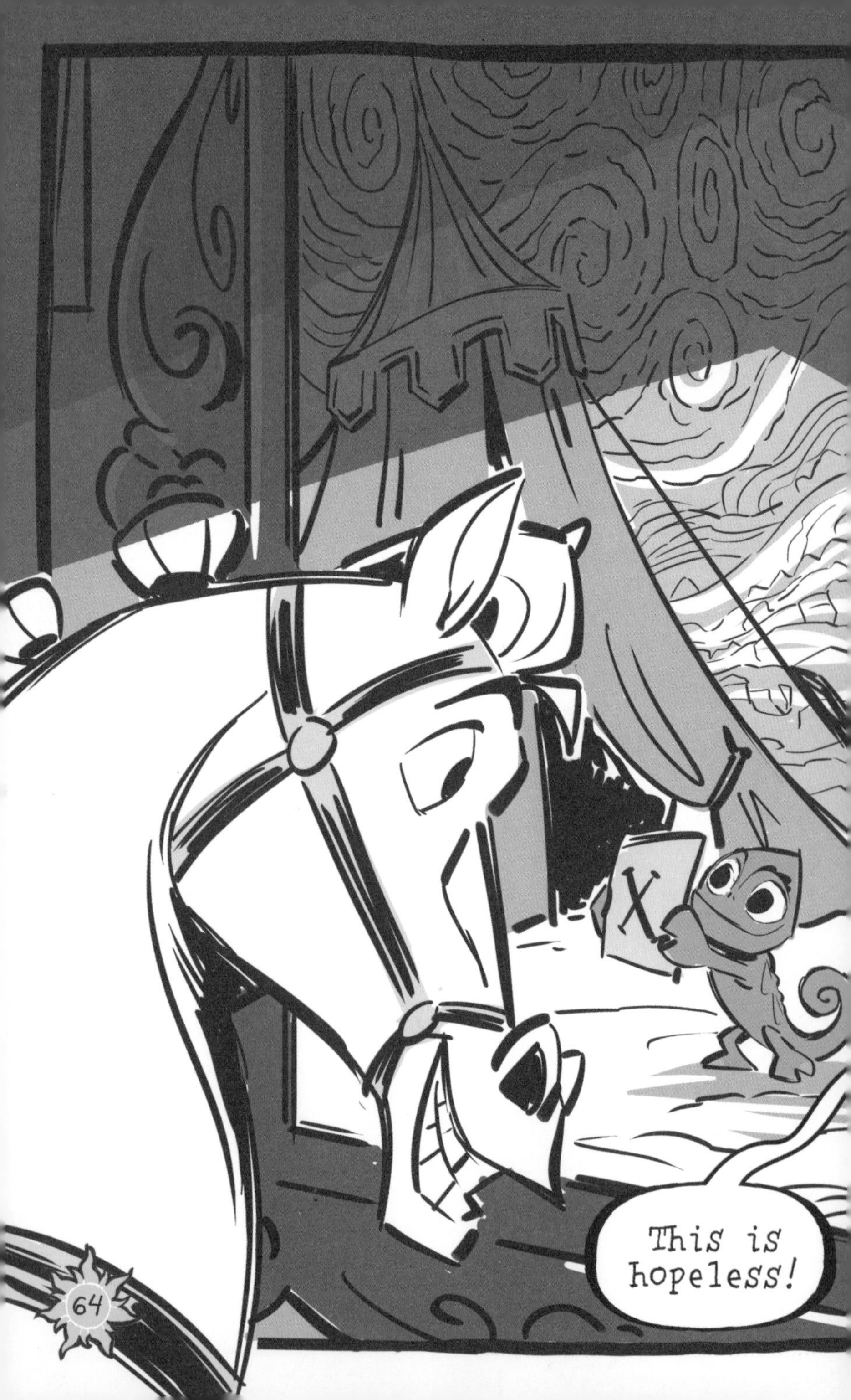
This is hopeless!

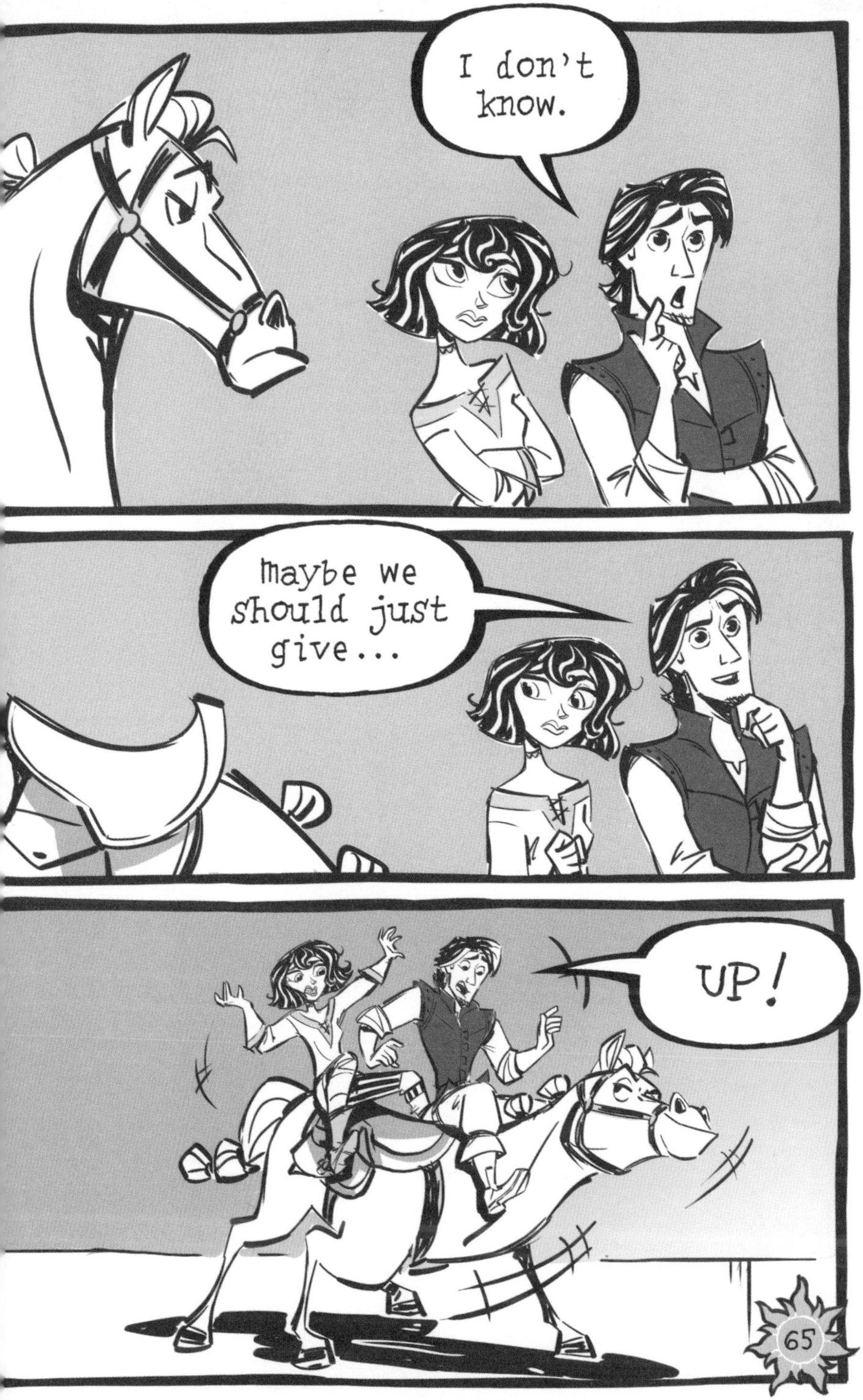
I don't know.
Maybe we should just give...
UP!

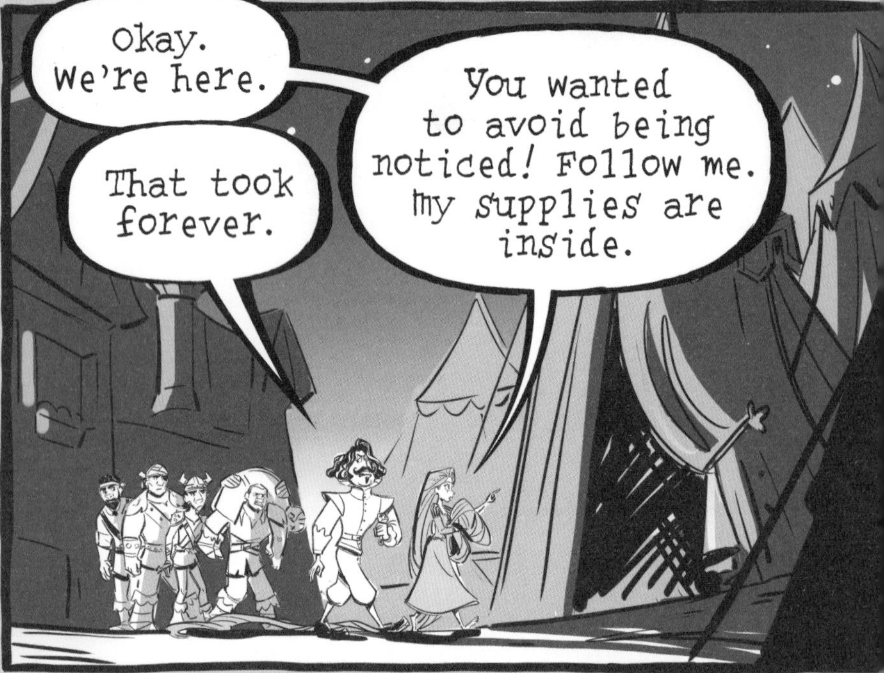
Okay. We're here.
That took forever.
You wanted to avoid being noticed! Follow me. My supplies are inside.
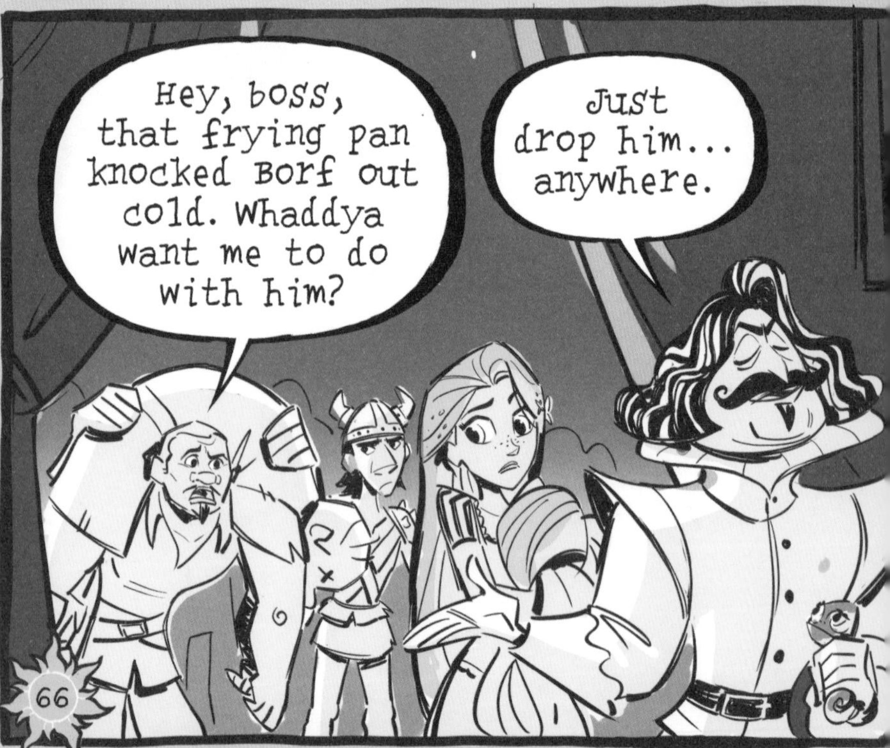
Hey, boss, that frying pan knocked Borf out cold. Whaddya want me to do with him?
Just drop him... anywhere.

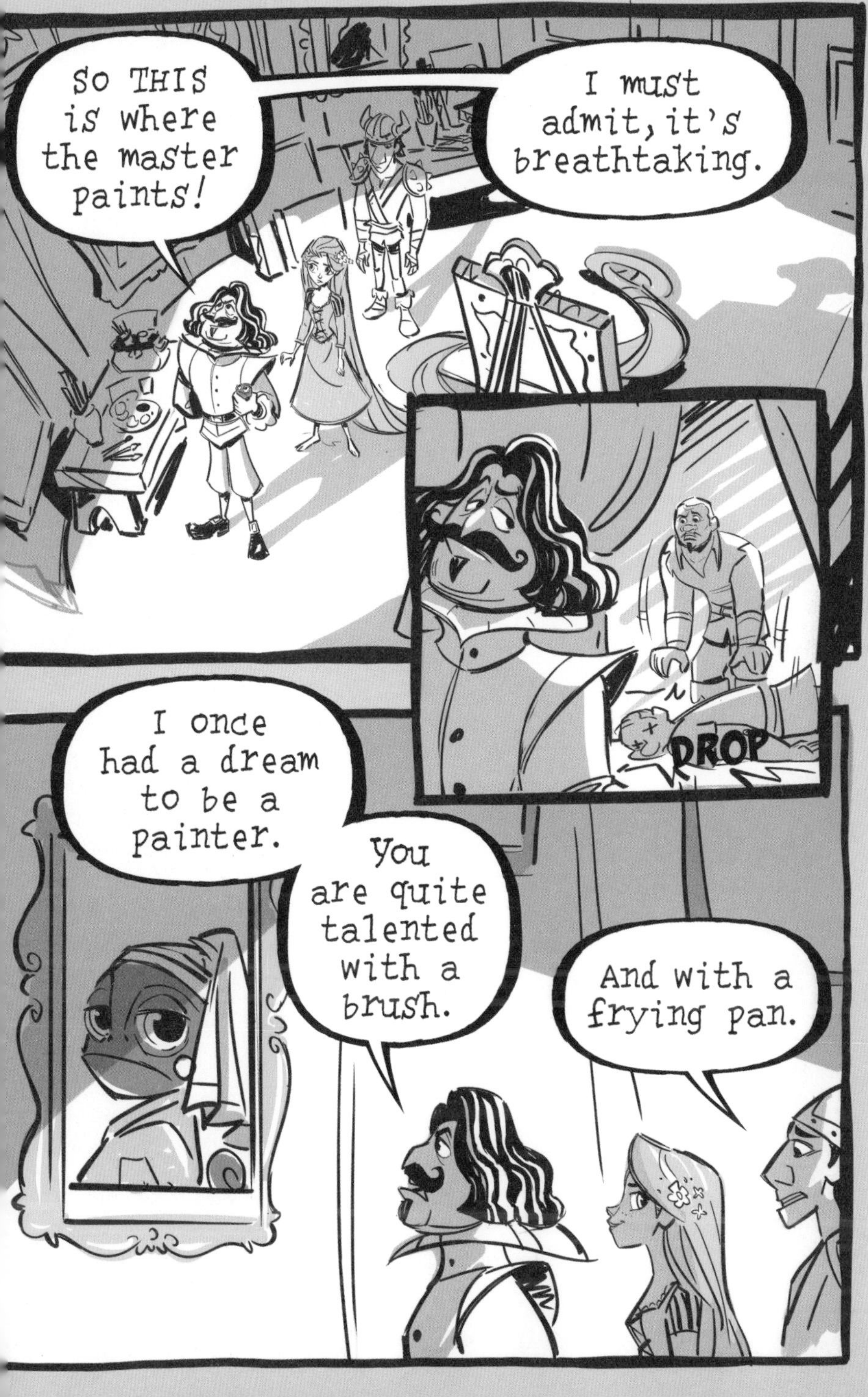
SO THIS is where the master paints!
I must admit, it's breathtaking.
DROP
I once had a dream to be a painter.
You are quite talented with a brush.
And with a frying pan.

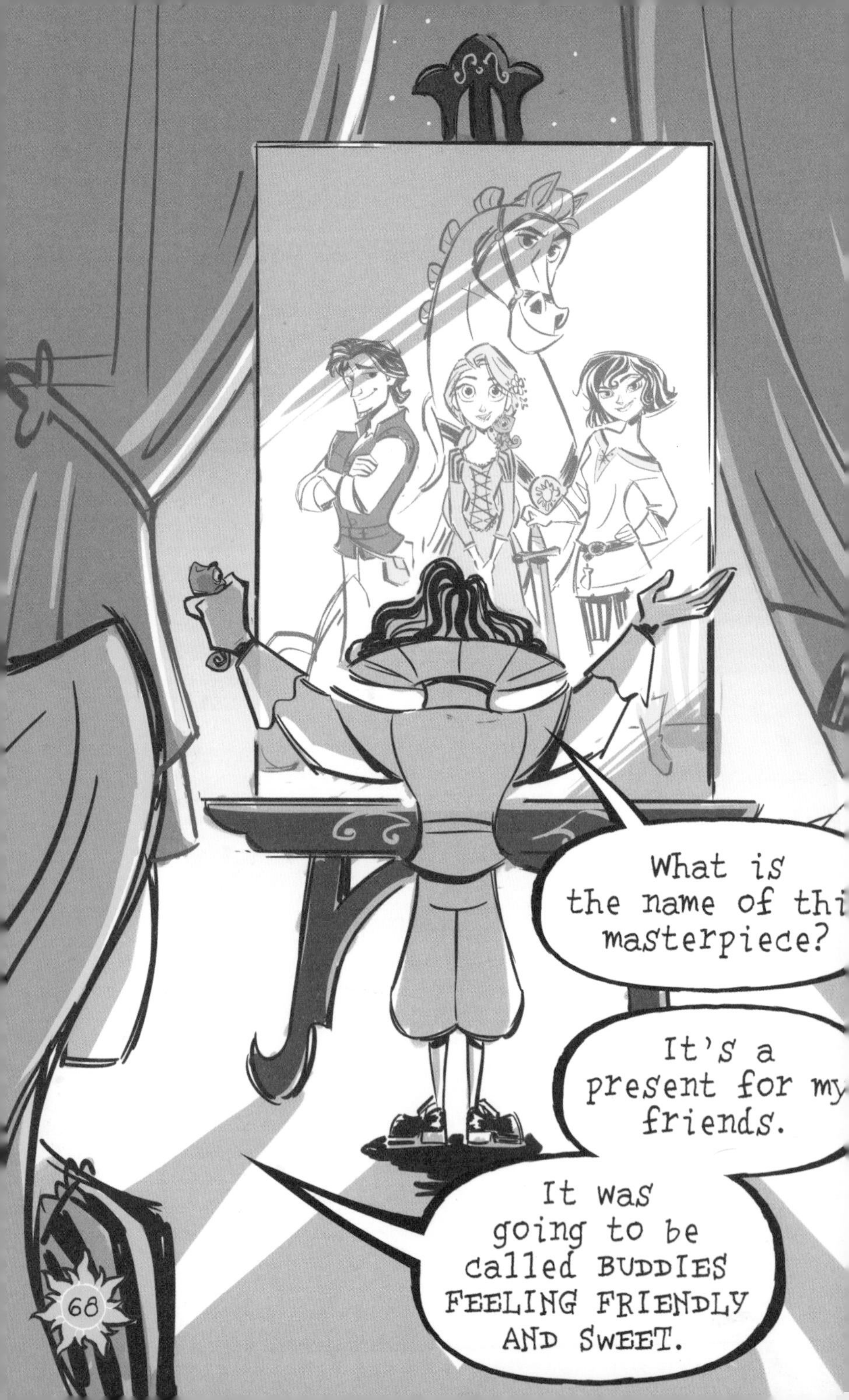
What is the name of thi masterpiece?
It's a present for my friends.
It was going to be called BUDDIES FEELING FRIENDLY AND SWEET.

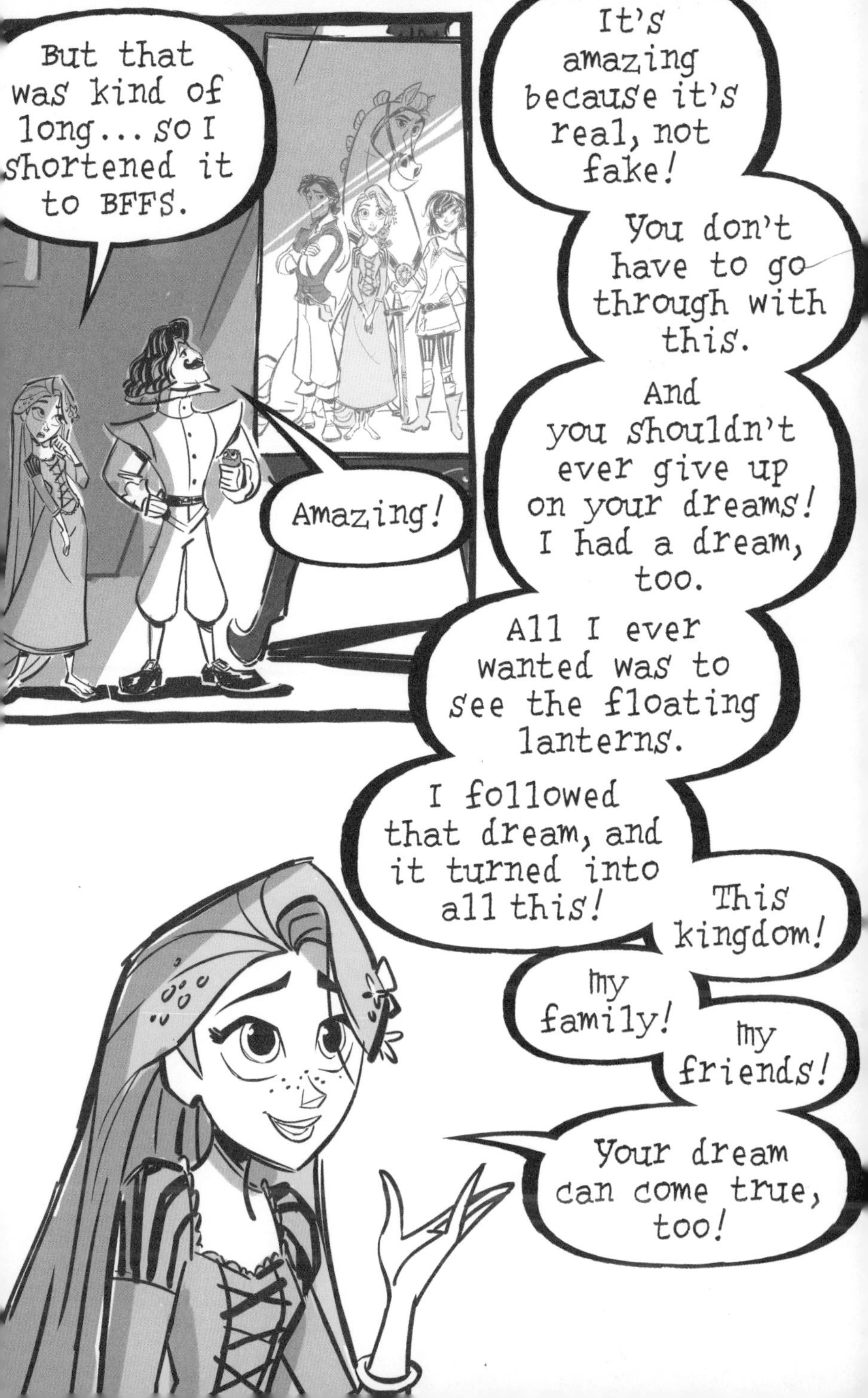
But that was kind of long... so I shortened it to BFFS.
Amazing!
It's amazing because it's real, not fake!
You don't have to go through with this.
And you shouldn't ever give up on your dreams! I had a dream, too.
All I ever wanted was to see the floating lanterns.
I followed that dream, and it turned into all this!
This kingdom!
My family!
My friends!
Your dream can come true, too!

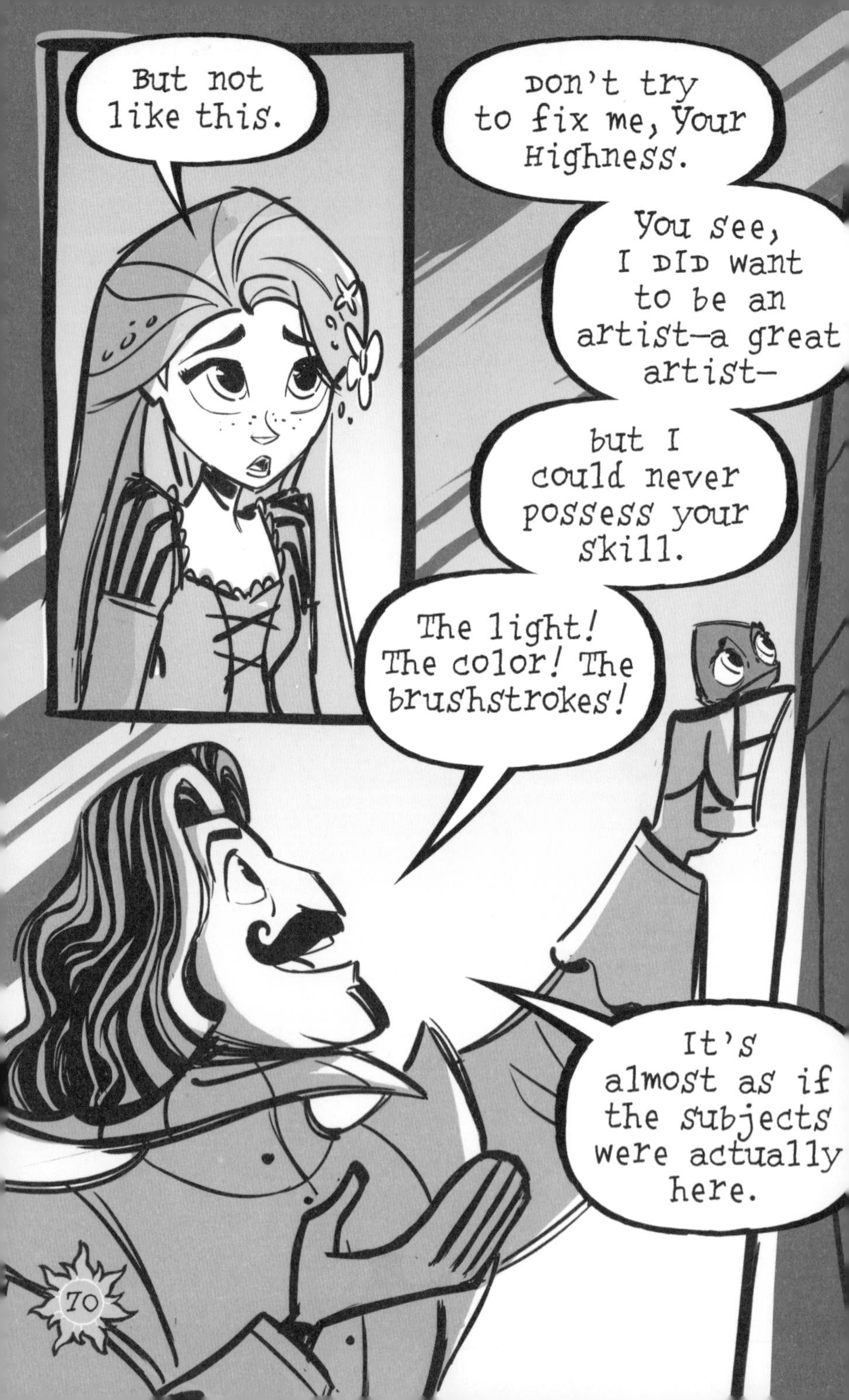

But not like this.
Don't try to fix me, Your Highness.
You see, I DID want to be an artist—a great artist—
but I could never possess your skill.
The light! The color! The brushstrokes!
It's almost as if the subjects were actually here.

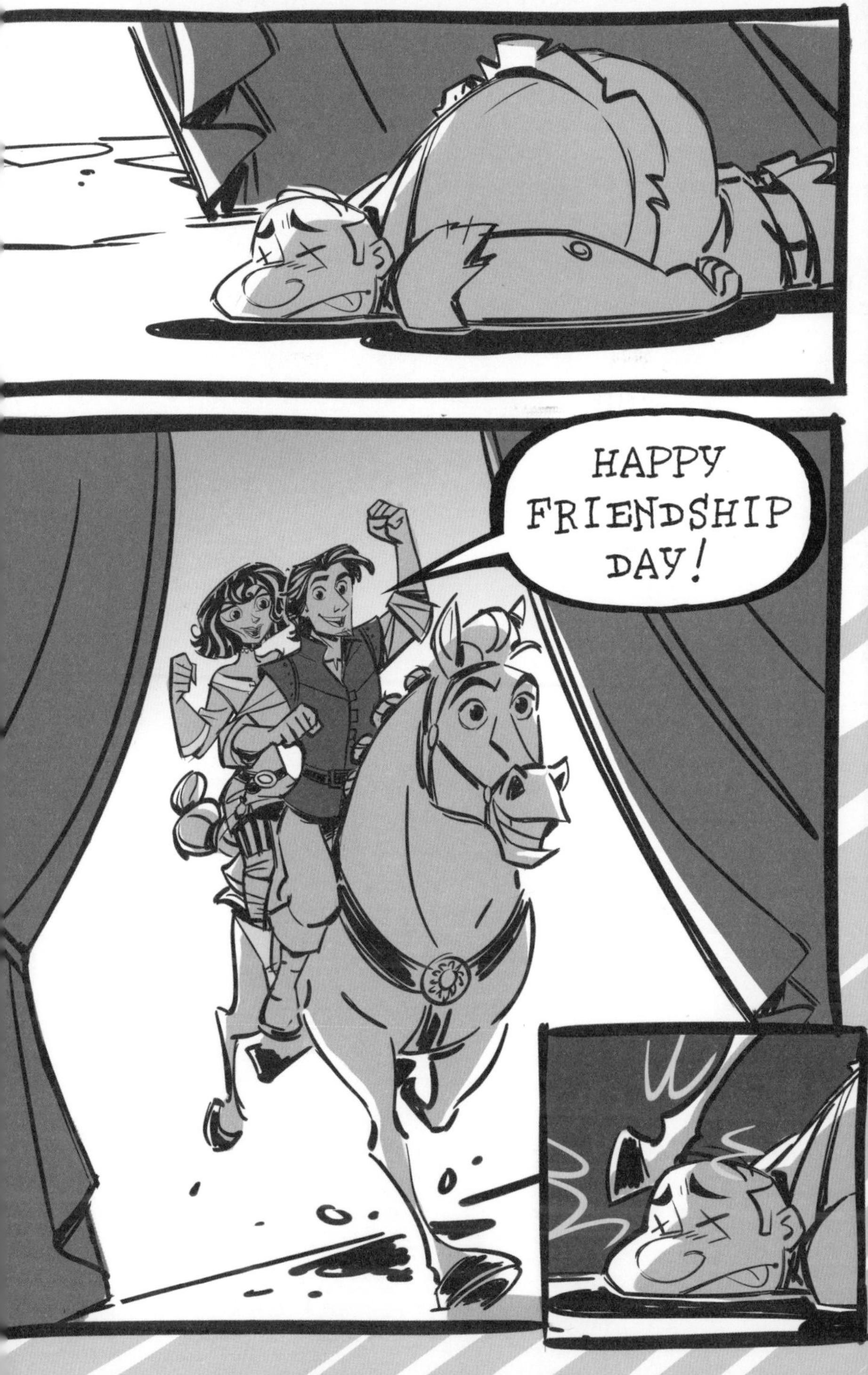
HAPPY FRIENDSHIP DAY!

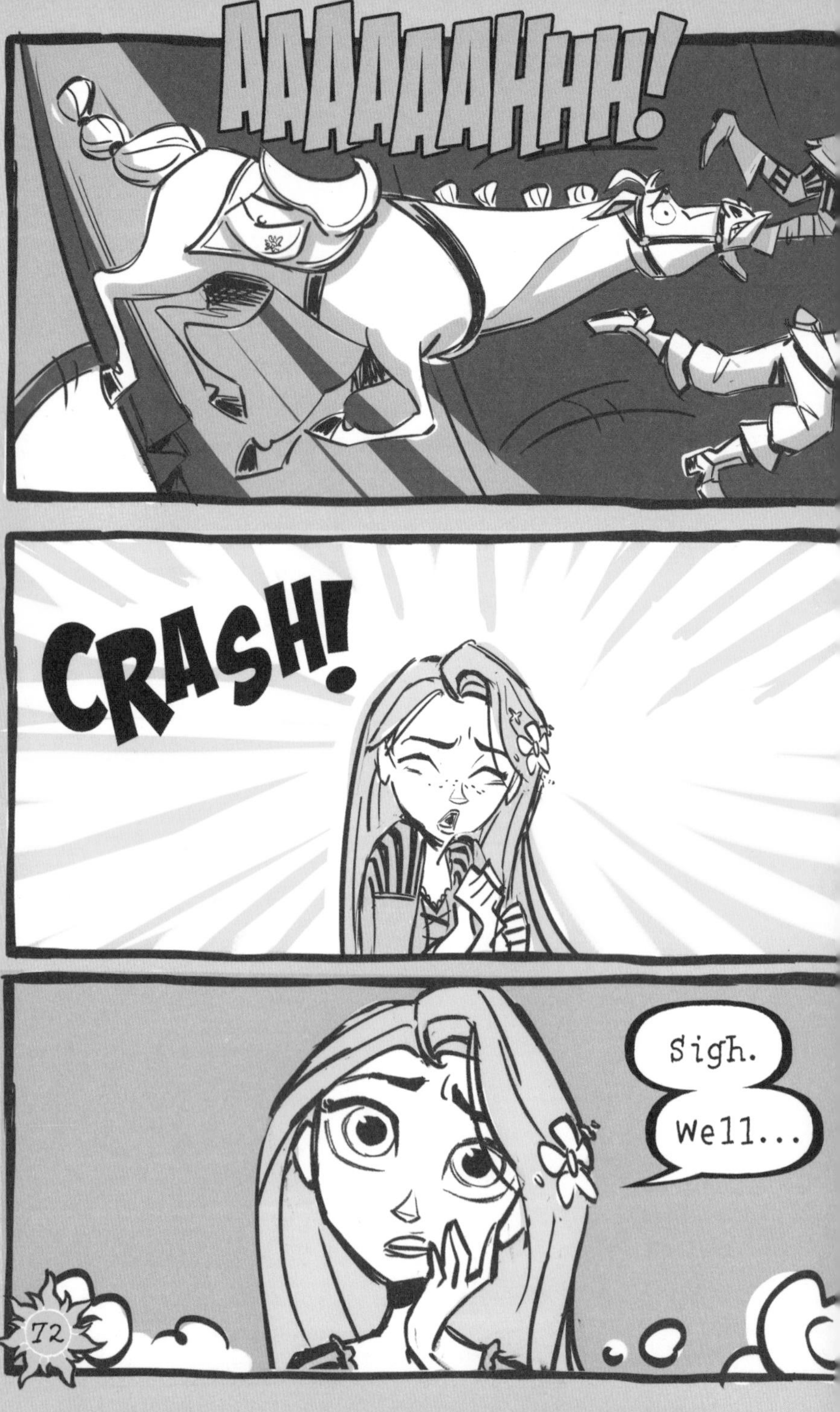
AAAAAAHHH!
CRASH!
Sigh.
Well...

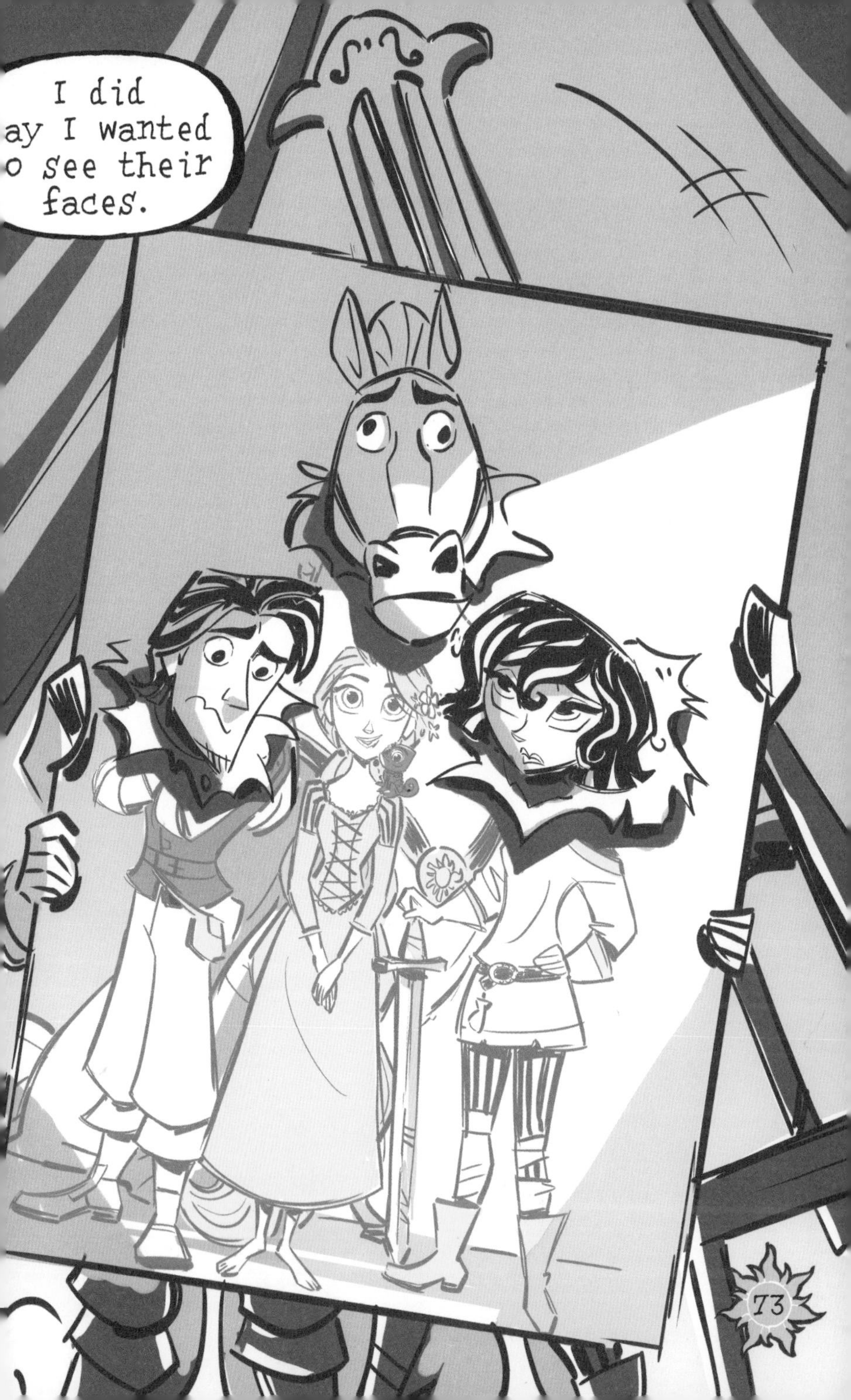
I did
ay I wanted
o see their
faces.

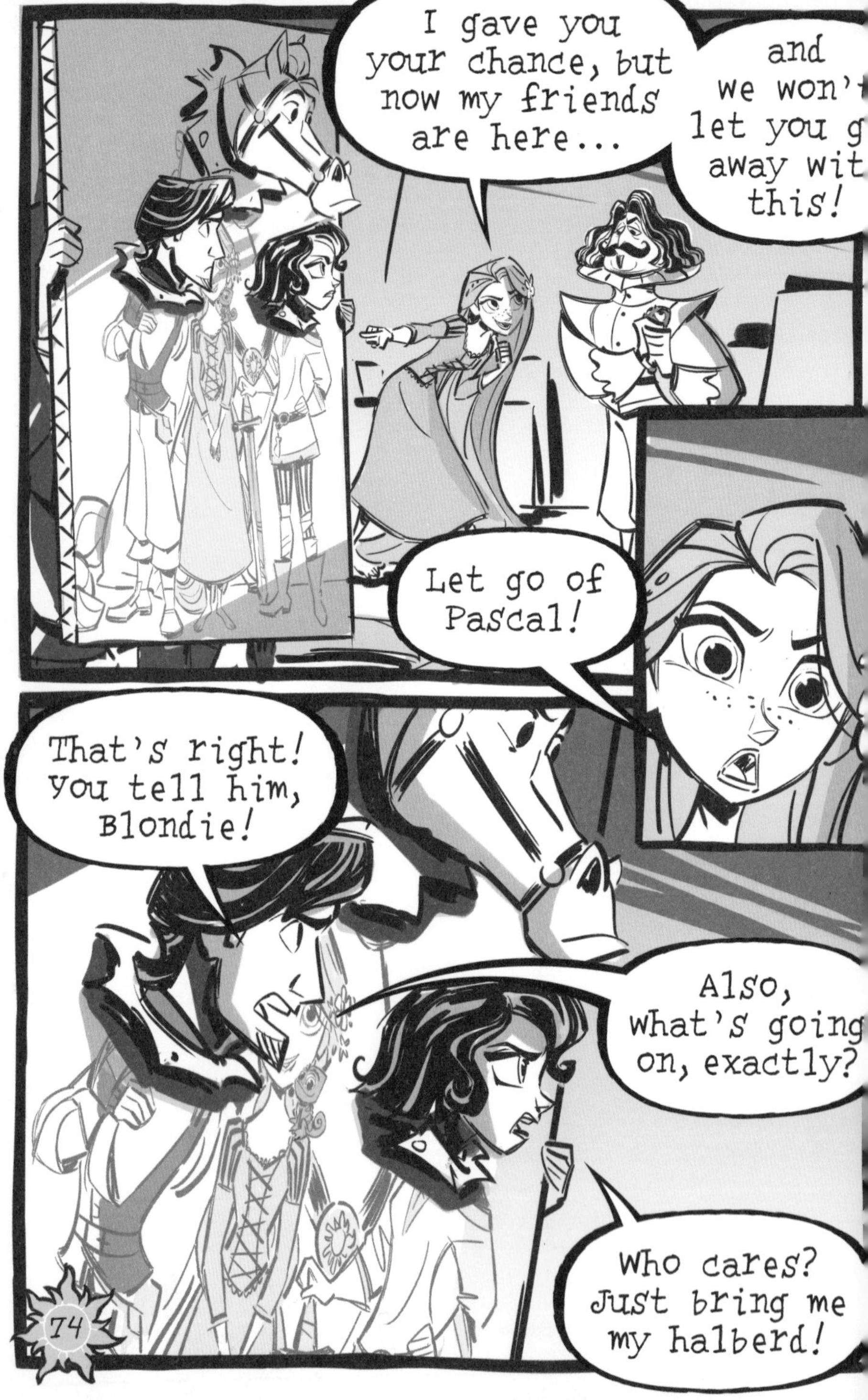
I gave you your chance, but now my friends are here...
and we won' let you g away wit this!
Let go of Pascal!
That's right! You tell him, Blondie!
Also, what's goin on, exactly?
Who cares? Just bring me my halberd!

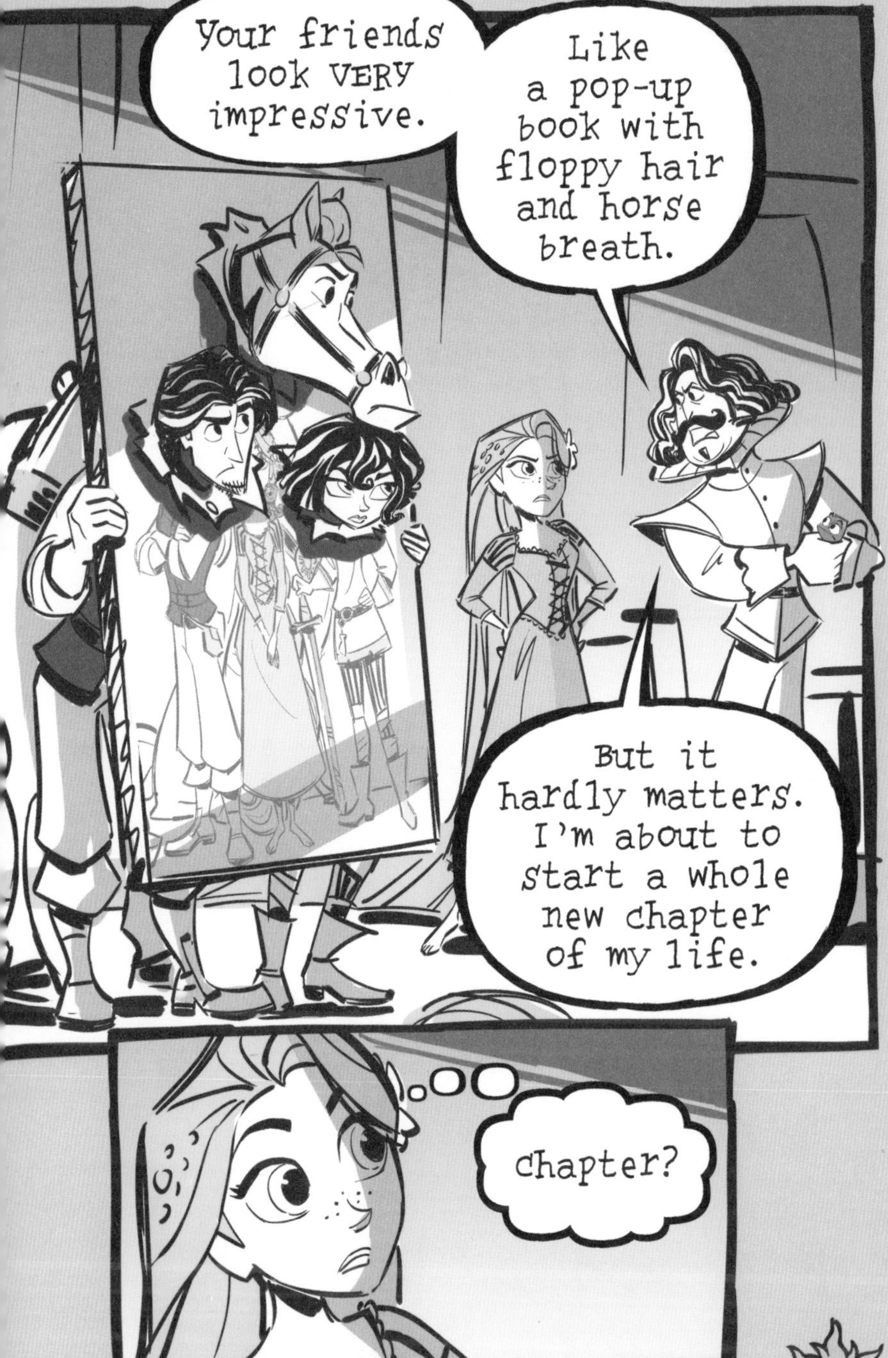
Your friends look VERY impressive.
Like a pop-up book with floppy hair and horse breath.
But it hardly matters. I'm about to start a whole new chapter of my life.
Chapter?

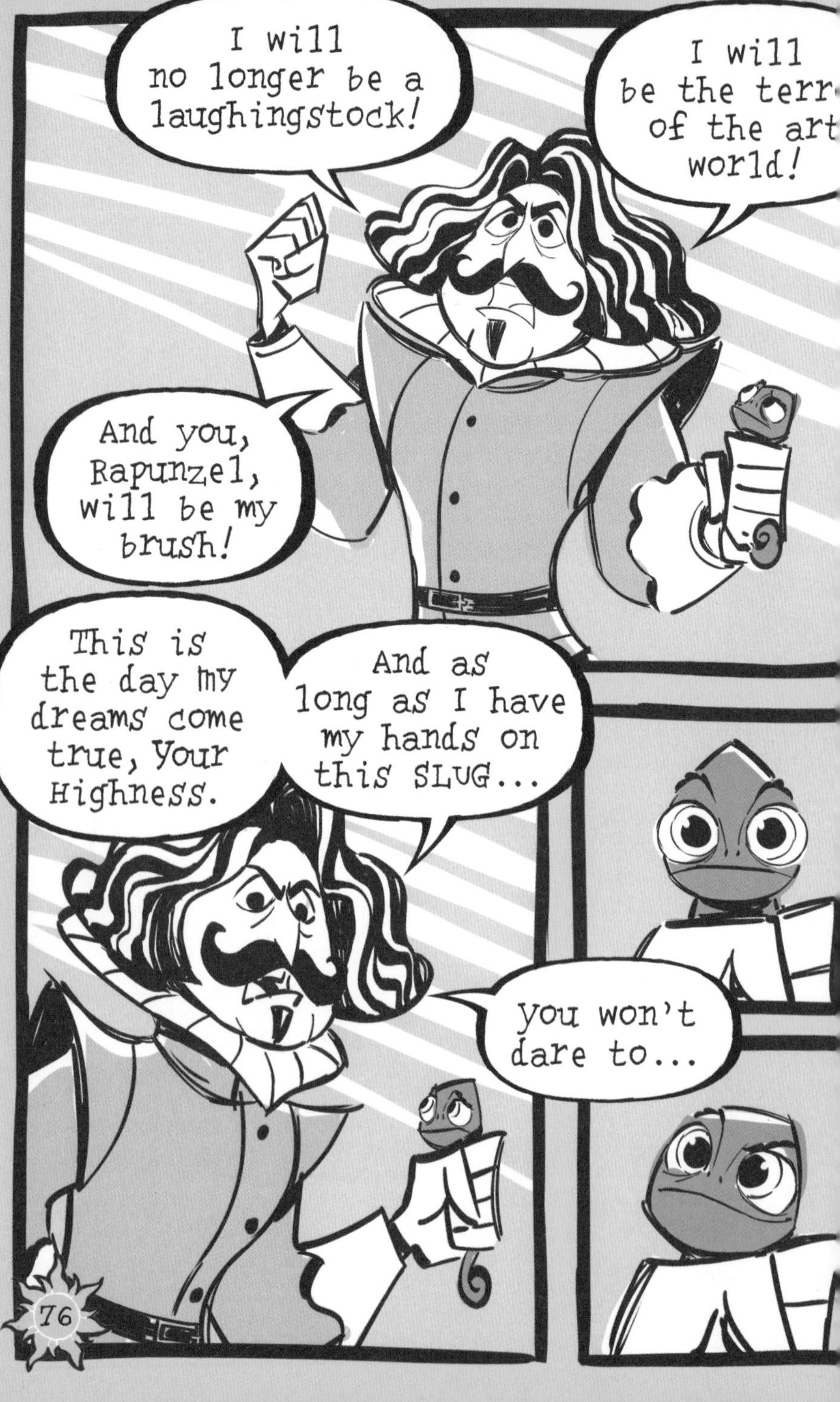
I will no longer be a laughingstock!
I will be the terr of the art world!
And you, Rapunzel, will be my brush!
This is the day my dreams come true, Your Highness.
And as long as I have my hands on this SLUG...
you won't dare to...

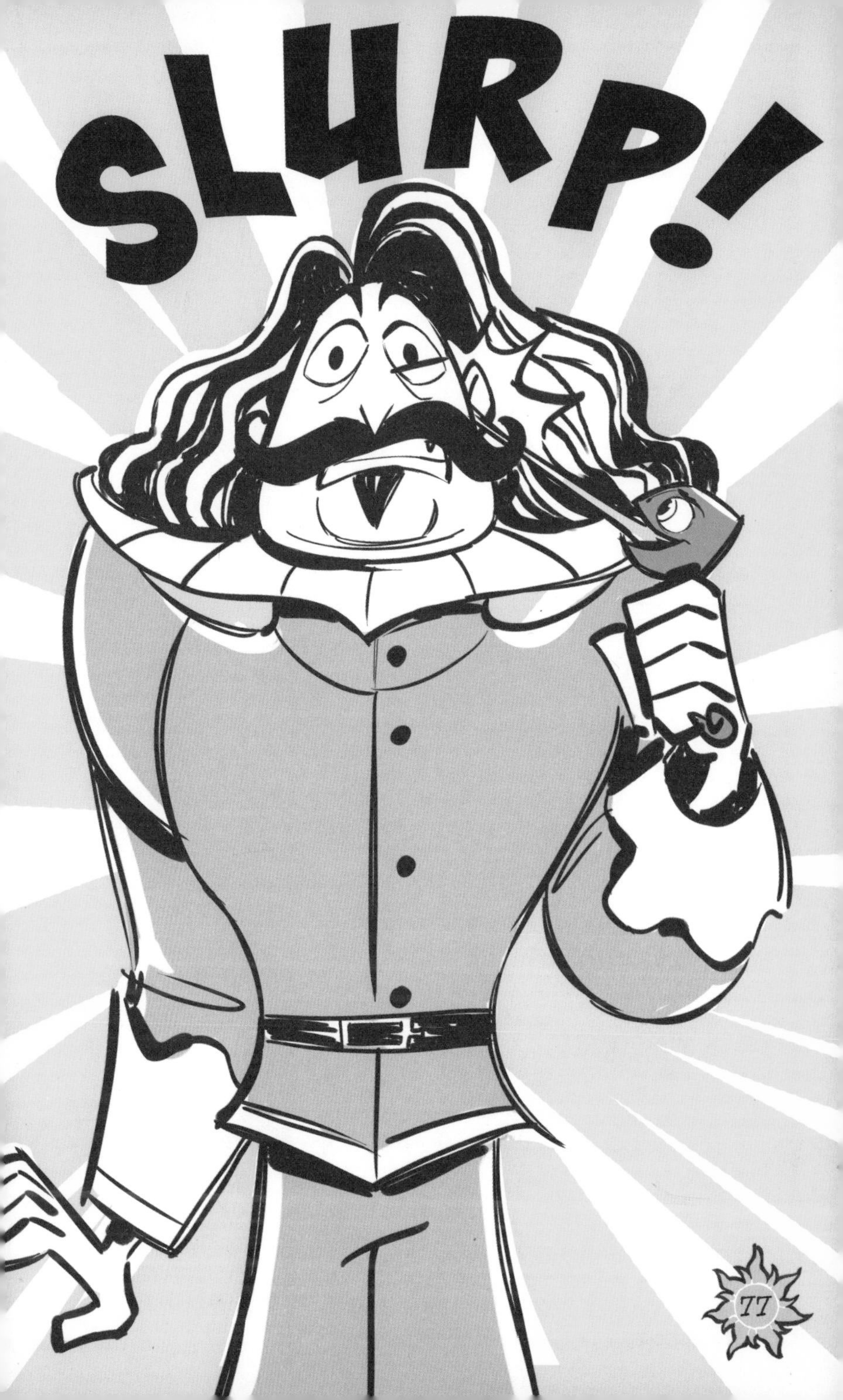
SLURP!

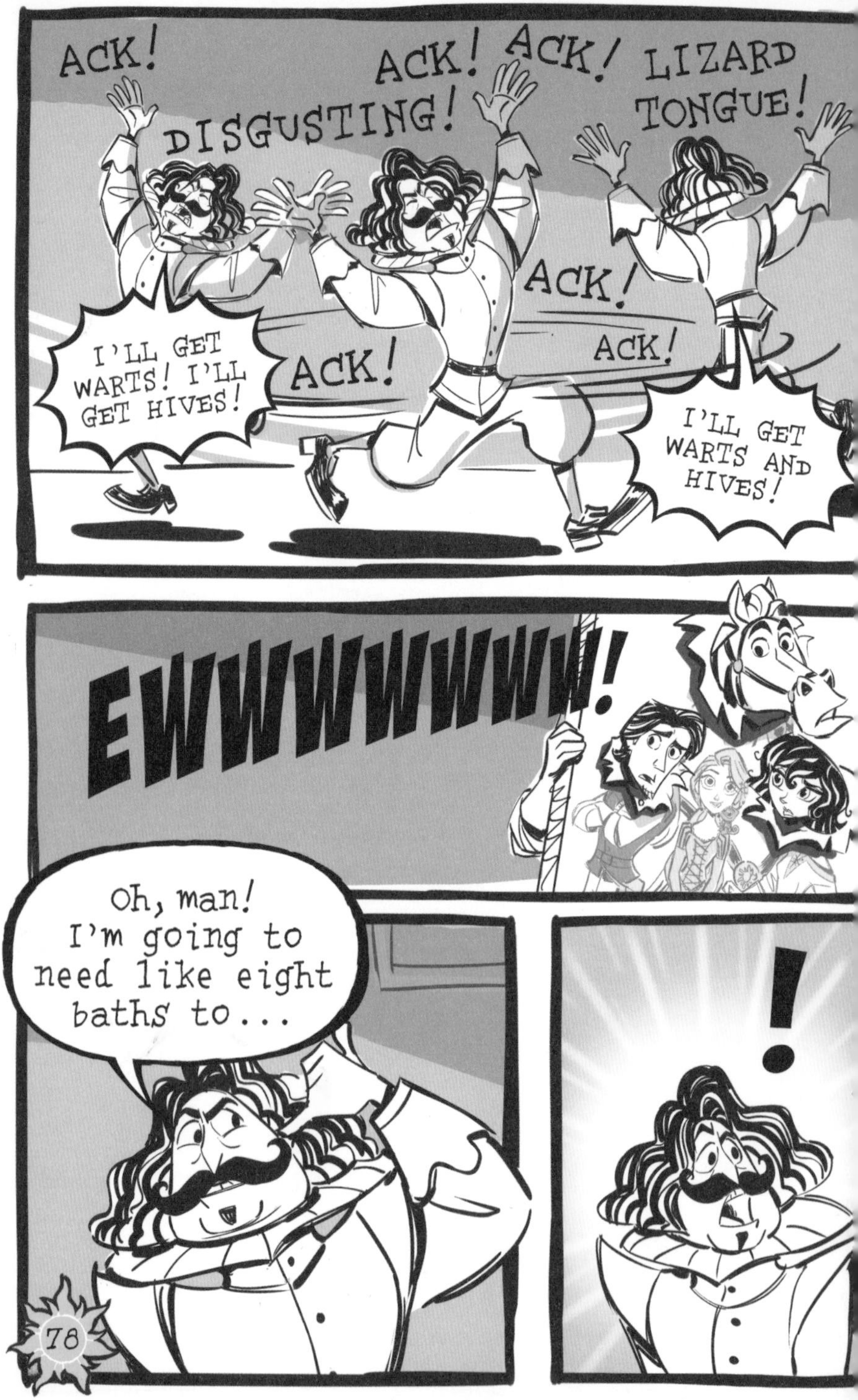
ACK!
ACK! ACK! LIZARD TONGUE!
DISGUSTING!
ACK!
I'LL GET WARTS! I'LL GET HIVES!
ACK!
ACK!
I'LL GET WARTS AND HIVES!
EWWWWWWWW!
Oh, man! I'm going to need like eight baths to...
!

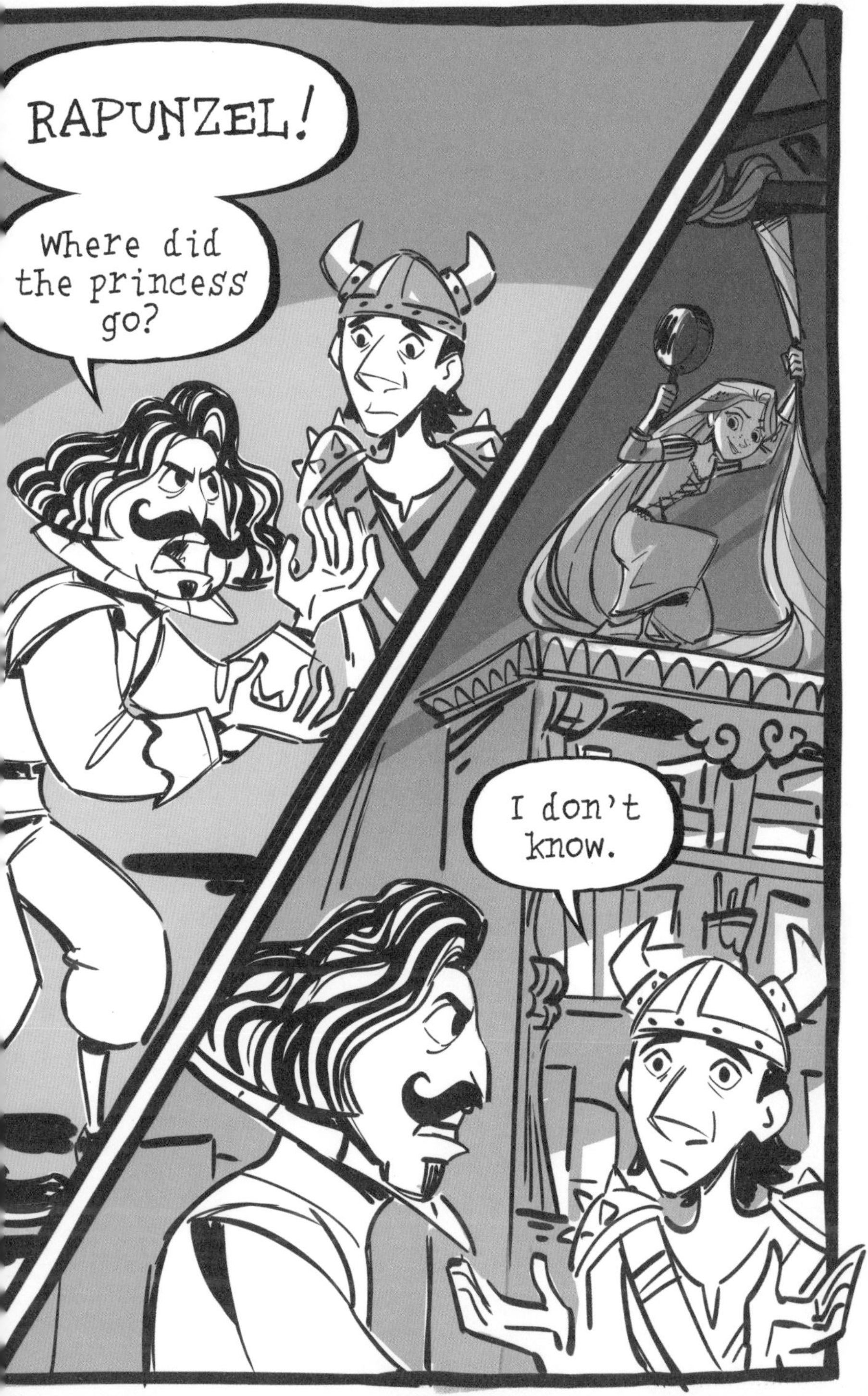
RAPUNZEL!
Where did the princess go?
I don't know.

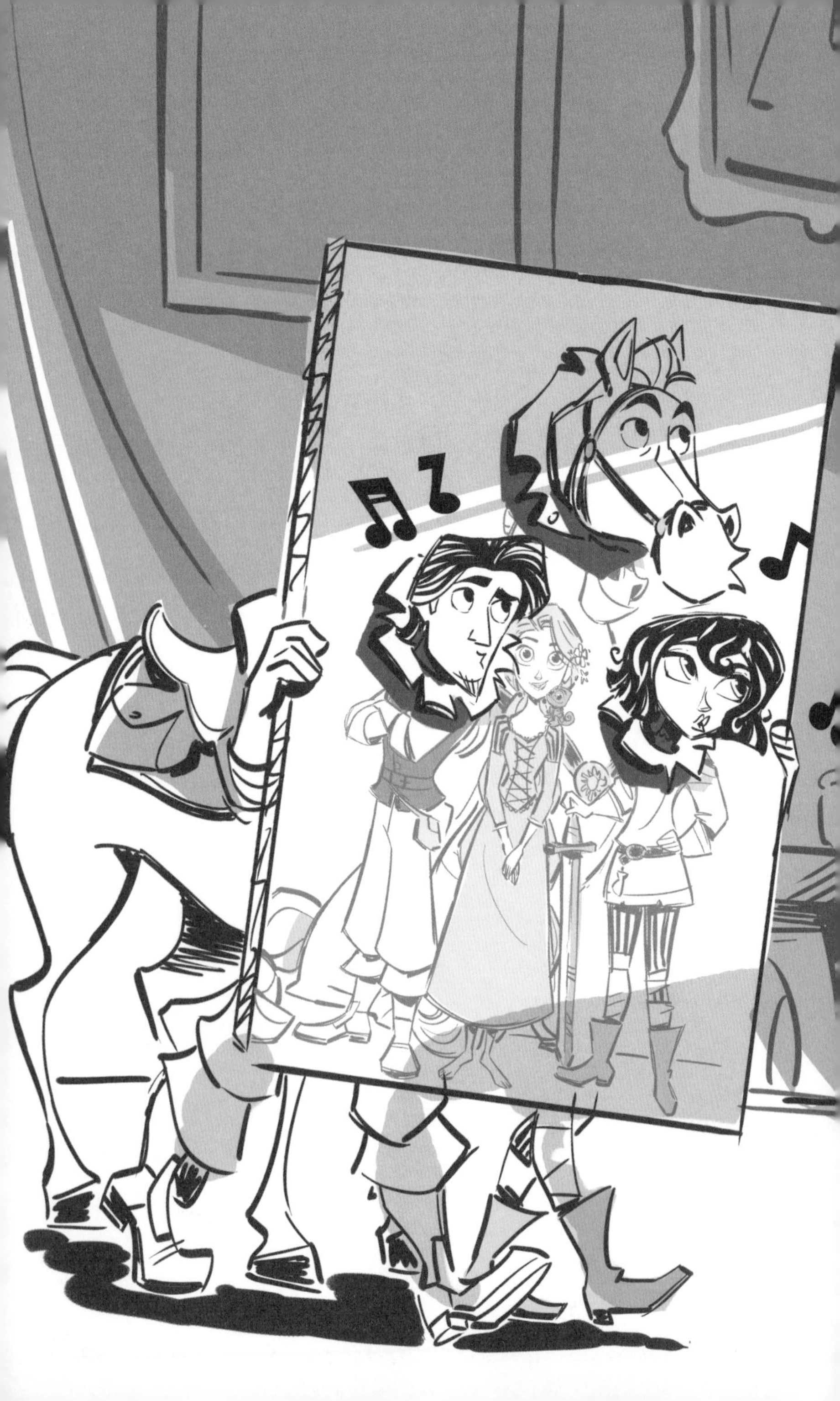

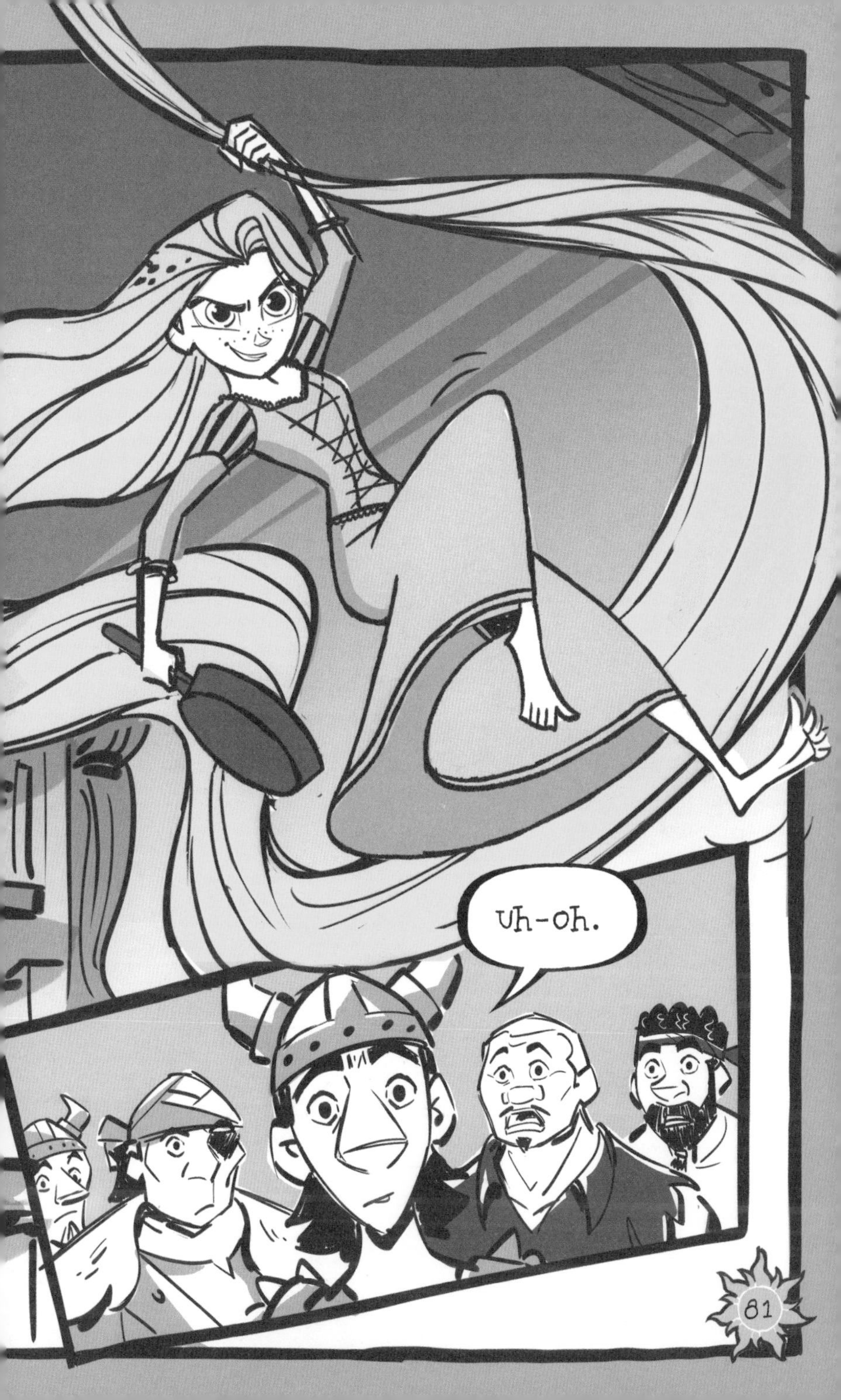
Uh-oh.

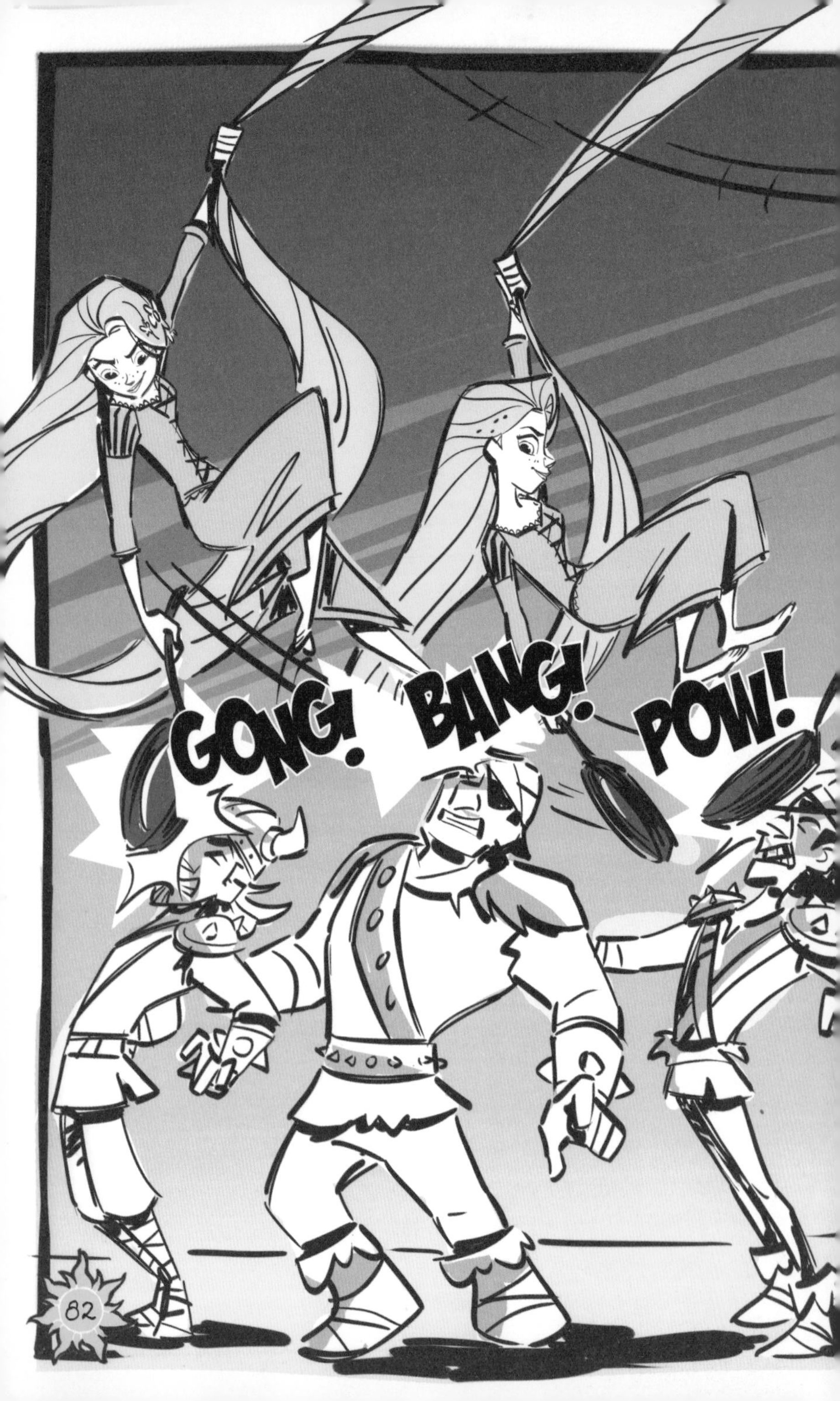
GONG!
BANG!
POW!

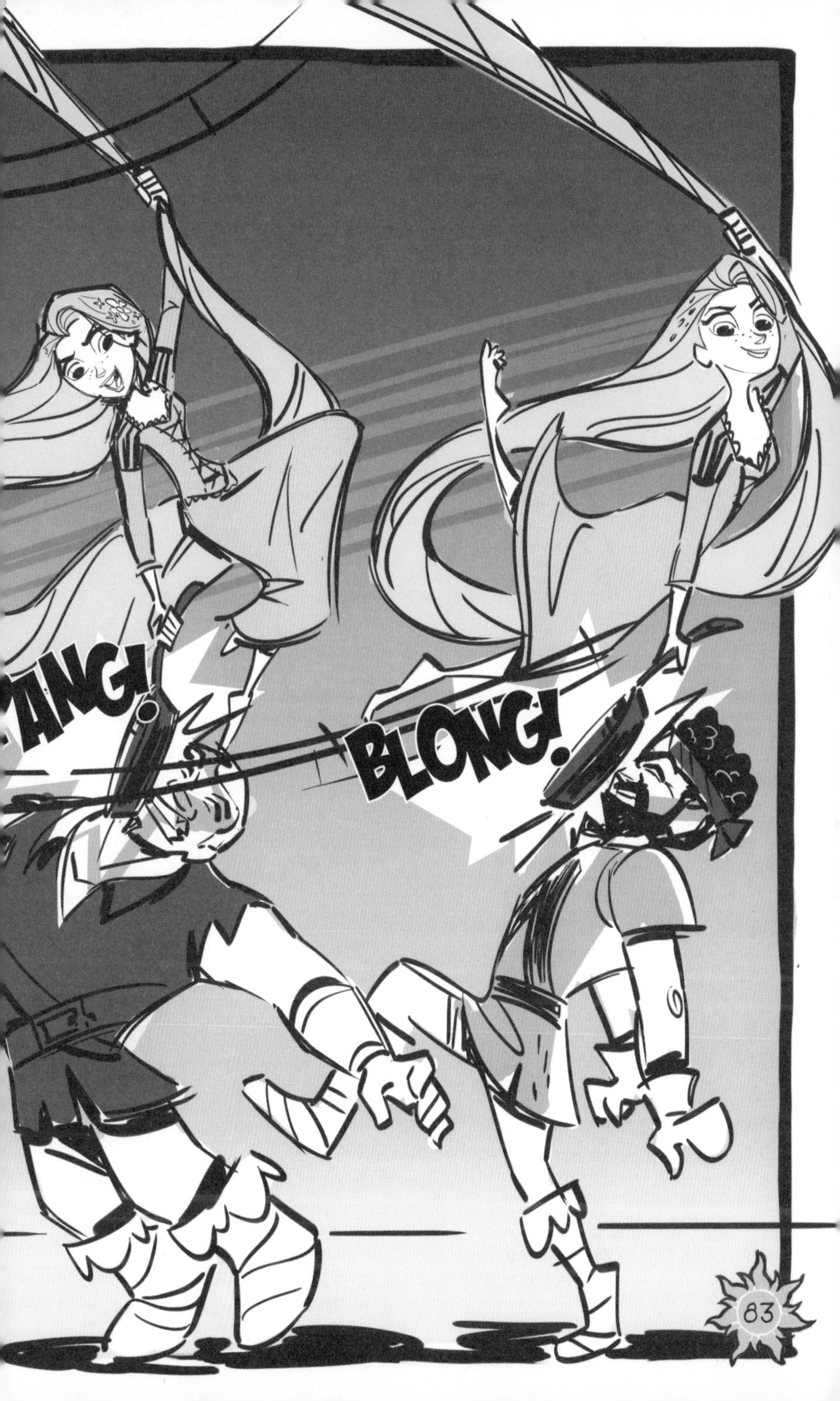
ANG!
BLONG!

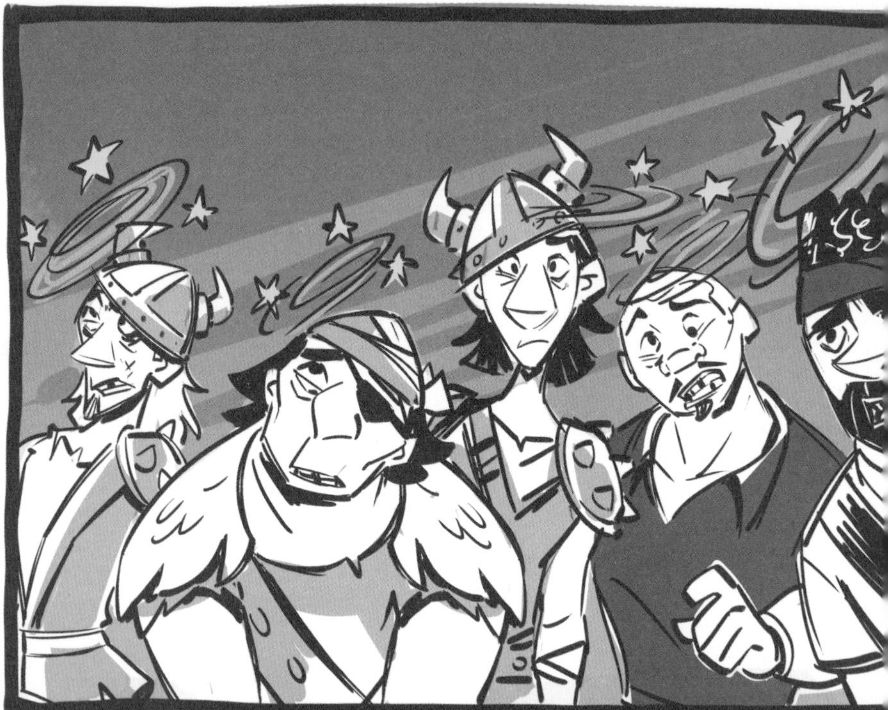

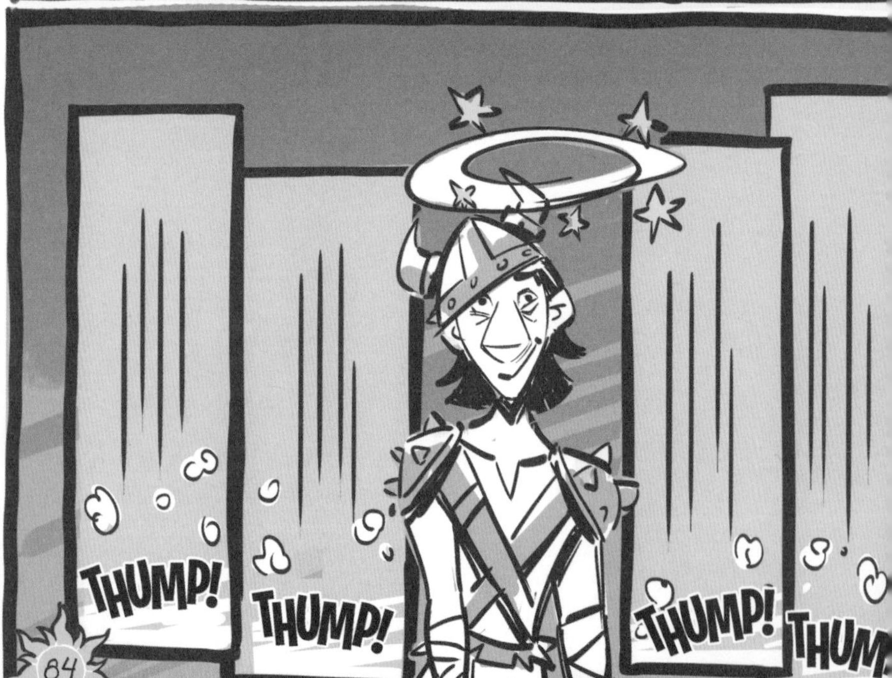
THUMP!
THUMP!
THUMP!
THUM

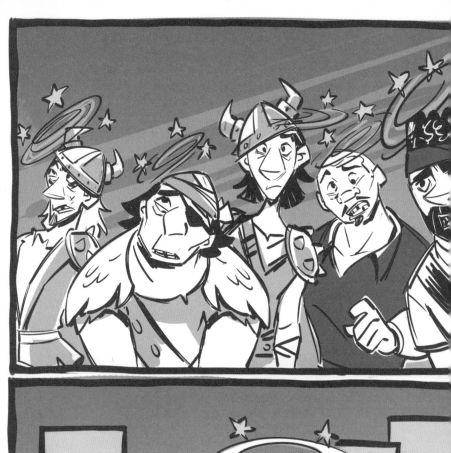

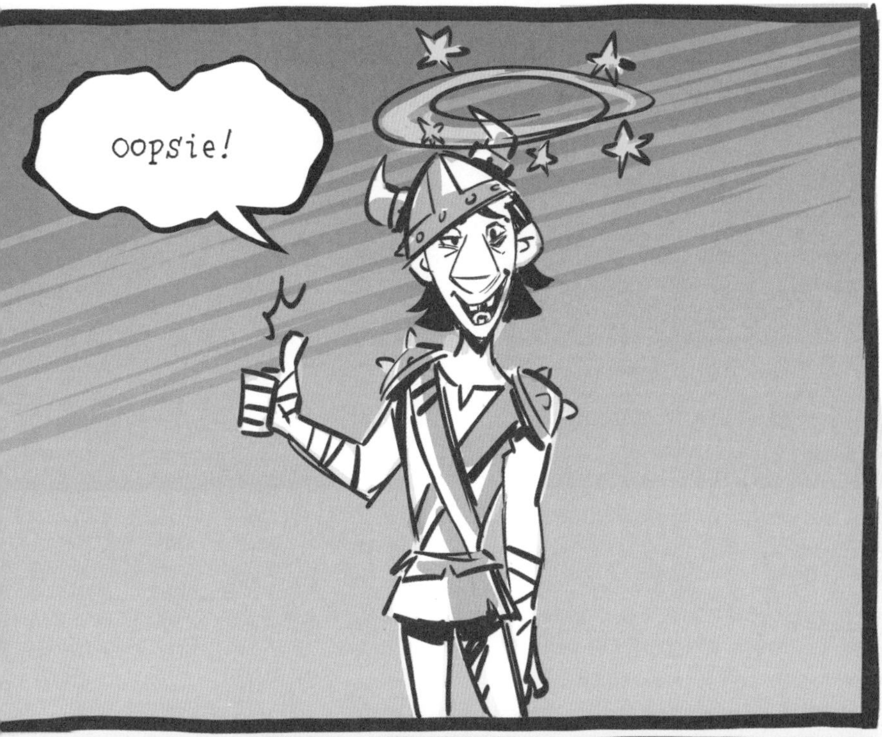
oopsie!

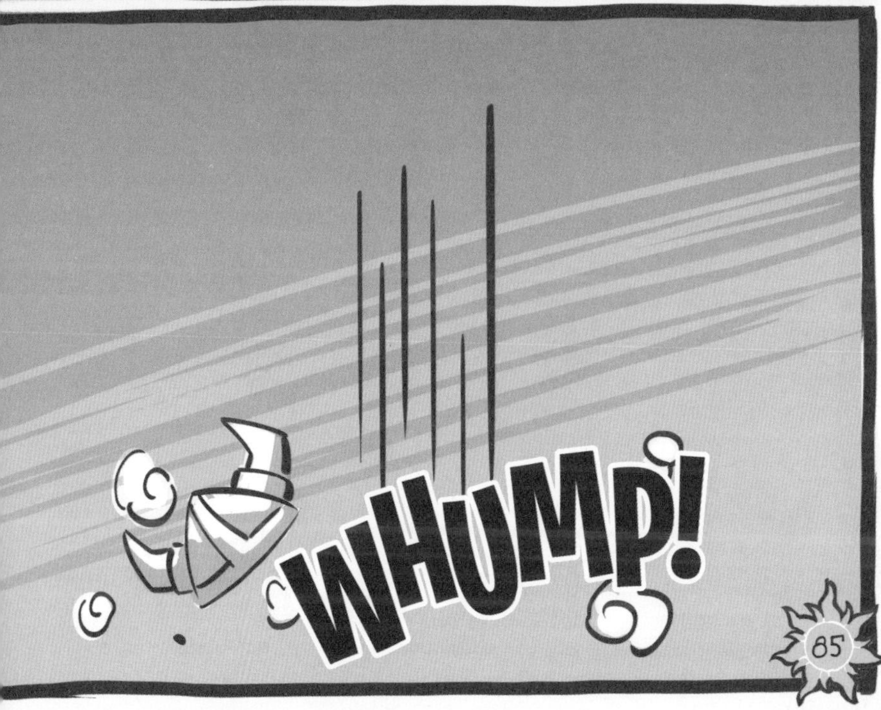
WHUMP!

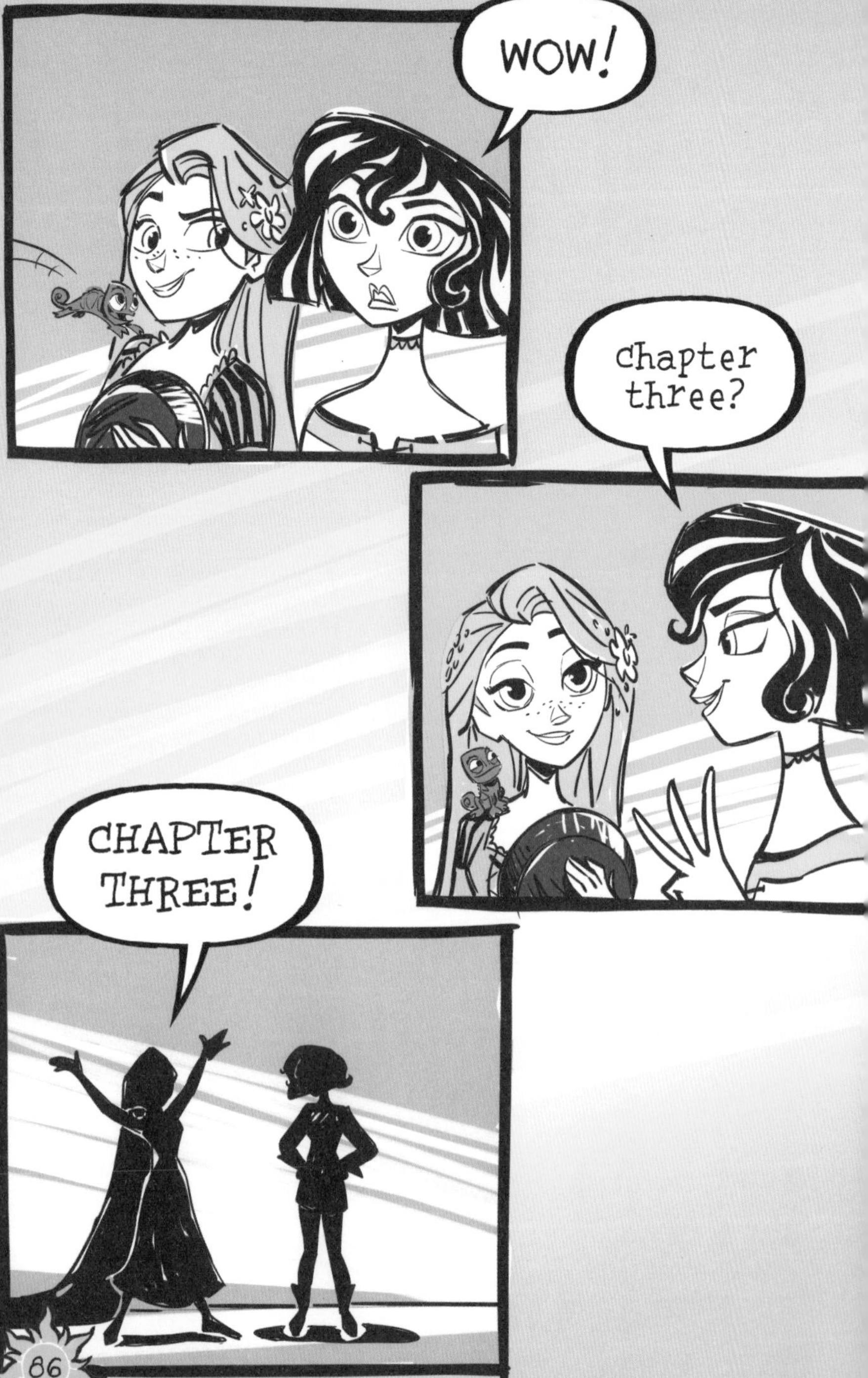
WOW!
chapter three?
CHAPTER THREE!

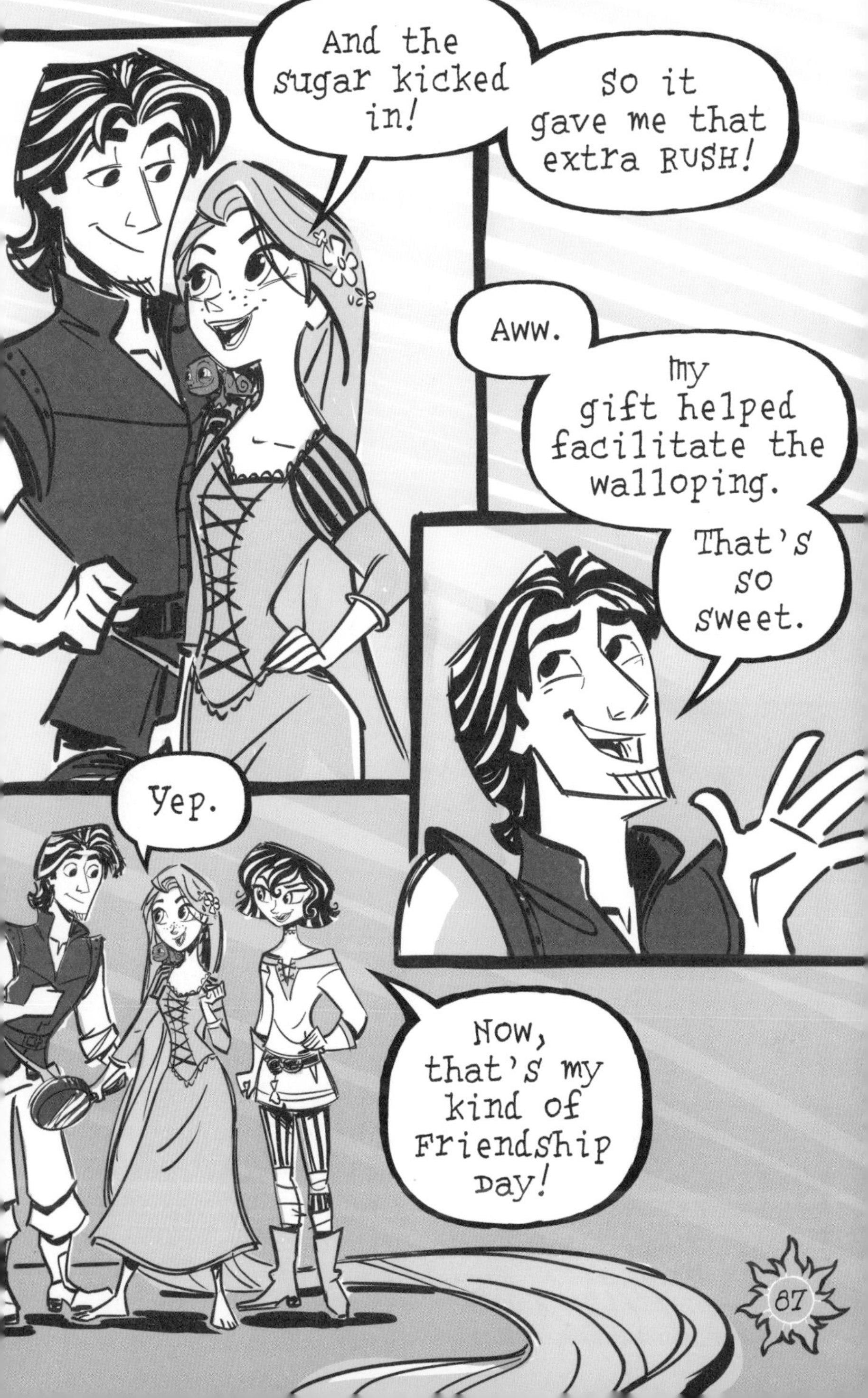
And the sugar kicked in!
So it gave me that extra RUSH!
Aww.
My gift helped facilitate the walloping.
That's so sweet.
Yep.
Now, that's my kind of Friendship Day!

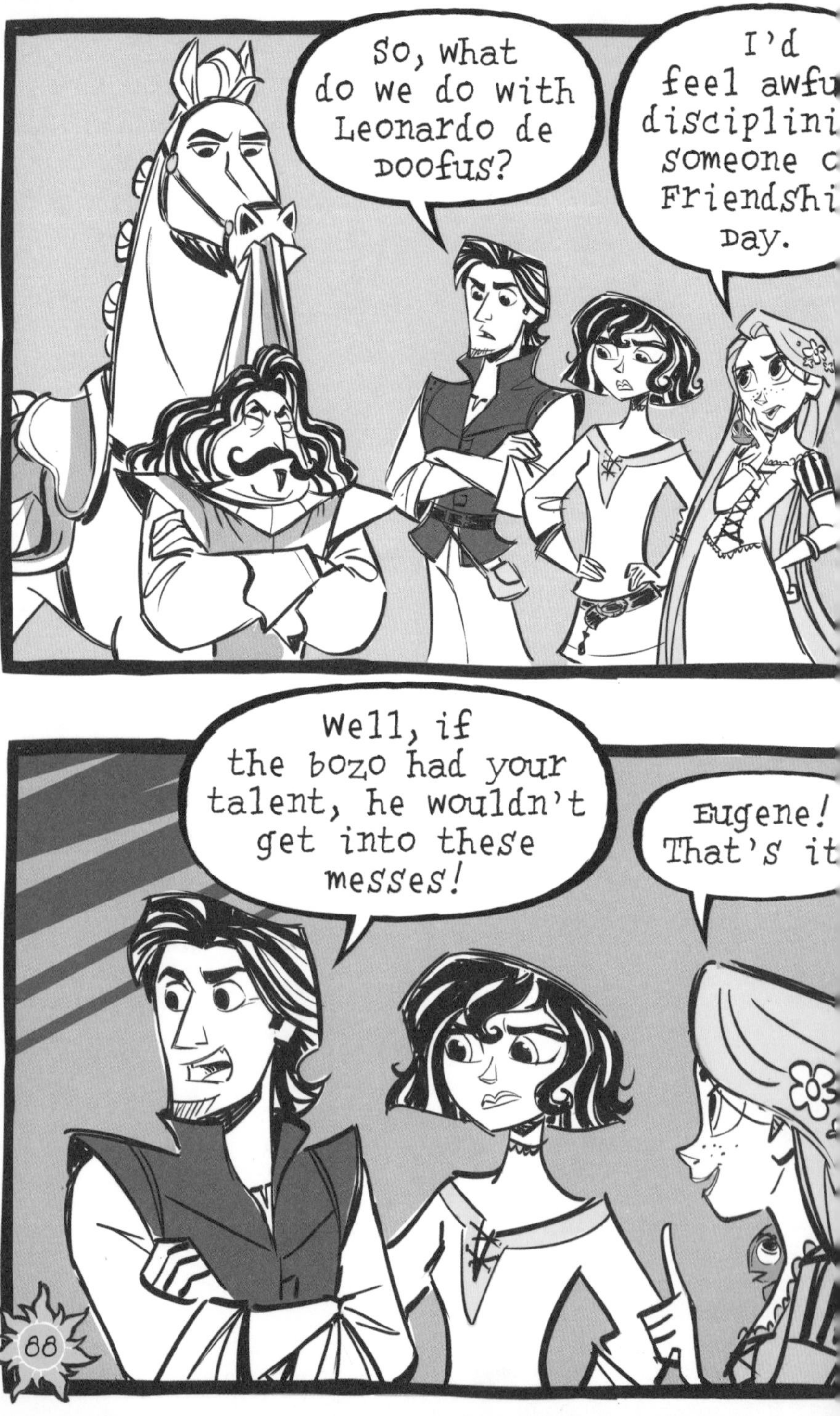
So, what do we do with Leonardo de Doofus?
I'd feel awfu discipli someone c Friendshi Day.
Well, if the bozo had your talent, he wouldn't get into these messes!
Eugene! That's it

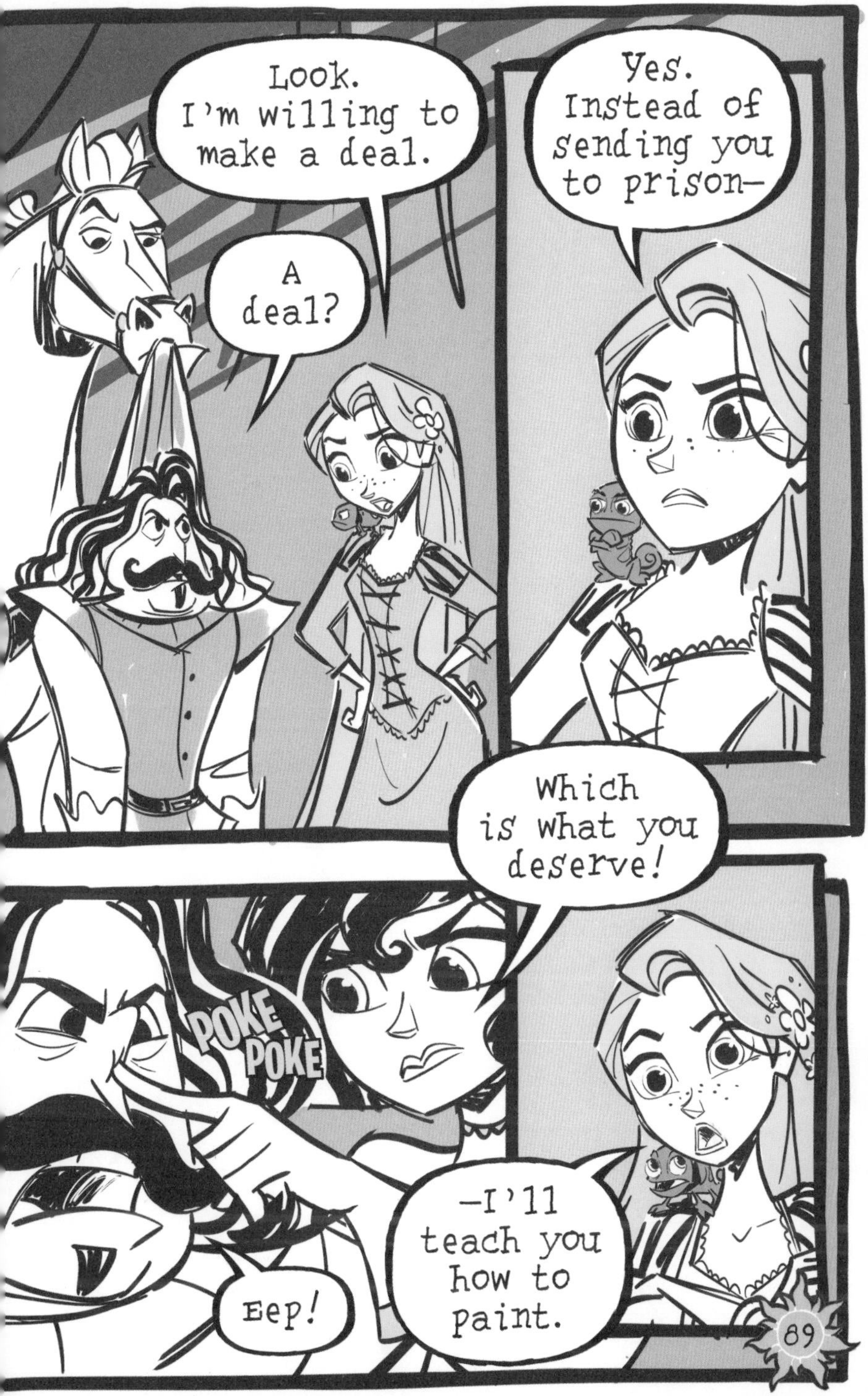

Look. I'm willing to make a deal.
A deal?
Yes. Instead of sending you to prison—
POKE POKE
Eep!
Which is what you deserve!
—I'll teach you how to paint.

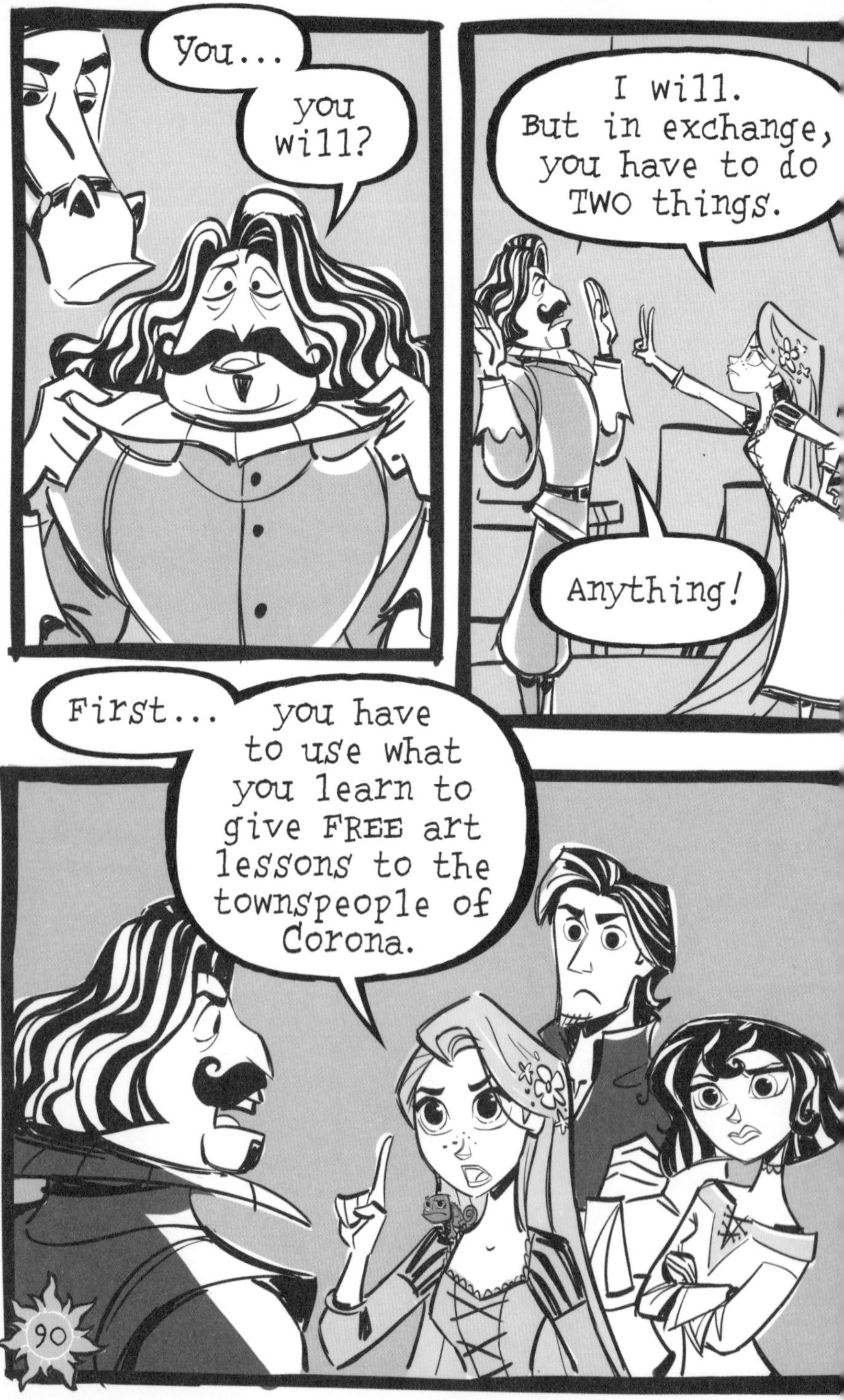

You...
you will?
I will. But in exchange, you have to do TWO things.
Anything!
First...
you have to use what you learn to give FREE art lessons to the townspeople of Corona.

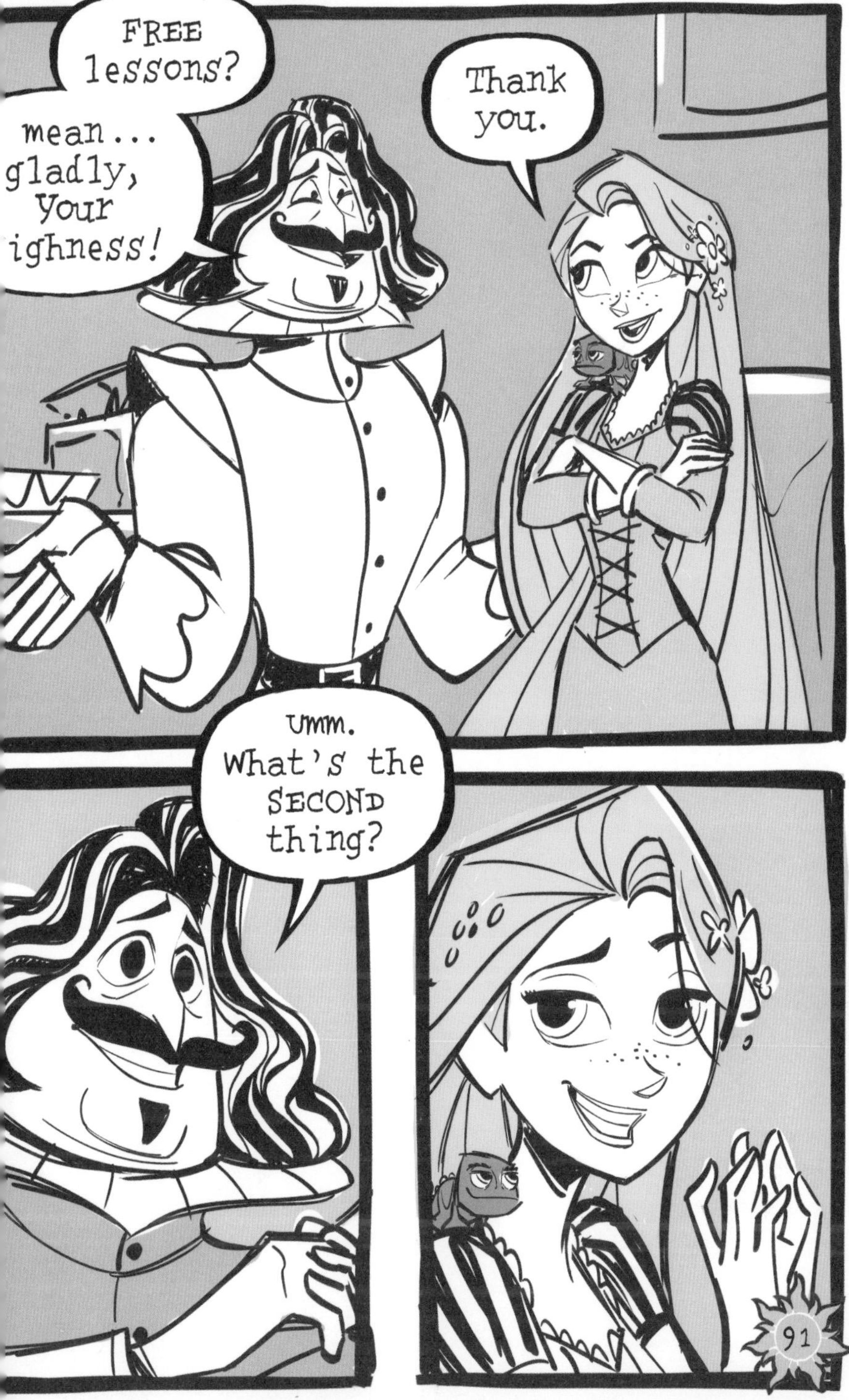
FREE lessons?
mean... gladly, Your ighness!
Thank you.
Umm. What's the SECOND thing?

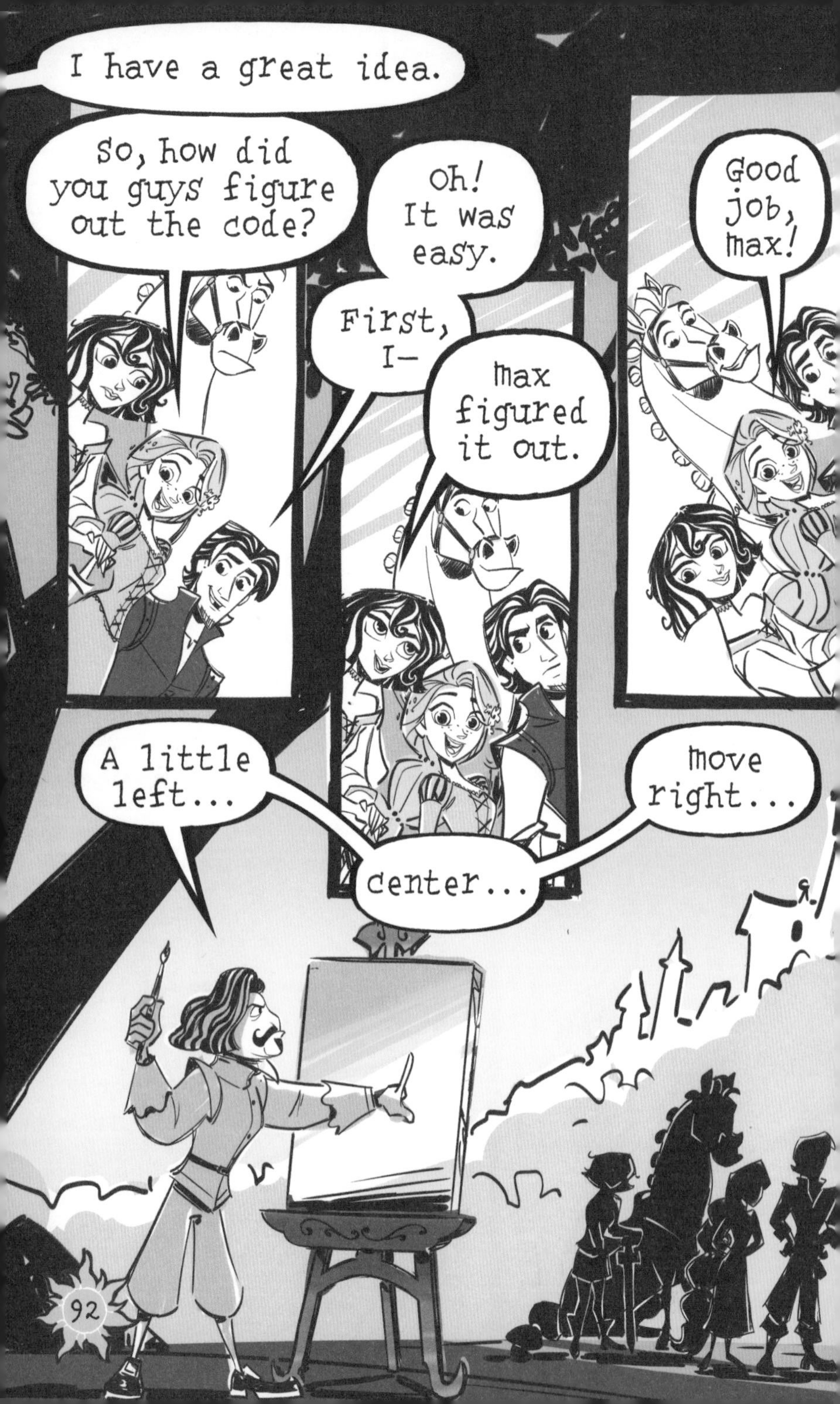
I have a great idea.
So, how did you guys figure out the code?
Oh! It was easy.
First, I—
Max figured it out.
Good job, Max!
A little left...
center...
move right...

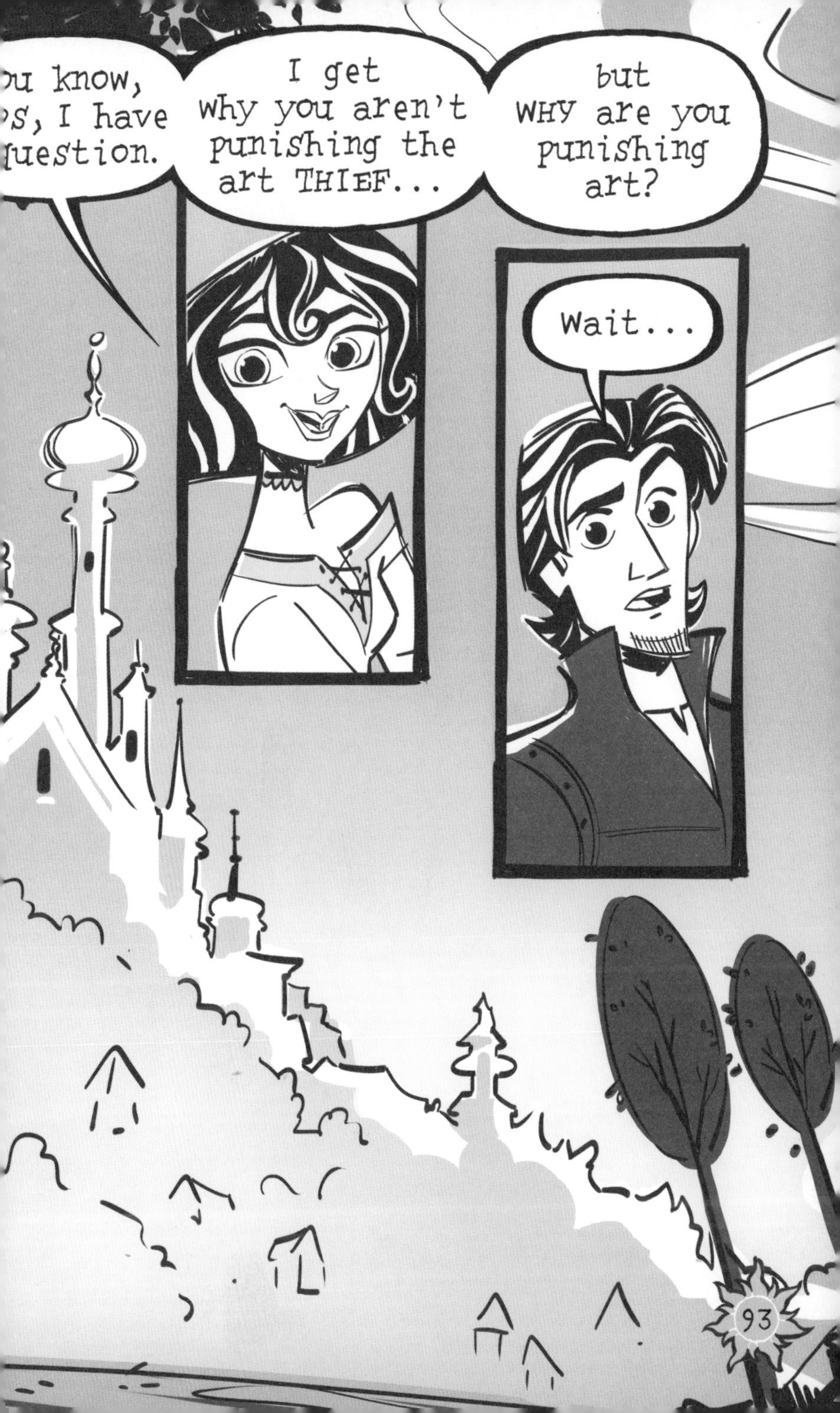

ou know,
s, I have
question.
I get
why you aren't
punishing the
art THIEF...
but
WHY are you
punishing
art?
Wait...

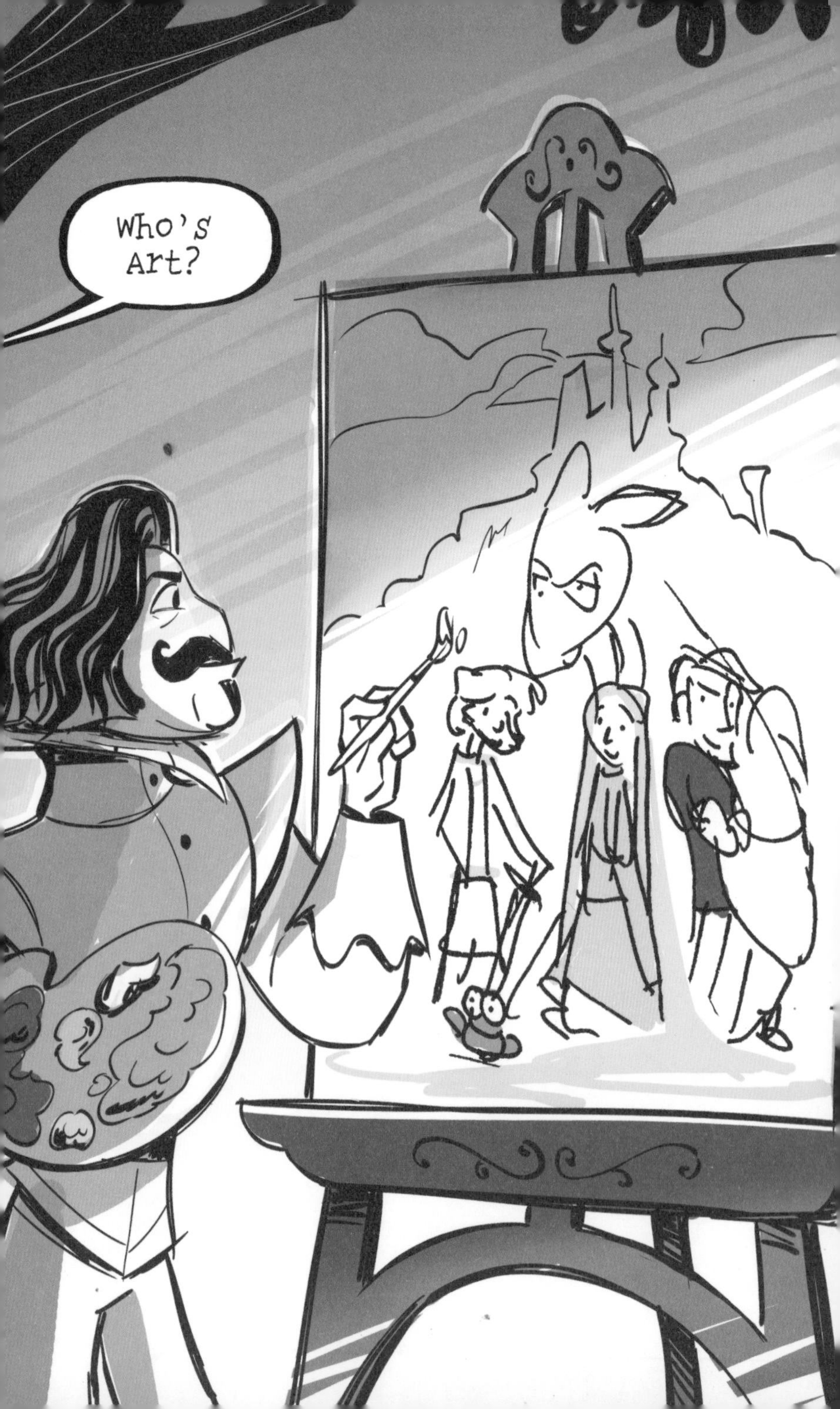
Who's Art?